499

MAD
MOUSE

MAD MOUSE

CHRIS GRABENSTEIN

CARROLL & GRAF PUBLISHERS
NEW YORK

MAD MOUSE

Carroll & Graf Publishers
An Imprint of Avalon Publishing Group, Inc.
245 West 17th Street, 11th Floor
New York, NY 10011

AVALON
publishing group incorporated

First Carroll & Graf edition 2006
First Carroll & Graf trade paperback edition 2007

Library of Congress Cataloging-in-Publication Data is available.

ISBN-13: 978-0-78671-936-5
ISBN-10: 0-7867-1936-2

9 8 7 6 5 4 3 2 1

Book design by Jamie McNeely

Printed in the United States of America
Distributed by Publishers Group West

This one's for my mom & dad.
She always knew I could do it.
He would've loved seeing you read it.

Thank You

To J. J., Eric, Don, Will, Michele, Karen, Betsy, Wendie, Grace, Beth, and everybody at Avalon who helped make my debut ride on *Tilt-A-Whirl* so much fun.

To our incredible families and friends.

To Bruce Springsteen for once again letting me borrow his words and Michele Slung for once again making my words better.

To the fantastic mystery booksellers and fans I've enjoyed meeting in bookshops, at Bouchercon, or on DorothyL.

To Jennifer Greene, who read the manuscript of this story before reading *Tilt-A-Whirl* and immediately demanded a copy of *Tilt*, too! To all my other early readers. I apologize for keeping you up all night.

To Michael Bradley, chief of the Long Beach Island, New Jersey, Police Department, who helps me make sure I get stuff right. To Heidi Mack for constantly updating my Web site and making it look so cool. To Jeanette and Parker (our cats) for keeping me company in the writing room and Buster (our dog) for helping me come up with the ideas in the first place.

And, last but not least, to my Down the Shore Family: Kathy, Dave, Meghan and Sam; Brenda, Warren, Heather and Maddie; Hugh and Susan; Bill and Jen. When I write these stories, I think of laughs on the beach and nighttime strolls to Skipper Dipper for soft-serve ice cream that melts all over your knuckles.

Then I think of those three pennies I lost that night we played "Left, Right, Center" with Dave's green dice.

I demand a rematch.

ONE

August 30th is National Toasted Marshmallow Day, so, naturally, we're celebrating.

Sure there's some debate: Is National Toasted Marshmallow Day August 14th or August 30th? We go with the 30th because it's closer to Labor Day. Besides, if you dig a little deeper, you'll discover that August 14th is also National Creamsicle Day, and we firmly believe Creamsicles deserve their own separate day of national recognition.

Five of my longtime buds and I are driving out to Tangerine Beach. Here in Sea Haven, New Jersey, the beaches get named after the streets they're closest to. On the way, we pass Buccaneer Bob's Bagels, Sea Shanty Shoes, and Moby Moo's Ice Cream Cove. In case you can't tell by the waterlogged names, this is your basic down-the-shore resort town: We live for July and August because our visitors go home in September and take their wallets with them.

I'm a part-time summer cop with the Sea Haven Police. That means I wear a navy blue cop cap and help elderly pedestrians navigate the crosswalks. This year I might go full time when summer's over, which is, basically, next week. They usually offer one part-timer a job at the end of the season. The chief gets to pick. We have a new one. We'll see. Anyhow, I put in my application.

Riding up front with me, twiddling her sparkly toes on the dashboard, is Katie Landry. She's a friend who I hope will soon become a "friend." Like the Molson billboard says: "Friends come over for dinner. *Friends* stay for breakfast." So far, Katie and me? We're just doing takeout. Mostly Burger King or Quiznos.

In the second row are Jess Garrett and Olivia Chibbs—a sleepy-eyed surfer dude and an African-American beauty queen slash brainiac. Jess and Olivia are already buttering toast and squeezing orange juice together. She comes home from college every summer to make money to cover the stuff her med school scholarships don't. Jess lives here full time. He paints houses when he's not busy goofing off.

Then there's Becca Adkinson and Harley Mook. Becca's folks run the Mussel Beach Motel, she helps. Mook (we all call him Mook) is short and tubby and loud. He's in the wayback, popping open a bag of Cheetos like it's a balloon. He's just in town for a week or two, which is fine. You can only take so much Mook. He's in grad school, working on his MBA.

According to Jess, that means "Me Big Asshole."

"Hey, Danny . . ." Mook hollers. "What's the biggest crime down here these days? Taffy snatching? Overinflated volleyballs?"

Mook's not funny but he's right: People typically come to our eighteen-mile strip of sand for old-fashioned fun in the sun. It's not the South Bronx. It's not even Newark. But Sea Haven *is* where I saw my first bullet-riddled body sprawled out on a Tilt-A-Whirl over at Sunnyside Playland. I remember that morning. It wasn't much fun.

"Traffic!" Becca says. "That's the worst!"

I'm driving because my current vehicle is a minivan with plenty of room for beer and gear. I bought the van "preowned," my mother being the previous owner. She sold it to me when she and my dad moved out to Arizona. It's a dry heat.

I'd say half the vehicles in front of me are also minivans, all loaded down with beach stuff. Bike racks off the backs, cargo carriers up top.

You can't see inside anybody's rear windows because the folding chairs and inflatable hippopotami are stacked too high. I have plenty of time to make these observations because our main drag, Ocean Avenue, is currently a four-lane parking lot.

"Take Kipper!" This from Mook. Now he's chugging out of a two-liter bottle of grape soda.

"Hello? He can't," says Becca. She points to the big No Left Turn sign.

"Chill, okay?" Katie teaches kindergarten so she knows how to talk to guys like Mook.

"For the love of God, man, take Kipper!" Now Mook's kneeling on the floor, begging me to hang a Louie. For the first time all day, he's actually kind of funny, so I go ahead and make the illegal left.

Oh—the streets in this part of town? They're named after fish. In alphabetical order. Only they couldn't find a fish that starts with a Q so Red Snapper comes right after Prawn.

As soon as I make the turn, a cop steps into the street and raises his palm.

And, of course, it's my partner. John Ceepak. He signals for me to pull over.

There's another cop with him. Buzz Baines. Our brand-new chief of police. Some people thought Ceepak should've taken the top job after what happened here in July. Ceepak wasn't one of them.

I'm not sure if Buzz is Baines's real name or if it's just what everybody calls him because he's really an Arnold or a Clarence or something. Anyhow, Buzz is the guy I hope will give me a full-time job next Tuesday. Today he's going to give me a ticket.

"Danny?" Ceepak is startled to see me behaving in such a criminal fashion.

"Hey."

Ceepak is a cop 24/7. He's 6'2" and a former MP. He still does jumping jacks and pushups—what he calls PT—every morning, like he's still in the army. He also has this code he lives by: "I will not lie, cheat or steal nor tolerate those who do." An illegal left turn? That's cheating. No question, I'm busted.

"Hey, Ceepak!" Becca sticks her head over my shoulder. She loves his muscles. Maybe this is why Becca and I don't date anymore: Where Ceepak's beefcake, I'm kind of angel food.

"Who we got here, John?" Baines hasn't recognized me yet.

"Auxiliary Officer Boyle."

I hear Becca sigh. Ceepak? He's handsome. Buzz Baines? He's handsomer, if that's a word. Sort of like a TV anchorman. You know what I mean, chiseled features with a lantern jaw and this little mustache over a toothpaste-commercial smile.

"Of course. Boyle. You and John cracked the Tilt-A-Whirl case."

"Roger that," says Ceepak. "Officer Boyle played a vital role in that investigation."

"Keep up the good work." Chief Baines winks at me. "And don't break any more laws."

"Yes, sir."

"Call me Buzz."

"Yes, sir. Buzz."

I hear Ceepak rip a citation sheet off his pad. It's all filled in.

"You're writing him up?" Baines asks.

"Yes, sir. The law is the law. It should be applied fairly, without fear or favoritism."

Baines nods.

"John, when you're right, you're right. Sorry, Danny. If you need help with the fifty bucks, come see me. We'll work out a payment schedule."

"Drive safely," says Ceepak.

"Right. See you tomorrow."

"No. Thursday's my day off."

"Oh, yeah. Mine, too."

Ceepak eyes our beer coolers. Marshmallows aren't the only things that get toasted at our annual beach party.

"Then have a cold one for me, partner."

"Roger that."

"But pace yourself. It takes a full hour for the effect of each beer to dissipate."

"Right. See you Friday."

"That'll work." Ceepak smiles. No hard feelings. He even snaps me a crisp "catch you later" salute.

I pull away from the curb, real, real slow. I can't see any signs but I assume 10 m.p.h. is below the posted speed limit.

I can't afford two fifty-dollar tickets in one day.

The late-night guy on the radio is saluting "The Summer of '96," reminding us what idiots we were back then.

"Tickle Me Elmo was under every Christmas tree and Boyz II Men were climbing the charts with Mariah Carey..."

Great.

He's going to make us listen to her warble like a bird that just sucked helium.

It's almost midnight. We're the only ones on the beach. Most of the houses beyond the dunes are dark because they're rented to families with kids who wake up at six A.M., watch a couple of cartoons, and are ready for their water wings and boogie boards around six fifteen. The parents need to go to bed early. They probably also need vodka.

I like the beach at night. The black sky blends in with the black ocean and the only way to tell the two apart is to remember that the one on top has the stars and the one below has the white lines of foam that look like soap suds leaking out from underneath a laundry room door.

Katie's sitting with the other girls around our tiny campfire, smooshing marshmallows and gooey Hershey bars between graham crackers. I bet she's the kind of kindergarten teacher who'd let you have s'mores in class on your birthday. She's that sweet, even though she grew up faster than any of us. Her parents died eight or nine years ago. Car wreck.

I need another beer.

I slog up the sand to the cooler. Mook and Jess are hanging there, probably talking baseball, about the only thing they still have in common. Mook wears this floppy old-man bucket hat he thinks makes him look cool. He has one hand jammed in the pocket of his shorts, the other wrapped around a long-neck bottle of Bud, his thumb acting like a bottle cap. The world is his frat house.

"Hey, Danny . . ." Mook shakes the Bud bottle. "Think fast."

He lifts his thumb and sprays me with beer. Now it looks like I just pissed my pants.

Mook's belly jiggles like a Jell-O shot, he's laughing so hard.

"Jesus, Mook." Jess says it for me.

I forgot about Mook's classic spray-you-in-the-crotch gag. One of his favorites. He also used to buy plastic dog poop at the Joke Joint on the boardwalk and stuff it in your hamburger bun when you weren't looking.

"Very mature, Mook." I wipe off my shorts.

"You're not going to arrest me, are you, Detective Danny?"

"No. I'll let you off with a warning. This time."

"You want a beer, Danny?" Jess fishes a long-neck out of the watery ice.

I check my watch.

"What's with the watch?" Mook saw me. "You're actually waiting an hour between brewskis? What a weenie! Your cop pal is a hardass. And that haircut! Who does he think he is? GI Joe?"

If Mook knew Ceepak like I do he'd realize: GI Joe probably plays with a Ceepak Action Figure. The guy's that good. I shake my head, ignore Mook, and mosey away with my beer.

Becca, Olivia, and Katie are sitting in short beach chairs, the kind that put your butt about two inches above the sand. I plop down with them.

"Someone please remind me why we hang out with Mook," I say.

Becca shrugs. "Because we always have?"

I guess that nails it.

On the radio, the deejay's yammering about *"Sea Haven's gigantic Labor Day Beach Party and Boogaloo BBQ. MTV will be broadcasting live. So will we . . ."*

They've been hyping this Labor Day deal all month. Come Monday, the beach will be so crowded, you'll be lucky to find enough sand to spread out a hand towel, maybe a washcloth.

"Here's another hot hit from the sizzling summer of '96!"

The radio throbs with "C'mon 'N Ride It (The Train)"—a bass-thumping dance tune from the Quad City DJs, the same people who gave the world "Whoot, There It Is." The choo-choo song was big in 1996, the summer The Marshmallow Crew first got together and somebody said, "You know what? We should do this again next summer!"

"Hey, let's dance!" Katie pops up, like she's ready to teach us all the hokey-pokey—the adults-only version.

The girls fling off flip-flops, kick up sand. Becca cranks up the volume on the radio, shimmies her blond hair like she's in a shampoo commercial. I attempt to get my groove thing going. Basically, when I dance, I stand still and sway my hips back and forth. Tonight, I also "move my arm up and down" as the singer suggests. Lyrics like that are extremely helpful for those of us who are dance impaired.

"Hey, isn't dancing on the beach against the law?" Mook brays like an annoying ass. Actually, the herky-jerky moves he is currently making should be ruled illegal. "You gonna haul us off to jail, Danny? Get your picture in the paper again?"

Ceepak and I got some press back in July. The wire services and magazines picked up the Tilt-A-Whirl story. I was semifamous for about a week. On top of being obnoxious, Mook sounds jealous.

Fortunately, any thoughts of Harley Mook drift away when Katie sashays over to dance with me instead of the whole group. She opens up her arms, swings her hips, invites me to move closer.

Then I hear these pops.

Pop! Pop! Pop!

Like someone stomping on Dixie cups up on the street.

I'm hit.

My chest explodes in a big splotch of fluorescent yellow.

Katie's hands drop down and fly behind her. She must be hit, too.

Pop!

A paintball hits the radio and sends it backwards. The batteries tumble out. The music dies.

Pop! Snap! Pop!

We're all hit—splattered with this eerie yellow-green paint that shines like a cracked glow stick. My sternum stings where the paintball whacked me.

"Danny?" It's Becca. She sounds hurt. "Danny?"

She sinks to her knees and brings a hand up to cover her eye.

It's fluorescent yellow and red.

The paint is mixing with her blood.

TWO

Call nine-one-one," I yell. "We need an ambulance."

Jess is on it. He whips out his cell phone while I check out Becca.

"Danny?"

She has her hand cupped over her eye. Blood trickles down her cheek, streaking through caked paint.

"It hurts."

"I know . . ."

"Motherfucking kids." Mook's right but not much help.

"Grab some ice, Mook."

"Danny—you're the cop. Go catch the little fuckers!"

"Go grab some ice," I say again.

"I'll get it," says Katie. She's keeping cool, like she must when one of her kids topples off the monkey bars.

"We need to cover the eye socket." Olivia takes a tiny penlight out of her purse to examine Becca's eye. "It's a blunt trauma injury."

"Is my eyeball bleeding?"

"You're going to be okay," answers Olivia. "Danny? We need to tape a protective cover over her eye to prevent further damage. Cut off the bottom of a plastic cup . . ."

"What about tape?" I ask.

"Don't need it."

I hear a rip.

Olivia is tearing some strips off her T-shirt.

Becca is rocking slightly to punch through the pain.

She shivers. I grab Jess's beach towel and drape it over her shoulders like a cape—a cape with a gigantic red-and-blue Budman plastered on it, the superhero of beer drinkers everywhere.

Katie returns from the cooler. "Here's some ice."

"Danny? I need that cup," Olivia says while she picks crud off Becca's cheek.

I race up to the cooler where we have a stack of Solo cups.

"The EMS guys are on the way," Jess says and closes his phone.

"Hey, Jess?" I shout.

"Yeah?"

"You and Mook head up to the street. Flag down the ambulance."

"Right."

"You should go after those fucking kids who did this!" Mook screams at me. His floppy hat is glowing. They tagged him with a headshot.

"Come on!" Jess gives Mook a shove and they run as best as they can with feet slip-sliding on sand.

"Here you go." I've managed to tear the cup bottom away from the sides pretty neatly, if I do say so myself.

"Owww."

Olivia spreads Becca's eye open, spotlights it, checks for debris. The eyeball's iris is purple on the bottom.

Olivia places my plastic circle over the injured eye like a pirate's eye patch. Katie hands her a strip of fabric and she ties a knot behind Becca's head.

I look at my friends and realize we look pretty ridiculous, like we've got some kind of glowing, yellow-green skin rash—the Neon Plague.

• • •

Jess meets the rescue squad ambulance up on the street. He sends the paramedics down to the beach to go get Becca.

"Where's Mook?" I ask.

"Off chasing the bad guys."

"You saw who did it?"

"No. Mook just ran up the road screaming, 'Come back, you motherfuckers.' "

"Yeah. That usually works."

"What seems to be the problem, fellas?" This bald guy stands in a driveway near the ambulance. He's what cops call a looky-lou—wants to take a look at whatever brought swirling roof lights to his street at twelve fifteen A.M. "Is somebody hurt?"

"Minor beach accident," I say.

"Friend of yours?"

"Yes, sir."

"Well, try to keep down the noise." The guy is probably fortysomething. Balding. He's wearing a T-shirt, shorts, and sandals. With socks. He's one of those dads who have to wake up in five or six hours when his kids start heaving Cheerios at each other. He shuffles back toward his rented beach house. "Some people are trying to sleep around here!"

Yes, and other people are trying not to go blind.

Jess and I hurry back down to the beach.

Becca lies down on the stretcher. The two burly guys from the rescue squad get ready to carry her away.

"I feel like Cleopatra." She notices the one paramedic's muscles. "What's your name?" she asks, half sitting up.

"Becca?" says Katie. "Down, girl."

The patient obeys. Olivia takes one hand. Katie grabs the other.

"And don't touch your eye," says Olivia.

"It hurts," Becca moans.

"I know, honey."

"You're going to be okay," Katie says. "Okay?"

"Yeah. Happy Toasted Marshmallow Day, everybody."

"Should we go find Mook?" I ask Jess.

"Fuck Mook," he replies.

"Better you than me," Becca groans. We all trudge slowly up the sand to the sea grass and the dunes and the pressure-treated boards that lead down to the dead end of Tangerine Street.

"Danny?"

It's Ceepak. He climbs off his eighteen-speed trail bike.

"I heard the call come in. Heard Becca's name."

"Hi, Ceepak." Becca sounds woozier.

Ceepak has a police scanner in his apartment. It's his favorite form of entertainment when he's not watching *Forensic Files* or listening to Bruce Springsteen CDs.

"Is she badly injured?" he asks.

"Eye trauma," Olivia says. "Possible hyphema."

Ceepak nods. "You noted a reservoir of blood in the anterior chamber?"

Olivia nods back.

"She needs to see an ophthalmologist. Stat."

Ceepak turns to the paramedics who have just secured Becca inside the back of their boxy ambulance.

"Guys? Light 'em up."

"Will do, Ceepak," says the muscle man. I think everybody in town who wears any kind of uniform or badge has heard about Ceepak. Knows he's a standup guy.

Ceepak gives them one of his famous two-finger salutes. "Appreciate it."

The paramedics hop in, spin their flashers, and race away.

I dig into my shorts for the van keys.

"We should follow."

A cop car crawls down Tangerine Street. No lights. No siren. Just the soft crunch of seashells under tires.

"Danny," says Olivia, "maybe you should stay here. Tell the police what happened."

"Yeah." I turn to Jess. "You good to drive?"

"Yeah." Jess never gets plotzed. Besides, the paintball incident was pretty sobering. I toss him the keys. They all hop into my van and take off after the ambulance. Ceepak and I will hang here because we speak Cop.

Well, Ceepak speaks it better than me, but I want to make sure we nail whoever the hell did this to my friends.

THREE

"Probably juveniles," Chief Baines says after taking a quick survey of the crime scene.

Everybody has a flashlight swinging around except me. The beach looks like it's hosting some kind of sand crab movie premiere.

"Punks with paintball pistols," Sergeant Dominic Santucci shares his opinion.

"More likely a rifle," says Ceepak.

"Because of the range?" asks Baines.

"Roger that. We can assume the shooter or shooters were positioned up there." He points to the road. "They knew no one would hear them approach." He points to the paint-spattered boom box lying dead in the sand. "The music was turned up to full volume." Now he indicates the footprints circling the charred remnants of our campfire. "Danny and his friends were oblivious to any intrusion because they were busy dancing." I haven't told Ceepak what we were doing. He can see it all in the sand.

Baines smiles. "Good work. I like the way you read a crime scene, John."

I still can't believe the new chief is the one who caught this call.

Apparently, he was riding along with Santucci on a routine night patrol as part of his "orientation process" when the ambulance call went out.

"Who do we like for this?" Baines asks Santucci.

"Well, there are these punks who hang out on the boardwalk. You know: tattoos, skateboards. Weird haircuts."

Santucci isn't much of a profiler. He's just described half the guys who cruise up and down the boardwalk all summer long.

"There's a paintball place on the boardwalk," I offer. "They might have a few names for us."

"Mmm-hmm." Baines thinks a minute. "The girl injured badly?"

"Blunt-force impact," Ceepak says. "Possible hyphema."

The new chief nods and thinks some more.

"Okay. Here's how we need to play this thing. Quiet. Almost like it didn't happen." Baines flashes his Ultrabrite smile my way when he sees my jaw drop. "Take it easy, son. We'll catch the bad guys. But summer's officially over in five days. We don't want or need any more headlines, not this year. So, we all do our jobs, but—we keep it quiet."

Baines is probably right. No need to stir up another panic. In the few weeks he's been in town, he's done a pretty incredible job of restoring faith in the local forces of law and order. Most folks, especially the visitors, have already forgotten what happened here back in July. I think that's why the town fathers hired Baines: He looks and sounds like he should be on TV telling you the truth, the handsome hunk sitting in the anchor chair. It's also why, from what I've heard, they're paying him a small fortune.

"Sergeant Santucci's theory is most likely correct," Baines continues. "I suspect we're dealing with some bored kids who think they're being funny."

Santucci points at my Hawaiian shirt. It looks like the flowers have exploded with neon-colored pollen.

"You got to admit, it *is* kind of funny." He snaps his gum, does his donkey laugh. "Especially on Boyle there."

Santucci has been busting my chops all summer long. If I go full time with the force, he can torment me daily, seven-to-seven, the whole twelve-hour shift. Longer if I pull any overtime.

"Chief?" says Ceepak. "We could look into this tomorrow. Both Auxiliary Officer Boyle and I have the day off. Might prove a valuable field training exercise. Help our minds stay active, help us keep our investigative techniques sharp."

Baines nods. "But you'll keep it on the q.t.?"

"Right."

Baines puts his hands on his hips and sniffs in some salty air.

"You sure you guys don't mind? Working on your day off?"

"I look forward to it, sir," says Ceepak. "I welcome the challenge."

I nod. "Me, too, sir."

"Fantastic. Here's how we play it: Ceepak and Boyle investigate. Meanwhile, we alert all units to be on the lookout. We see a bunch of kids crammed in a car looking like they're looking for trouble, we pull them over."

"That'll work," Ceepak says. "Provided, of course, we have probable cause."

"Oh, we always have probable cause," Santucci sneers, like he thinks the whole Bill of Rights is a lousy idea dreamed up by a bunch of dead guys with their faces on coins.

"I look forward to hearing what you two dig up," Baines says to Ceepak. "Might help me decide which summer cop to hire next week." Now the chief gives me this meaningful glance.

Great.

The Case of the Perilous Paintballs is going to be my final exam, the homework assignment I need to ace to win full-time employment with the Sea Haven Police Department.

If we don't crack this case by Labor Day, I may have to find a job pushing carts around the parking lot at Wal-Mart.

FOUR

Everyone's gone, and I'm dancing on the beach again.

Well, not quite everyone. Ceepak's still here.

I'm doing a solo number without any music to show him my approximate location during the paintball bombardment. The campfire's long gone and he's shining his Maglite on me.

"I was here . . ."

"Facing the street."

"Right. Katie was facing me. She took a hit in her . . . you know."

I don't want to say "ass" or "butt."

"Her gluteus maximus." Ceepak helps out. He looks up toward the beachfront homes on the far side of the dunes. "The shots were probably fired from the street. Or off one of those balconies."

I look to the left and right of our entrance to the beach. There are three or four houses on either side. Modern jobs. All windows and right angles. They look like vinyl-sided shoe boxes stacked on top of each other, and, since this is beachfront property, every level has its own balcony or sun deck. Some of the houses even have widow's walks—a platform up on top of the roof. I think they call it that because that's where the widows of ship captains used to hang out and hope their husbands weren't really dead. Probably cursed god and the ocean some while they were up there, too. The higher elevation made it easier to scream at heaven.

"Danny? Focus."

"Right."

When I drift off like that, Ceepak usually reels me back in.

"Where was your radio located?"

"There." I point to the trash barrel. "Propped on top."

He takes one more look at the boom box lying in the sand on the ocean side of the trash barrel.

"Confirming that the shots came from the west."

"From one of those balconies?"

Ceepak crouches.

"I don't believe so. You say the paintball smacked you square in the chest."

"Like somebody heaved a medicine ball at me."

"I'd like to do a more comprehensive trajectory analysis, but judging from your impressions of the incident and the position of the radio, I'd say the shooter operated at street level. Perhaps firing from a car window."

Ceepak stands. His face, as usual, doesn't say much, but I think he's relieved we're not dealing with some kind of rifleman up on a rooftop. He saw enough of those back in what the soldiers all call Bagh-nasty-dad. Snipers, mostly. Ceepak went in with the first wave, the guys hunting for the weapons of mass destruction nobody ever found because they never actually existed. Later, he was in this convoy that was almost blown up by one of those roadside bombs the locals like to hide inside everything from rusty oil drums to tricycle tubing. When the bomb blew, Ceepak's Humvee gunner went ballistic. Did some horrible stuff to several civilians. I think that's when Ceepak decided to rotate stateside when his tour and bounce-backs ended. Decided he'd pack up his medals and say so long to the army, which, up to that point, had been his whole life.

I hear him suck in some night air.

The way Ceepak squints up at those balconies and widow's walks? I know he's seeing bad guys with rocket-propelled grenades and AK-47s. He lost a lot of buddies back in the "sandbox." Every now and then, he talks about it.

Every now and then.

"Come on," he says. We start working our way up the sand. "The midnight gang's assembled and picked a rendezvous for the night."

Now he's mumbling Springsteen lyrics. It's one of Ceepak's auto-focusing techniques. He remembers every song the Boss ever wrote — even ones Bruce has probably forgotten.

"They'll meet 'neath that giant Exxon sign that brings this fair city light."

This one's a classic. "Jungleland." But I don't see any Exxon sign. The only light is off in the distance, about a half block up Tangerine. One of those orange-ish street lamps, its hazy beacon a dance club for the big flappy bugs that only come out at night.

We reach the dunes and seagrass. Ceepak crouches in front of a bench made from pressure-treated two-by-eights. It faces the ocean right where the beach ends and the rolled-out dune fencing starts. Nothing special. Just a place to sit and shake sand out of your shoes.

"See something?" I ask.

"Yes."

"What?"

"Too many footprints."

Ceepak stands up and dusts some sand off his pants.

People stop here to put on their sneakers or flip-flops or whatever before walking down to the street. You walk barefooted on hot asphalt in August, your feet are going to talk to you about it. Ceepak realizes it's such a high-traffic zone there's no way we're going to pick up any usable footprints or clues.

"We need to talk to some people." He nods at the dark houses. "Find out if anybody saw or heard anything besides your music."

"Right." We had the radio blaring pretty loud, especially during the dance number. Mook was sending up his own personal noise pollution long before that. I'm sure some of the neighbors would give me an earful if they knew it was *my* Toasted Marshmallow Day party that disturbed their peace.

We crest the dune and walk down the short stretch of planks to the street. Ceepak hunkers down again. I do the same thing. Sometimes, it's like we play Simon Says.

He pulls a magnifying glass out of one of the pockets in his cargo pants. All I have in my shorts is a beer-bottle opener.

"Same story here."

"Tire tracks?"

"Dozens," he says.

He points to the sweeping arcs of tread marks and I see what he sees: Car after car drove down the dead-end street, dropped off the kids, unloaded all the beach stuff—much of which also had wheels: little red wagons, rolling ice chests, beach carts. We've got tire tracks on top of tire tracks.

"Nothing." Ceepak bites his lip, shakes his head. TMI. Too Much Information. Nothing stands out. It all blends in.

"I don't believe paintball weapons expel shell casings." Ceepak pulls out a notepad and jots something down. "I believe they act more like a cannon, propelling the ball out of the chamber. The ball stays intact until it strikes its target."

"Yeah." As one of the targets, I know how it strikes. I also know how it hurts.

"I need to do some research. But first, we need to knock on a few doors."

It's almost one A.M. I'm sure the neighbors are going to *love* us.

"What about the q.t.?" I ask.

"Come again?"

"You know. The chief told us to keep this thing quiet. If we start asking questions, people will wonder what happened." I point to my yellow-green chest.

Ceepak nods. Slow. Up and down, up and down. He's thinking.

"You make a valid point, Danny."

"We'd have to tell them something."

"Yes. But, I am disinclined to disseminate misinformation."

The Code. He will not lie. If we want witnesses, now is probably the best time to talk to people—while memories are fresh. But if they ask us questions and we truthfully answer them, this thing could spin out of control fast.

"Perhaps we should do a little legwork first. I suspect the chief and Santucci are correct. This is most likely the work of teenagers who pose no imminent threat."

"Right. The kind of guys who play mailbox baseball."

"Excuse me?"

"You know—you drive around, lean out the window, and whack people's mailboxes with a baseball bat."

"You've done this sort of thing?"

"Me? No. I've, you know . . . heard about it."

"I see."

I'm not lying. If I was, Ceepak would know and then he'd never trust me again. That's how The Code works.

"I'd like to visit this paintball arcade you mentioned," he says. "On the boardwalk?"

"Sure. No problem."

Ceepak punches the digiglo button on his Casio G-shock watch.

"Let's regroup at oh nine hundred hours."

"Pancake Palace like always?"

"Perhaps some place closer to the boardwalk."

"How about The Pig's Commitment? You know, over on Ocean and Oyster. Catty-corner to King Putt Golf."

"Roger that."

Suddenly, he turns around and walks a few steps back toward the beach. I do the same. We walk up the half-buried planks, reach the crest of the dune, and stand behind that shoe-changing bench. Down on the beach, our little circle of chairs is still there. The trash barrel. In my mind, I can see Katie dancing.

Ceepak crouches one more time.

He looks at the back of the bench. We didn't think to do that when we came up from the other side. We were just staring down at all those footprints that weren't going to help us.

Ceepak fishes out his flashlight and shines it on the back of the bench.

There's a splat of green-yellow paint, like somebody slammed a neon egg against it with their palm, smooshed the shell and let all the yolk dribble down.

"Any prints in the paint?" I ask.

"Negative. The perp wore gloves. See the blurring here? The smudging?" He swings his light to the right.

Next to the paint splotch there's this pushpinned plastic sleeve with something inside it. It looks like a baseball card. Only, when I look close, I see it's not. It's a trading card that shows a superhero in a purple diving suit with a black mask over his eyes.

The Phantom.

FIVE

The Pig's Commitment is probably the most popular restaurant on Ocean Avenue.

It's open twenty-four hours a day so it's great for breakfast, lunch, and dinner, especially if you like bacon and barbecue. Pork, as you might guess, is the common denominator all day long.

The owner, Grace Porter, an elderly and elegant black lady who swears she improvises her secret rib sauce recipe every time she whips up a batch, named the place after her favorite joke. You know—the one about the chicken and the pig and a plate of scrambled eggs with bacon. The chicken is involved. The pig is totally committed.

I'm a little early because I need coffee. Jess had swung back by the beach with my van around two A.M. He told me Becca was doing fine. Great news. The emergency room doctor didn't think there would be any permanent damage and sent her home with some drugs and a higher-quality eye patch. Then Jess and I had to pack up our beach chairs and coolers and stuff. My head didn't hit the pillow until sometime close to three thirty. Maybe four.

Like I said, I need coffee.

Grace brings it over in one of those plastic thermal pots that hold about a half gallon and you can pour yourself.

"Here you go, Danny. You look like you need it."

"Thanks, Grace."

Even though she spends most of her day in a kitchen with fattening food, Grace Porter at age sixtysomething is as thin as one of the mint toothpicks they keep near the cash register up front. She's wearing one of those cool Kofi hats with tribal squiggles all over it and this blousy mudcloth dress. She looks like a jazz musician or, as she likes to call herself, the Queen of Cuisine.

"Will you be eating alone this morning?"

"No. Ceepak's joining me."

"Mr. Ceepak? How wonderful. I'm looking forward to finally meeting our local hero." She studies the silverware next to the empty place setting. I see water spots and dried egg yolk on fork tines. So does she. "Excuse me." She scoops up the offending cutlery and hustles off to find a clean fork and maybe have a word or two with her busboy.

I check my watch. Eight fifty-three. Ceepak will march through the front door at eight fifty-nine at the latest. My man is always on time. I sip some coffee and look around at all the porker paraphernalia. The walls are covered, the shelves crammed. Ceramic pigs, plastic pigs, piggy banks of all kinds, pig-shaped cutting boards, pigs on tin signs for overalls, a weathervane with a winged flying pig.

"Danny?"

The voice interrupting my pig appreciation comes from a man in the booth underneath the weathervane. He has oiled-down silver hair, glasses, bright-green shorts and a rugby-striped polo shirt that sort of matches the shorts. I think he used to go to church with my parents. Weese. Right. Mr. Weese.

"Hello, Danny."

His wife. Mrs. Weese. He's tall and lanky; she's short and stout. A classic case of Jack Sprat–itis. There's a younger couple in the booth with them. The guy is kind of tall, and even though I figure he's only my age or maybe a little older, he has this receding hairline coupled with wavy, swept-back hair that makes him look like he might sing country music, only he's wearing clunky glasses with a paper clip pinned through one hinge, and country stars seldom do that. He's sitting next to a short girl with dark hair and a sour face. She looks like somebody just poured last month's milk into her coffee.

"You remember our son?" Mrs. Weese says with a big, proud smile. "You remember George?"

"Of course." I'm glad Ceepak isn't here. I'm lying through my teeth. I don't remember George Weese at all.

"He's visiting. With his wife."

I guess the wife doesn't rate her own name.

"We're grandparents," says Mr. Weese.

"Boy *and* a girl!"

"Twins?" I ask.

"No. Nine and twenty-three months."

Wow. Georgie Boy and Sourpuss have been busy. If we were playing that Milton Bradley board game *Life*, their little car would have four pegs in it. Two blue. Two pink. Me? One peg. And I'm nowhere near that Getting Married space.

"How about you?" asks Mrs. Weese.

"Me?"

"Any children?"

"No." I almost add, "None that I know of." But then I remember these were my *parents'* friends, not mine.

"What's stopping you?" Mrs. Weese gives me a country club smile — the kind some queen flashes to her peasants. Now I remember. He runs a bank. She sells real estate. The Weeses play golf, live in a huge house, and love to remind everybody how rich they are.

"Danny doesn't have time to settle down," says Mr. Weese. "He's a hero. That awful murder and everything. Read all about it. Sent George the clippings."

George, whom I'm supposed to know, sort of grunts in my general direction. I get the feeling he's not so crazy about his parents. I'll bet he's glad he has to visit Sea Haven only once or twice a year.

"Way to go, Danny." Mr. Weese gives me a stubby thumbs-up.

"Just, you know, doing my job." I've heard a lot of cops say that in the movies. TV too. Figure it might work for me.

"Still just a part-time job?" Mr. Weese asks.

"Yeah."

"Well, we need to skeedaddle." Mr. Weese stands up so everybody can fry their eyes on his green shorts. "Anybody need to use the facilities? George?"

"No. Thanks."

"You sure, son? It's a ten-minute drive back to the house."

"I'm fine."

"How about you, Natalie?" he says to his daughter-in-law. "Need to powder your nose?"

She shakes her head no.

"You kids sure?"

"Yes, Dad."

Mr. Weese leads the way to the cash register. George and his wife slouch out behind Mrs. Weese. They *so* don't want to be here.

I return to my coffee. It's good. Strong. Loaded with Colombian caffeine.

Someone taps me on my shoulder. Mr. Weese. I guess he circled back.

"Give me a call after Labor Day." He flicks a business card on the table. He's not a banker but a mortgage broker, whatever that is. "If interest rates hold steady, I might have some telemarketing slots opening up."

"Sure. Thanks."

He tugs on his belt. It's white. He's wearing monogrammed tan knee socks that blend in with his skin.

I want him to go away, but he just stands there, sucking on a toothpick.

"Good morning, Danny."

Thank God. Behind Weese I see Ceepak.

"Enjoy your breakfast." Mr. Weese gives his belt a final hike and walks away. He jingles change in his pocket and studies the bill from breakfast. "Grace?" he calls up to the register. "I think you over-charged us on George's milk. He ordered a small. I know the girl brought him a large, but we *ordered* a small."

Ceepak sits down. "You okay, Danny?"

"Yeah. Now. Thanks."

"Sorry I'm late."

I check my watch. Nine-oh-one. Wow. I let it slide.

"I swung by the Mussel Beach Motel," he says. "Checked in with Becca's folks. They say she's fine. She has a contusion coupled with ecchymosis."

I think that means she has a shiner.

"But no permanent damage."

"Yeah. Jess told me. Last night."

"Excellent."

Ceepak is always bright and chipper first thing in the morning. Me? I'm more your nocturnal type.

He opens a pants-pocket flap and pulls out that plastic-sealed trading card of the Phantom we found last night. He's tucked the clear sleeve inside another plastic protector. I wonder if he's checked the first pouch for fingerprints yet? Probably.

"Mr. Ceepak?"

It's Grace.

"Yes, ma'am?"

"I'm Grace Porter. Welcome to my establishment."

Ceepak stands to shake her hand. The guy's classy that way.

"I am very pleased to make your acquaintance."

Grace has brought some clean silverware to the table and places the rolled-up paper napkin in its proper position on the left. I know. I used to be a busboy.

"What would you like for breakfast, Mr. Ceepak? My treat."

"You don't have to—"

"If I *had* to, I probably wouldn't."

"Yes, ma'am," Ceepak says with a grin. I can tell he digs Grace because she's totally his type: a no-bullshit straight shooter. He

CHRIS GRABENSTEIN

glances down at the laminated menu. "May I please have corn flakes and fresh fruit?"

Grace glares at him for a second.

"No, you may not. This is not 'The Corn Flake's Commitment.' "

"Right. How about bacon?"

"Certainly."

"And some sausage? Maybe the ham. And let's see . . . scrapple. That sounds awesome."

"Very good. How do you like your eggs?"

"You tell me."

"Scrambled. With onions, green peppers, and jack cheese."

"That'll work."

She pours Ceepak coffee from a fresh pot I know she brewed especially for him. She sees the sealed photograph of the guy in the purple diving suit.

"Is that the Phantom?"

"Yes, ma'am."

"He operated in Africa, if I'm not mistaken."

"That's right."

"Tell me—why did he wear that mask?"

"Excuse me?"

"Why'd he wear that Lone Ranger mask over his eyes? Everybody had to know who he was."

"How so?"

"He was the only white man for hundreds of miles in any direction. I'm certain even the elephants knew his secret identity."

Ceepak grins like crazy. His dimples wiggle up and down.

"Yes, ma'am. I suppose you're right."

"Tell me, Officer Ceepak, are you on duty today?"

"Is there some problem?"

"Nothing of earth-shattering significance."

"I'd like to help if I can."

"It's nothing really. A young man, who thinks he's funny, vandalized my property last night."

30

"Where?"

"Out back."

"Let's take a look."

"But your coffee will go cold."

"You can bring me a warm-up. Let's go see what we can see. Danny?"

I gulp one last swig of java.

"Let's roll," I say.

Grace escorts us to the kitchen. There's all sorts of sizzling going on and the rich, greasy smell of bacon dripping off the walls. I'm drooling.

"Out this way." She leads us past the sputtering skillets. "I know it's that one boy. The one with the spiky blond hair and tattoos up and down his forearm. I've seen him out back here before. Probably sizing up his opportunity, casing the joint, as you gentlemen might say."

She pushes open the screen door and we're out behind the building in a small parking lot big enough for two cars and one Dumpster. She walks past the cars, turns around, and points at the brick wall.

For years, the whole back wall of her two-story building has been a local landmark. That's because it's covered with this billboard-size cartoon of a pink pig, with chubby cheeks and a big smile holding a knife and fork, licking his chops in anticipation of eating, well, a friend, I guess.

"See what he did? I wonder, Mr. Ceepak. Could you visit this child? Teach him what is considered unacceptable behavior in civilized society."

I look down at the pink pig's crotch. Somebody has given him balls. Two splotchy blue balls. Somebody shot Grace's big pig with a paintball gun.

SIX

E xcuse me," Ceepak says after he burps.

When he ordered it, he didn't know scrapple was chopped pork and cornmeal mush, seasoned then fried. He'll probably remember all day long. Scrapple has a tendency to repeat on you, and we totally wolfed down our breakfast so we could hustle over to the boardwalk and nab our paintball Picasso. Seems the alleged artiste was busy last night. First The Pig's Commitment, then my annual beach party. Or maybe vice-versa.

Anyway, we figure our perp must strut his stuff at the paintball booth on the boardwalk. People there might be able to ID him for us.

In Sea Haven, the boardwalk runs along the beach for about a mile or two, all the way from Oyster Street north past Anchovy. It's one of the town's top attractions, especially for the under-twenty-one crowd. One side is mostly open to the sand and ocean; the other is cluttered with booths and arcades. There are food and souvenir shacks and games of chance like Whack-A-Mole and The Frog Bog, where you hammer these tiny green seesaws to see if you can flip a rubber frog onto a lily pad. I never can.

The boardwalk is also where the big Labor Day blowout will

CHRIS GRABENSTEIN

take place on Monday—the day before I either become a full-time cop or start training for an exciting career in mortgage brokering with Mr. Weese.

"Excuse me."

If Ceepak keeps saying that every time he burps, he'll wear himself out. Mr. Cereal-and-Fruit isn't used to scarfing down so much early-morning grease. Me? I'm an old pro at digesting partially hydrogenated oil of all types. Most of my meals involve some sort of deep-frying or lard.

As we climb the steps up to the boardwalk, I can see the distant silhouette of the little roller coaster at the end of a pier jutting out into the ocean. It's what they call a Mad Mouse—a tight track with wicked sharp turns. Instead of a train of connected cars like a bigger roller coaster, it has tiny, individual cars shaped like mice. The undercarriage of each one is designed to make you feel like you hit the turns before the wheels do and every time you fly into a curve, you think you're going to rocket off the edge and die. Just when you recover, the little mouse car whips into another turn, throws you another curve, and you think you're about to die all over again.

It's a blast.

Near the north end of the boardwalk is another wicked ride: the Tower of Terror. You can see it no matter where you are because it's twenty stories tall. Basically, it's an open-air elevator that hauls you up, then drops you like somebody snipped the cable. The one time I took the plunge my stomach ended up somewhere behind my eyeballs.

It's Thursday. August 31st. A practically perfect end-of-summer day. Not too muggy, especially for the last day of August. It rained Tuesday night, but I don't think it will today. Maybe we'll get a thunderstorm later. We usually do. The clouds are towering up on top of each other like puffy popcorn balls. I can even smell the popcorn. Hot. Buttery. They sell tons of it on the boardwalk.

As we march up the steps, I'm hit with a cool breeze and the wafting aromas of not only fresh popcorn but sausage-and-pepper sandwiches, curly-cut fries, onion rings, charbroiled burgers, fried

34

clam strips, cotton candy. I figure this is what heaven must smell like. At least the boys' side.

"Have you any idea who this young man Grace mentioned might be?" Ceepak asks.

"Don't think so."

"Well, he should be easy to spot," Ceepak says. "What with the large tattoo ringing his forearm."

I just smile.

We join the crowd walking the boards, and just about everybody has a tattoo somewhere. This is a great place to show them off because the idea at the beach is to be buck naked except for your underwear. That's what swimsuits are. Drip-dry underwear.

Some guys have your classic scary tats up on their shoulders. Spider webs and skulls and angry ladies biting knives. Others have Thai tribal etchings scrolled around their biceps. Then there are the girls with naughty little drawings or Chinese letters peeking out from under their bikini bottoms, front and back.

Scanning the inked-up passersby, Ceepak decides its time to narrow our search.

"Where's the paintball arcade?" he asks.

Paintball Blasters is a politically incorrect shooting gallery right across from the Mad Mouse pier.

The gimmick is the targets. You get to splatter life-size photographs of folks like Osama Bin Laden, Adolf Hitler, O. J. Simpson, Saddam Hussein, and, of course, Britney Spears. Or Michael Jackson. They're all strung up on a clothesline about twenty feet back on the firing range

When you get tired of defacing America's current crop of evildoers, you can take a shot or two at this garbage can lid that pops open to reveal a red, white, and blue bull's-eye target. Then, when that gets boring, you can blast away at a rusty old Pontiac down in the sand underneath the dangling targets. Looks like the windshield is a popular spot to splatter.

"Ten balls for five bucks," the burly guy running the place says when Ceepak and I step up to his counter. He's reading a newspaper and doesn't look up. "Thirty for ten."

"Are these Trippman 98s?" Ceepak asks.

I can tell Ceepak did his paintball homework last night on the Internet. The burly guy puts down his newspaper.

"What?" He snuffles his nose and sounds like he might hock a loogie. "Am I supposed to be impressed here or something? You know the name of a gun?"

"I was merely inquiring."

"Huh." The paintball proprietor turns back to his paper.

"Who's your best?" Ceepak now asks.

"What?"

"Who's your top gun?"

"Me." He proudly snorts some more wet stuff back into his throat.

"Who besides you?"

"Depends. What category? Kid? Adult? Local? Tourist?"

"Juvenile. Boy. Spiky blond hair. Tattoos on his forearm. Sound familiar?"

"Why should I tell you?"

Ceepak smiles.

"Because I'm a better shot than you."

"What?"

"I believe you heard me the first time."

"You sayin' you're better than me, slick?"

"That's right."

"Bullshit."

"My friend never lies," I say.

Ceepak pulls out a ten-dollar bill.

"That's for my first thirty shots."

"You challenging me?"

"Yes, sir."

"I don't give away prizes or nothing. You want prizes, go over there, grab a squirt gun, and pop a clown's balloon."

"I don't want a prize. I want information. About the boy."

"T. J.?"

"Is that his name?"

"Maybe."

Ceepak picks up a rifle.

"Let's shoot. If I win, you tell me where I find T. J."

"And if I win?"

"You keep the ten bucks."

"What? No fucking way. I get the ten bucks for renting you my fucking gun."

"Right you are." Ceepak pulls out his wager—a crisp fifty-dollar bill he tucks under the barrel of the rifle to his left so it won't blow away.

I turn around and see we're drawing a small crowd.

Ceepak's rival hops up on the counter and swings his feet over.

"You're on, ace."

Ceepak takes up his rifle and checks out the sighting down the barrel.

"You want Saddam?"

"Fine." Ceepak's cool with Saddam. They've tangled before.

"I'll take Osama. We both fire thirty rounds. Most headshots wins. Agreed?"

"Agreed."

"Hey, Joey?" The arcade guy is yelling down to some old geezer I hadn't seen before. He's off to the side of the range, dressed in a sleeveless Italian-grandpa undershirt, chewing on the stub of an unlit cigar. He sits on a stool behind a plywood partition. Must be the target master.

"What?" Grandpa grumbles.

"Hang me a clean Osama and Saddam."

"Why?"

"Because I fucking told you to is why."

"Yeah, yeah, yeah." He spits out the cigar stub and drags some clean cardboard targets out to the clothesline.

"You ever use glow-in-the-dark paintballs?" Ceepak asks while they wait.

"Nah. Too expensive."

"What about T. J.?"

"Maybe. I don't know. I'm not his fucking mother."

"You two ever talk about it?"

"Maybe. Once. He said he wished he had this special hopper that pumped UV rays into the balls so they glowed or something. Sounded expensive as shit."

"Set!" Grandpa hollers and shuffles back to his stool, picking up his wet cigar butt on the way. I see that the plywood wall he sits behind has been pelted, too. I guess when you get bored nailing the targets you can always try to nail a live geezer.

"Crank it up!"

I hear an air pump hammer—like on a power washer. The guns are pressurized.

"Send him flying!"

A motor whirrs. A chain clicks on a pulley. All of a sudden, the Saddam Hussein target slides back and forth, while Osama stays still.

"Saddam moves around a lot." The guy chuckles, sure he's hooked another sucker. "Before we nabbed him, he was always running from one spider hole to another."

"Does your target move as well?"

"Nah. Osama's just sitting there, hiding in his cave."

"I see."

"Hey, pal—you're the one who picked Saddam."

"Actually, you picked him for me."

"What? You think I'm cheating or something?"

"I don't think it. I know it."

"Oh, so now you want out? You just want to talk big, flash your cash, then back down?"

"No," Ceepak says. "I just want to be clear." He puts the tiny rifle stock up to his shoulder.

"Thirty balls, pal."

"Thirty. Roger that."

"Fire at will."

I hear that pop, pop, pop again, only now it's in total stereo. Like everybody on both sides of the boardwalk is stomping on paper cups. I also hear a lot of thwacks, paint splatting on pressboard.

The guy who runs the booth? He's good. A couple of his shots miss Osama's head. Some splatter on his robe below the neck. One or two whoosh past the turban altogether. But he's basically nailing his target. I'd say about two dozen paintballs explode dead center on Osama's nose and obliterate his face in no time flat. Like I said, the guy's good.

But he's no John Ceepak.

Every single one of Ceepak's shots hits Saddam smack in that bushy mustache. No misses. No near misses. All thirty shots hit the exact same spot on the moving target. He's just stacking whacks on top of each other.

Those medals Ceepak got in the army? A couple were for marksmanship.

SEVEN

T he Ring Toss," the arcade guy mumbles.

"Excuse me?" Ceepak puts down his air gun.

"T. J. He works mornings up at the Ring Toss."

"I know where it is," I say.

This superskinny guy in chocolate chip desert camo shorts, a matching T-shirt, and what they call a boony hat steps out of the crowd.

"Wanna shoot again?" he says to Ceepak.

"No, thank you."

"You army?"

"No, sir."

"But you used to be, right?"

"Yes, sir."

"Figures."

When I say this guy's skinny, I mean he's a six-six skeleton, like somebody who just crawled out of a tomb.

"Army asshole."

"Sir," Ceepak says, "I need to leave. Perhaps you should consider doing the same."

"Perhaps you should consider kissing my ass," he says and grins. His teeth are bony too, like he doesn't have any gums. "You army creeps make me sick!"

Ceepak points at the guy's camo getup.

"You served?"

"No." The smile slams shut. He fidgets with that hat. "They wouldn't take me. But I could take you, man. I could take you down."

I start to feel sorry for him. Under that boony hat, I figure he's got a few loose lug nuts.

Now he jabs a bony finger at me.

"I could take you down, too, punk."

I want to smack the guy's hand, get that gnarly finger out of my face.

"Danny?" says Ceepak, poker-faced. "We need to move along."

"Right."

We walk away.

"We need to maintain focus on our mission."

"Yes, sir. The Ring Toss is just another block up."

We reach W-A-V-Y's live boardwalk broadcast booth. Music thumps out of humongous outdoor speakers. When the song fades, the deejay yammers.

"Hey, this is Skeeter—burning up the Jersey Shore on W-A-V-Y. I'm joined by a very special guest . . ."

Springsteen? Southside Johnny? Bon Jovi?

"Sea Haven's own—Mayor Hugh Sinclair."

Oh. Him.

"Great to be here, Cliff."

Cliff Skeete and I went to high school together. We even tried to run this party-music deejay business for a couple of months. It didn't pan out. There was this incident at a wedding. All I can say in my defense is that I was very hungry and the cake had excellent frosting.

Cliff catches my eye and gives me a wave. They wave a lot at W-A-V-Y, the "Crazy Wave of Sound for Sea Haven and the Jersey Shore," as they say between songs. Constantly.

"I hope everyone's having a sunny, funderful day," says Mayor

Sinclair. He says that all the time. It's the town's official slogan even though it's stupid. "Skeeter, I want to personally invite you and all your listeners to the World's Biggest Beach Party and Boogaloo BBQ!"

I think this newly dreamed-up Labor Day deal is supposed to be some kind of mass hypnosis designed to make us all forget what happened at the Tilt-A-Whirl back in July. I know it won't work on me, but I'm always up for a good party. This one should be awesome. Big-name bands. Cheap, greasy food. Girls in teeny bikinis. I think they're having a "Best Tan" contest. Maybe they'll need an extra judge. Maybe Skeeter will put in a good word for me.

Up ahead, I see "The Lord of the Rings Toss." Of course it's not in any way officially tied to the movie. Somebody just ripped off the poster art and used it for their plywood signs. They've even painted in some characters who sort of look like Gandalf and the Elf guy with the arrows.

A kid, probably fifteen or sixteen, works inside the game shed. He's the one who pulls plastic rings off these two-liter soda bottles filled with black water. The rings are gold, just like Frodo's, only Frodo's wasn't spray-painted.

The kid has bleach-blond dreadlocks pulled back by a wide white headband that makes the dreads stick up like a feathered headdress. He's bare-chested and wears droopy shorts that show off the elastic waistband on his underpants. He has about two dozen rubber rings stacked up to his elbow on his left arm. The right forearm is wide open, showing off a swirling tattoo. I think it's some kind of sea creature wrestling with a mermaid.

The barker, the Ring Toss boss, sits out front, trying to draw a crowd. He has on one of those Madonna microphone headsets so everybody can hear how bored he is.

"Win a bunny for your honey," he drones. "Win a Tweetie for your sweety. Take home a SpongeBob for your heartthrob."

He doesn't seem any too thrilled by his own pitch or prizes.

"You know, Danny," Ceepak whispers, "many of these carnival games are inherently dishonest."

Since Ceepak will not lie, cheat, steal, or tolerate those who do, I can tell he considers Mr. Ring Toss Boss a potential Code Violator. To me, though, it's a borderline case, since Ring Toss is, technically, what they call an "amusement." You pay your money, you take your chances.

"That must be T. J." I nod toward the bottle boy.

"Roger that."

Ceepak steps up to counter.

"Six rings for a dollar, sir," the barker mumbles. "Score two, you're an Elf, win any prize on the bottom shelf." He points. The bottom shelf is filled with brightly colored crap. Key chains and plastic flashlights and whistles. Crap.

"How much for the plush pig?" Ceepak points to a stuffed hog on the top shelf. He lays into the word "pig" so T. J. is sure to hear it. "The *pig* in the Harley Davidson outfit?"

"The Harley Hog?"

"Yes, sir."

"That's top-shelf merchandise. That'll cost you six rings."

"Six rings on six bottles?"

"Ring six, win any prize you picks."

Ceepak nods. He understands the rules. "I'll take six rings."

"You need to ring six bottles to win big, need six to take home the pig."

"Maybe you should buy more rings," I suggest.

Ceepak smiles.

"I've studied the game."

"Really? You can study Ring Toss?"

"You can study anything, Danny, and you'll always learn something."

Duly noted. He lays a dollar on the counter.

"T. J.? Fix him up," the barker says to blondie.

The kid counts out six rings.

Ceepak studies T. J.'s hands.

"I see you used thin skins. Did they warm in your pockets prior to loading?"

The kid looks at Ceepak.

"Here's your rings," is all he says. Then he sort of shuffles to one side. I catch him checking out his hands before he buries them deep inside the pockets of his droopy shorts.

"What's a thin skin?" I ask Ceepak.

"Inexpensive paintball. They have a tendency to burst prior to loading."

"Win a bunny for your honey!" The barker is back at it. He's lost interest in us. The next sucker with a couple of bucks to toss his way is all that counts.

Ceepak squats under the counter, puts himself level with the bottle tops.

"I've done some preliminary research, and my findings suggest that children win this particular game more often than adults."

We're drawing another crowd.

"Children, you see, operate closer to bottle level. Therefore, their release point is better, their throwing arc relatively low."

Ceepak flings his first rubber ring. It wobbles around a bottle neck and slides down.

"If I use a topspin release . . ."

He flicks another. It rings a bottle.

". . . coupled with a sidearm throwing style . . ."

Dink! Another one.

". . . much like that utilized when flinging a Frisbee . . ."

Dink. Dink. Five in a row.

". . . I significantly increase my chances of victory."

Dink. Six for six. We have a winner. The small crowd goes wild. They applaud and whistle and laugh. Ceepak stands up, and everybody else pushes forward. They all want to play now that he has showed them how to win.

"How the hell did you . . . ?" The barker looks half pissed off, half amazed.

"Sometimes you just know what you know," Ceepak says and turns to T. J.

"We're closed!" the barker yells at the crowd. Guys shove money in his face. "Closed!"

"What about my pig?" Ceepak asks. "I want to give it to a friend. Perhaps she'll display it in her restaurant."

"T. J.? Grab Professor Squat here his Harley Hog."

The kid takes down the pig, hands it to Ceepak.

"I know what you did, T. J."

T. J.'s pale face goes about as pink as the pig. "I didn't do any-thing."

"Your fingernails."

The kid flips his hands over, looks at his nails.

"Is blue your usual color?" asks Ceepak.

I see it now. There's blue crud under the kid's nails. One of those thin skins must've burst in his hands. He is *so* busted.

"Is that the douchebag who splattered us?" I look over my shoulder. It's Mook. Where'd he come from?

"Back off, Mook," I say. "We've got it under control."

I see Mook jerk his arm up and down. He's shaking a bottle of Fanta grape.

"Douche bag!"

Mook spews a purple gusher at T. J.'s crotch.

"Fuck!" T. J. steps back, throws up his hands.

"Drop it!" snaps Ceepak.

Mook drops the bottle and holds up his hands in mock surrender. The crowd hoots.

"We're closed!" the barker screams. "Closed!"

This isn't going the way Ceepak planned.

"That's enough," he says. "Move along. Show's over."

The crowd disperses.

Mook swaggers up to the counter.

"Gotcha, punk! Gotcha good!"

"Sir?" Ceepak says.

"What?"

"Move along."

"I'm with Danny!"

"Danny? Tell your friend to leave. Now."

"Mook?"

"What?"

"Go."

"Fuck you, Danny. Okay? Fuck you."

Mook talks tough but walks away. Backwards, and with a swagger. Then he flips me the finger—the junior high school version with fingers one and three in the bent knuckle position flanking a fully extended middle digit. Extremely mature.

"I apologize for that," Ceepak says to T. J.

"Shit." The kid is staring at his wet pants.

Ceepak pulls out his fifty-dollar bill. "I hope this will cover the cost of any replacement clothing." Ceepak picks up his Harley Hog.

We turn around to leave. Our crowd has moved on to other boardwalk amusements.

All except one fan.

That creepy guy in the camo shorts. Mr. Bones. He hangs back in the shadows under a pretzel cart awning.

He smiles that bony smile.

Then, he flips me the finger, too.

EIGHT

The Mussel Beach Motel is a cozy little cinderblock box on the sandy side of Beach Lane.

Becca's mom and dad own and operate the place, and the family occupies rooms 101 through 103. I've always thought it would be so cool to live in a motel. You could get a bucket of ice anytime you wanted and your toothpaste cup would always be sealed in plastic, your toilet seat Sanitized For Your Protection.

But Becca tells me the ice machine moans all night long and clunks out cubes so it sounds like an avalanche, and sometimes she has nightmares about rockslides and gravel trucks. Not to mention Becca's the one who sanitizes all the toilets.

I drop by to see how she's doing. Ceepak has gone to the house—that's what we call the police station—to report our findings to Chief Baines. I guess I've aced my final exam.

On the way over to the motel, I grabbed Becca a box of saltwater taffy. The Sea Haven variety comes in a white box with striped letters on the front. There's also this drawing of a beach chair, a sand bucket, and a starfish. Actually, it's the same box they use anywhere that has a beach.

"Thanks, Danny," Becca says, sucking on a peppermint tube.

"You feel okay?"

"Yeah. How do I look?"

"Like Ray Charles."

Becca has on this huge pair of Ray-Ban Daddy-O sunglasses despite the fact that we're sitting inside in the lobby.

"You seeing Katie today?" she asks.

"I might, you know, drop by the Landing."

During her summer school break, Katie works at Saltwater Tammy's, a candy shop in Schooner's Landing, this multilevel mall of shops built around a tall ship, a schooner, I guess. The sails have "Schooner's" and "Landing" painted on them like huge, flapping billboards.

"She likes you, you know," Becca says.

"Well, I like her, too."

"I mean she *likes* you." Becca punches my thigh.

All of a sudden, I feel like we're back in fifth grade: "Katie Landry told Becky Adkinson to tell you . . ." We should pass notes or at least text message each other.

"You two make an extremely cute couple."

It's been a while since I've been in a couple, cute or otherwise.

"She has her break at three thirty. Be there." Becca pops another stick of taffy in her mouth, the blue one, whatever flavor blue is. "And thanks for the taffy!"

Three twenty P.M. I sit on a bench in Schooner's Landing across from the entrance to Saltwater Tammy's.

The candy shop has huge plate-glass windows, so I can see bins of bright-colored goodies. Gummi Bears. Jelly Bellies. Spearmint Leaves. Pinwheel lollipops that stand on the counter like funky sunflowers. It's Willy Wonka land in there. The display case is crammed with malted milk balls, chocolate-covered pretzels, chocolate-covered coconut clusters. Ladies with wide bottoms and shorts that strangle their dimpled thighs waddle out the door with white paper sacks and say, "Just one more piece, then I'm saving the rest."

So far, no one I've watched has saved anything.

I don't see Katie. She might be in one of the side windows dipping apples in caramel goop or working the taffy-pulling machine.

Schooner's Landing, tucked into three square blocks, has its own tiered boardwalk and ramps. The buildings are all designed to look like sea shanties or New England cottages. There's a big lighthouse at one end of the top level and a pretty decent seafood restaurant called The Chowder Pot at the other.

Three twenty-two.

I figure I'll "drop by" in about five minutes. While I wait, I watch this old lady on a bench toss chunks of her soft pretzel to some gulls. At the same time, five jocks thunder past like the front line of the Giants. They trample the pretzel crumbs. Smoosh 'em flat.

Three twenty-four.

It's time to pretend to be "just in the neighborhood so I thought I'd drop by."

"Danny?"

It's Katie. She comes out of the candy shop, smoothing down her shorts, fluffing up her hair. She doesn't have to. She looks great.

"What're you doing over here?"

"I was just, you know . . . in the neighborhood."

"Cool."

"You wanna go grab a coffee or something?" she suggests.

"Hey, cool. Yeah."

"Cool."

"Yeah."

If we manage to remember some words beyond "cool" and "yeah" when we hit the coffee shop, we might actually have a conversation.

Sun Coast Coffee is up on the third level. Katie and I sit outside under an umbrella. She has a cappuccino. I'm doing a double espresso.

"So, what'd you do on your day off?" she asks.

"Hit the boardwalk. I think we found the kid who paintballed us last night."

"Really?"

"Yep."

"Awesome. I've got bruises on my butt!"

I think about saying, "Can I see them?" but don't.

"We got a lucky lead this morning. The same kid vandalized the Pig's Commitment."

Katie's eyes sparkle. "The blue balls?"

"You saw it?"

"Yeah. I know it's terrible."

"But kind of funny?"

"Yeah."

"I thought so, too. But don't tell Ceepak."

We both sip our coffees. Katie gets some froth on her lip and licks it away with a flick of her tongue and a giggle. She's in uniform today. Sleeveless white top with Salt Water Tammy's stitched over her left breast, not that I'm staring at her breasts which, okay, I guess I am. I quickly shift my gaze over to the marina. Up here on the third floor, you get a great view of the whole bayside of the island. This is where the older people like to live, the ones who dig sailboats and sunsets more than the beach and surfboards. I can see a new development of condos under construction up past where the yachts are docked.

"Danny?"

"Yeah?"

"You look nice today," she says.

"Thanks. You, too."

"Oh, you like a girl in uniform, huh?"

"Yeah."

"Me, too."

"You like girls? Not that there's anything wrong with that."

"No," she laughs. "I like it when, you know."

"When I wear my uniform? My cop cap?"

"It's not so much the hat. It's, I don't know. You're doing something worth doing."

"Directing traffic? Writing parking tickets?"

"Protecting people."

"Yeah, well—I think it's cool what you do, too. Teaching kids."

"You think you'll go full time?"

"I put in my application. We'll see. Sometimes, there's a lot of politics involved . . . only one slot."

"Yeah."

We sip and sort of smile at each other for a while.

"You know what makes summer so great, Danny?"

"What?"

"It's like dessert. You only get it after you put in a fall, winter, and spring. If it was summer all the time."

"We'd be in Hawaii."

"Yeah. I think Hawaii would be boring. Nothing to do but nothing to do, you know?"

"Yeah. I like working," I say, sort of surprised to hear myself say it. "I mean lately." I cannot tell a lie, and not because Ceepak would bust me if I did. Katie knows my history. Until now, work had been what I did during the day to pay for the fun I had at night.

Katie gives me her softest smile, melting my heart faster than a Good Humor bar dropped on August asphalt.

"Relax, spazz!"

My head whips right. It's this new instinct I've developed ever since I started working with Ceepak. My radar's always up.

"We're goin' for a ride!"

It's those five muscle boys I saw downstairs. The football team. They're pushing this scared kid in a wheelchair up the ramp from the second level. The kid's head is sort of droopy and tilted sideways. One of his arms seems frozen in front of him, limp at the wrist, dangling like it's dead. Palsied.

"It's Jimmy," Katie says. She sounds scared. "Tammy's son. He's . . . you know . . ."

"Let's go on a roller-coaster ride!" The lead jock races ahead of his buddies, shoves Jimmy's chair up the ramp fast—makes him pop a wheelie.

"No! Stop!" The kid sounds like he's going to cry.

I look at all the shoppers standing around licking ice cream cones or nibbling monster chocolate chip cookies. Nobody's doing much besides shaking their head.

I stand up. I don't have a gun. I don't even have my badge or cop cap. It's my day off. I don't know what I think I'm going to do. I just know that these knuckleheads are totally freaking out the poor kid.

"Ready?" the biggest guy hollers down the slope to his buddies.

"Ready!" they holler back. "Send the retard down!"

The one who's holding on to it is about to let go of the wheelchair, about to send Jimmy rolling back down the ramp.

"Stop!"

I run over, push him aside, and grab the wheelchair handles.

"Hey, man! What the fuck?"

"I'm with the police."

"Then arrest this little retard. He blocked traffic, took up the whole fucking ramp."

The guys down below thump up the incline. They have me and Jimmy surrounded.

"I'll take care of this," I say.

The big boys move in tighter.

"You gonna arrest him?"

"We'll help you roll him over to the jail, dude."

"Kid's a retard. He should stay inside."

"Yeah, he's scaring away the ladies."

"Okay, guys." I try to channel Ceepak. "Thanks. Now, why don't you move along?"

"I got a better idea," the biggest one says. "Why don't *you* go fuck yourself? We were just having some fun, right retard?"

Terrified, trembling, Jimmy nods.

"We were just about to give him a free rolly-coaster ride."

"I can't let you do that," I say.

"Retards like rolly-coaster rides."

"Leave him alone."

"Make us." The circle shrinks. I wonder if I'm cut out for this job I just told Katie I like so damn much.

A menacing wall of sweaty meat surrounds me. I could use the wheelchair to bulldoze over a couple of them but that would probably leave Jimmy traumatized for life or, at least, pretty bruised.

"We were just having fun. Right, spazz?"

"Maybe you should go have it somewhere else."

It's Ceepak.

He's behind me licking an ice cream cone. The football boys take one look at him, and, suddenly, they aren't so menacing anymore.

"You heard Officer Boyle," he says. "You need to move along. You need to do so in an expeditious manner."

"What?"

"Leave. Now." Ceepak tosses what's left of his waffle cone into a trash bin and wipes his sticky hands with a paper napkin. He crumples the napkin into a tight wad and tosses it into the can, too. When he crushes stuff, you can see the veins and muscles and tendons rippling in his arms. You have to figure his fists will be somewhat furious.

The five guys step backwards in virtual lockstep. Like they're not really leaving even though they actually are. It's the tough dude retreat, the fadeaway admission of defeat.

"Watch your back," one of them remembers to hiss at me. "Watch your back!"

"You okay, Jimmy?" Katie's beside him now. She's kneeling in front of the wheelchair so she can look Jimmy in the eye, so he can see her familiar smile.

"I want ice cream."

"Then we'll go get you some, okay?" Katie looks back at us. "Thanks, Danny. Mr. Ceepak. You guys are the best."

She takes the wheelchair in hand, turns it, and waves, as she heads down the ramp with Jimmy.

I wave back.

"That's Katie?" Ceepak says.

"Yeah."

"Nice lady."

"Yeah. Real nice."

I'm glad Ceepak approves. He has high standards for everything. Women included.

"Becca suggested I might find you here," Ceepak says. "She told me to wait until fifteen forty-five."

That's army talk for three forty-five P.M. I guess Becca wanted to give Katie and me fifteen minutes alone.

"What's up?" I ask.

"Not much. Just wanted to report in on my conversation with the chief."

"And?"

"Are you free tomorrow evening? He'd like to take us out to dinner. I suspect he wants to discuss something with you."

"The job?"

Ceepak refuses to rise to the bait. I never actually thought he would.

"Not knowing, can't say," he says.

It doesn't matter.

It's The Job.

It's mine.

NINE

Friday morning. September first. I feel like a full-time cop already. I'm working sewer duty. Or maybe it's water main duty. Basically, I'm acting like a human traffic light—signaling cars to slow down and move into the center lane of Ocean Avenue so these backhoes can dig up the street and pull out eight-foot-wide sections of concrete pipe.

I hope it's a water main. I don't want to think about an eight-foot-wide tube of sewage, even if it is buried underneath a ton of asphalt.

You've got a lot of time to think about stupid stuff when you're a human traffic light and it's 92 degrees in the shade—of which there is absolutely none in the middle of Ocean Avenue. The heat makes me loopy. If I weren't wearing my cop cap, I think my head would melt.

Ceepak isn't directing traffic this morning. He's working with the bosses on the battle plan for Monday and the World's Biggest Beach Party and Boogaloo BBQ. I guess they want to make sure security is tight but loose—in other words, that we're all over the place but nobody notices. Every cop on the force, me included, will be on the clock Labor Day. The full-time guys probably score double overtime. I hope that's me next year. Double overtime sounds nice, especially when you think your head is about to melt.

I'd gone by the house this morning for roll call. Dominic Santucci was in the lobby standing next to the gumball machine. Why the police station has a gumball machine, I don't know. It's not like people on the street say: "I need some gum. Let's go see if the cops have any." Maybe the gumballs are just for Santucci. He sure chews a lot of them. He likes to chomp while he sizes you up.

"I hear you're going on a date tonight," Santucci said smugly. "You and the new chief." He likes to think he's in the know on departmental scuttlebutt.

"Yeah. Sorry your boy won't be joining us."

"My boy?"

"I figured, you know, you recommended someone else for the job. One of the other guys. One of the losers?"

"It ain't over till the fat bastard sings. Capeesh?"

Santucci tends to mangle his clichés like that, but I let it go, set my snicker on its silent mode.

Anyway, what he probably doesn't know is that dinner is scheduled for seven P.M. at Morgan's Surf and Turf. That's a swanky restaurant up Ocean Avenue, across the street from the big green water tower.

I'm working this dusty sewer-pipe detail with Skip O'Malley, another summertime cop. I know Skip applied for the full-time job like I did, but he's only twenty-one and hasn't helped solve any major crimes this summer.

I don't mean to gloat. I guess Ceepak somehow just managed to make me feel like I've got the job in the bag.

I turn around and see O'Malley at the other end of our detour — directing traffic with one hand, yakking on the cell phone he holds in the other. I know he's got this serious girlfriend so his phone is constantly glued to his ear. They talk so much I don't know what they talk about since they never seem to do anything except talk to each other.

A black Ford Expedition comes up Ocean. It's the chief's car. I see him behind the wheel.

I pivot and watch it cut this amazingly dangerous U-turn right in front of me. I would definitely write it up for a tire-squealing stunt like that but, like I said, it's the chief's car. He pulls off to the shoulder on the far side of the intersection.

I stand up a little straighter and flick my traffic-signaling wrist like a pro, like one of those white-gloved guys you always see on *America's Funniest Home Videos*, only I don't do the little dance.

I watch Ceepak climb out of the passenger side and stomp across the intersection—after waiting, of course, for the WALK signal to give him permission.

"Danny." He acknowledges me as he marches past.

I just nod gravely and keep signaling my traffic. From the totally serious look on my face you'd think I'm trying to move motorists around a nuclear power plant meltdown, not a water-pipe installation. I do, however, crane my neck enough to see where Ceepak is going.

To jump in O'Malley's face.

Ceepak has his hands on his hips and leans in to give Skipper an earful. I see O'Malley close up his cell phone and clip it to his belt. He's fifty feet away, but I can see him go so bright red I wouldn't be surprised if all the cars down there slam on their brakes. With his big Irish head, he's starting to look like a stoplight.

Yeah. I gotta figure Skip O'Malley won't be offered the full-time job even if his father is on the town council, which, of course, he is.

I don't mean to gloat.

I'm just looking forward to dinner.

Thankfully, I was able to head home and grab a quick shower after work. Protecting bulldozers all day left me looking like some kind of rusty sand man, dusted with whatever red crap the backhoe scraped off the pipes down in that ditch.

After my shower, I made a couple of quick phone calls. Reached my folks out in Scottsdale. Told them what was up. Mom was proud. Dad was busy in the garage, tinkering with his golf cart. It's what they drive instead of cars at their condo complex. Knowing my dad, he's souping up the battery-powered engine so he can race guys to the 7-Eleven.

Next, I called Katie. She wished me luck and said to say "hey" to Olivia. Our friend is a waitress at Morgan's. Katie also recommended I stay away from the crab pie that Morgan's is famous for. "Too much butter. It'll clog your arteries."

Wow. She's already worried about my arteries. Wow.

I told her I'd swing by tomorrow morning with a full report on my big night. She'll be at the taffy shop early because Tammy has to take Jimmy to his Saturday morning physical therapy appointment on the mainland. She also said she had something special she wanted to give me. A surprise.

I put on my blue button-down shirt.

It's the only one I own. Soon I'll probably have to buy a tie. Growing up can be expensive.

Morgan's Surf and Turf is crowded. This is one of those places the adults visiting the island go on that one night of their vacation when they hire a babysitter or get Grandma and Grandpa to look after the kids.

Morgan's is classy. The napkins here aren't paper and the place-mats don't come with crayons. The waiters and waitresses, even the busboys, all wear black pants and white shirts. Of course, everybody has on a different kind of black pants and a different kind of white shirt, so the uniform is sort of catch-as-catch-can. One dude may have on black Dockers, another black cargo pants, and nobody seems to iron their white shirts, because ironing usually involves steam, and very few folks want to be pumping steam in August. But all in all, the staff at Morgan's Surf and Turf still looks classier than the folks at Rudy Tootie's Root Beer.

I think I'm thinking about this stuff because I'm nervous, standing up front near the bar, waiting for Ceepak, waiting for the chief—my new boss.

My boss. I'm getting The Job.

"Hey, Danny." It's Olivia, dressed in black pants and a white blouse, looking classy, carrying a black-and-gold wire basket of crackers. "What're you doing here?"

Morgan's is not where my buds and I typically hang. We're more the Sand Bar types, a bayside beer joint more famous for its party deck than its food. In fact, Olivia usually joins us over there when her shift ends here.

"I'm meeting Ceepak," I say. "And Chief Baines."

"Wow. The Job?"

"Yeah. Think so."

"Way to go, Danny Boy."

She kisses me on the cheek and hustles off, carrying that basket of cellophane-wrapped crackers to its final destination. They've got Waverly Wafers at Morgan's, not just saltines. Like I said, the place is classy.

"Danny?"

It's Ceepak. He wears a white shirt, gray slacks, and navy blue blazer. He looks like someone who might wave a wand over you at the airport.

"Hey."

"The chief called. Said he might be running a little late."

"Should we wait at the bar?"

Ceepak shakes his head.

I get it. You really don't want to be sitting at the bar, knocking back a few cold ones when the chief of police strolls in to offer you a full-time job on the force.

"Let's see if we can be seated at our table," Ceepak suggests.

"Hi, guys."

It's the hostess.

"Just two?"

"No," says Ceepak. "We'll be three altogether."

"Oh. Well, we can only seat complete parties."

"Of course. We'll wait over here." Ceepak moves to this leatherette bench near the front door. Rules are rules. "Chief Baines should be along soon," he says to the hostess. "He's running a little late."

"Oh. You're with the Baines party?"

"Yes, ma'am."

"Mr. Baines made a reservation."

"Different set of rules?" Ceepak asks.

"Whole different rule book." She grabs a stack of menus. She's pretty and more like Ceepak's age. I think she irons her blouse, too. And—she's wearing a black skirt with black stockings. Very unbeachy. But definitely classy.

"Follow me."

"With pleasure, ma'am," Ceepak says.

Is he flirting? I believe he is. He's certainly smiling. His dimples kick in like crazy and his eyes most definitely twinkle.

The hostess looks at Ceepak over her shoulder, hugs that stack of menus closer to her chest. She dimples back at him.

Okay. This could get interesting.

TEN

I'm Rita," she says after we sit down, taking the cardboard Reserved sign off our table. "I'll be your server tonight."

"I thought you were the hostess," Ceepak says. I'm wondering if he'll march back up front if Rita proves to be a hostess impersonator and, therefore, not properly authorized to seat us at this table.

"I am. I mean, I was. I was covering for Norma."

She gestures toward the front where I see a little old lady in a ruffled white blouse and ankle-length black skirt, her bluish hair sculpted into a stiff bubble. She leans against the sign that says "Please Wait For Hostess To Seat You," trying not to knock it over. When Norma's shuffling people to tables, I bet you do indeed wait a while to be seated.

"Norma had to powder her nose," Rita whispers.

"I see. Nice of you to cover for her."

Rita places menus in front of us.

"I do my best," she says.

"It's all any of us ever *can* do," says Ceepak.

Rita stops. Not only do we not get the whole Welcome-to-Morgan's routine, I think Ceepak just made her forget tonight's catch of the day.

"Would you like some water?" she asks, going with the part of the script easiest to memorize.

"Water would be wonderful."

I figure Rita is thirty, maybe thirty-five. I know Ceepak is thirty-four. Rita has a big swoosh of blond hair that's too long to be in style, looks more like that Farrah Fawcett poster from the '70s, the one they still sell on the boardwalk. Her eyes tell me she's probably somebody's mom because they look tired, maybe even sad. I figure her kid is a teenager. I remember my mom's eyes when my brother and I were teenagers—she looked like we never let her sleep. I also figure Rita is a single mom. Maybe it's the way she looks when Ceepak is polite, like maybe her first guy wasn't so nice.

"Would either of you gentlemen like a cocktail?" she asks.

"No, thank you," I say.

"Not right now," says Ceepak. "Maybe later?"

The way he says it? I swear it sounds like he's asking Rita out on a date.

"Sorry I'm late." It's Chief Baines. "I had to meet with the mayor." He yanks out his chair, sits down.

"Would you care for some water, sir?" Rita asks.

"Sure. Put it in my Scotch." The chief winks at Rita. "You guys order drinks?"

"Just water," I say, letting him know what a good boy I am.

Our host crinkles his brow. "You sure you don't want a beer, Danny? I was going to propose a toast."

"A beer would be good," Ceepak says.

Okay. Twist my arm.

"Sure. I'll have a Bud."

We clink glasses, do our toast, and the chief offers me a full-time job starting Tuesday, the day after Labor Day.

"Of course, we'll want you to take some classes at the community college and some training seminars offered by the state police."

I nod and act like I was already planning on signing up for

Criminology 101 this fall even if I went back to busing tables or working at Wal-Mart or that telemarketing gig with the mortgage broker.

Next, Baines tells me Ceepak has requested that he and I partner up.

"You're lucky. An experienced officer like Ceepak can teach you a lot." Baines tilts his glass in his direction.

"He already has."

And I mean it.

Now it's time to order. Ceepak and the chief go with Morgan's world-famous cheese-covered concoction of lumpy crabmeat swimming in congealed cream sauce the consistency of wet cement, the dish Katie warned me about.

I order the prime rib. I'm sure it'll clog my arteries, too, but I'm only twenty-five, and I figure I have years to repent for such youthful cholesterol sins.

Silverware scrapes across plates. The chief happily demolishes his crab pie and tells us stories about where he used to work. Florida. He asks Ceepak about Iraq, but all Ceepak says is, "It was something."

That's as far as he'll go tonight.

So, we move on to a new topic. Labor Day and the big beach blowout.

"I think we're ready," the chief says. He puts away a huge slug of scotch and water. Licks his lips. "As ready as we'll ever be."

After our main courses, Rita comes by to wonder if we'll be having dessert and coffee.

The chief can't. He has to run. He's got a meeting with some MTV folks at the Sea Spray Hotel. He's looking pretty pleased with himself.

He stands up. So does Ceepak. So do I.

"Rita?" The chief signs the credit card slip. "If these two gentlemen order anything else, just add it on. And make sure you give yourself a nice tip."

"I'm sorry, sir—I can't do that."

"Oh?" The chief flashes her a dazzling grin. I think he uses those Crest Whitestrips.

"I mean—I can't fill in the tip amount. That wouldn't be right."

I think I just heard Ceepak's heart skip a beat, and it has nothing to do with cholesterol-clogged arteries. Sounds like Rita has Ethics, maybe even a Code.

"Why don't you just put what we've had up till now on your charge slip," Ceepak suggests. "Then, if Danny and I order dessert, I'll pick up the tab. I'd like to treat my new partner this evening, as well."

"Fair enough." Baines scribbles some numbers in the boxes on the credit card slip and signs it. Ceepak and Rita smile at each other. I enjoy having everybody else pay for my food and booze.

"Catch you guys tomorrow," Baines says.

"Roger that."

We sit back down. Rita pulls out her pad.

"Can I get you anything else?"

"Danny? How about another beer?"

"Are you having one?"

"Is it possible for one to call a cab should that prove necessary?" Ceepak asks Rita.

"Of course. Another round?"

"No. I'd like a Sambucca."

"Very good, sir." She's impressed.

"And a slice of the Mississippi Mud Pie."

"Excellent choice."

"I'll try that too," I say.

"Would you like a scoop of ice cream on the pie?"

"Of course," Ceepak says. I think he wants to stay here all night. "Chocolate ice cream."

"Try the caramel crunch," Rita whispers. "It's fantastic."

Ceepak smiles. Nods. "Caramel crunch. That'll work."

Rita is writing up our drink and dessert order when T. J. walks into the restaurant. What's he doing here? Shouldn't he be out defacing signs and maiming people with paintball blasts? Now he's wearing a Burger King uniform like he works there, too. He heads straight to our table.

"Mom?" He's talking to Rita.

"Hey. What's wrong?"

"Nothin'. I just forgot my keys."

Rita looks sort of embarrassed to be interrupting our dinner with her personal life. "I'm sorry . . ."

"No problem," says Ceepak.

"I'll get my keys," she says to her son.

"Thanks."

"Did you eat dinner?"

"Half a Whaler."

Rita nods her head toward a small table near the back of the dining room.

"Go sit down. I'll have the kitchen fix you some real food."

Ceepak stands up.

"Is this your son?" he asks.

"Yes. I'm sorry. This is T. J. Thomas James."

Ceepak sticks out his hand. T. J. takes it. They shake.

"I'm John Ceepak. This is my partner, Danny Boyle."

I stand up, shake the kid's hand, wonder whether he's had time to scrub that blue paint out from under his nails.

Ceepak doesn't lie about meeting T. J. earlier. But he doesn't rat him out to his mother, either. Rita beams. She's proud to see her boy being treated like such a man.

"Go grab a seat, hon."

"Okay, mom."

I polish off my second beer and then hit the head. While I'm gone, Rita brings dessert.

When that's done and there's nothing on our plates but Mississippi mud stains, Ceepak calls Rita back to the table so he can order coffee.

T. J.'s at the staff table inhaling a salad and some fried shrimp smothered with ketchup. I can see that his mom makes him drink a glass of milk, too.

Ceepak pays for dessert and the second round of drinks.

"Should I call that cab?" Rita asks.

"Danny?"

"I'm good to go."

Ceepak looks at his watch. It's almost ten P.M. He's been timing my beers. Plus, I've had two cups of coffee. I can see Ceepak's internal calculator doing the math.

"No, thank you, Rita." I guess I made it under the wire. "Everything was wonderful. Best meal I've had since moving to the island. And it was definitely a pleasure meeting you."

Rita blushes. "I hope we'll see you in here you more often."

I can't tell whether she's speaking on behalf of Morgan's or herself.

"I'd like that. Danny?"

"Thank you, ma'am. Everything was great."

"Thank you. Oh—and congratulations on your new job."

"Thanks."

Ceepak and I head toward the front door.

"Danny?"

It's Olivia.

"Yeah?"

"Can you guys hang for a second? The kitchen made key lime pie tonight. It's Jess's favorite."

"Then I definitely need to take him a slice."

"Thanks."

"Is he home?"

"No. Working."

"No problem."

"You want some, too?"

I never say no to cake or pie.

"Totally."

Our buddy Jess is a painter, and in the summer he likes to work at night, while it's cool, while he's not dripping as much as his brush.

"He's at that house on Maple," Olivia says.

"Still?"

"Yeah. Do you guys mind waiting?"

"Not at all," says Ceepak.

"Cool. Thanks."

"We'll hang out front," I say, since we're kind of blocking the flow of traffic near the door.

"Great."

Ceepak and I head outside.

Morgan's parking lot is still full. Their crab pie really is famous. I guess word about how lethal it is just hasn't gotten around.

"Good place," Ceepak says.

"Yeah."

"Top-notch seafood." He fiddles with the loose fiber on the dock rope Morgan's has strung between pier pilings along the walkway to their front door. On top of each post is an antique-looking brass lantern, the kind you'd find on a ship. Some of the pier posts have nets or lobster traps tied off on them. It's all very nautical. In a bogus kind of way.

Ceepak gazes up at the starry sky and the silhouette of the huge water tower across Ocean Avenue. At night, the water tank resembles a Tootsie Pop for King Kong.

"That was nice," I say.

"Great meal."

"No. I mean how you didn't bust T. J. in front of his mom."

"Here you go, guys." Olivia comes out and hands me a white paper bag. I unroll the top to peek inside

"Did you wrap the pie up with foil and make it look like a swan?"

I hear two pops.

Olivia's white shirt explodes with green paint.

The bag flies out of my hands and smacks me in the ribs.

"Down!" Ceepak shouts. He grabs Olivia's shoulders and throws her behind a car.

I hear a third pop. My hair goes sticky.

Ceepak shoves me down behind one of the piers. I see him tuck and roll. I hear a snap and feel a rush of wind zip past my head right before some glass shatters behind me.

That wasn't a paintball.

That was a bullet.

ELEVEN

Stay down!"

Ceepak scrambles across the parking lot, using the cars for cover.

"Olivia?" I grunt.

"Yeah." She doesn't sound so good.

"You okay?"

"Yeah. I think. Yeah."

"Stay down."

"My knees are bleeding."

"Stay down, okay? Stay behind that car." I kind of crawl forward. It's hard to breathe. My lungs ache when they push out against my ribs. I check my shirt. No blood. Just bright yellow-green paint. Pretty soon, I won't have anything left to wear.

I drag myself over to the closest car—a big Lincoln in the handicapped spot up front. There's an empty patch of asphalt with blue stripes for unloading wheelchairs. From here, leaning up against the car, I can cover Olivia and see Ceepak. He's all the way across Ocean Avenue and scaling the chain-link fence surrounding the base of that big water tower. I never thought about the water tower as a potential sniper nest before. Just that giant Tootsie Pop.

I figure Ceepak's back in Iraq. Chasing rooftop shooters, looking for bad guys with rocket-propelled grenades. I look to the left of the water tower. There's a two-story house on the corner. The first floor is a shop. A nail salon. They'll paint palm trees on your fingertips. Upstairs is somebody's house or apartment. They have a deck and a widow's walk on top of the roof. I look north. Another house where the first floor is retail space. That house has a dormer, an extra window pierced into the roofline, turning the attic into a bedroom, or somebody's shooting gallery.

Right across from Morgan's, there's nothing but a fenced-in lot for the base of the water tank. I can't remember if there are ladder rungs welded into the tower. We never climbed up to spray-paint our high school team colors on it like they do in Iowa or wherever. We were too busy drinking beer and surfing.

It's dark, but there's some moonlight. I hear the rattle of fence against pole and see Ceepak clear the curled concertina wire up top with a sideways swing of his legs like he's a gymnast doing that pommel horse deal in the Olympics. Pretty impressive. I hear him land hard on the gravel on the other side.

"That was delicious."

A couple comes out of the restaurant. The man pops wedding mints in his mouth.

"Get back inside! Now! Move!" I scream. I think the guy choked on his mints when I yelled. "Go! Close that door!"

The guy takes a look at me. He looks horrified. I touch my moist head and figure it out: in the dim light of the pier lamps, it must look like my brain is gushing blood.

He makes a move toward me.

I hold up my hand.

"I'm fine. Go back inside, sir. Please. You could get hurt out here."

"Do it," Olivia moans.

The guy swings his head right.

"Ohmigod." He sees the dark wet splotch covering the front of her blouse. Now he must think he's looking at a weeping chest wound, the kind you see in the movies when someone's been blasted with a shotgun at point-blank range.

Our friend finally gets the picture and pushes his wife back toward the door.

"We'll call the police!"

"We are the police," I want to say, but I don't. I go with "Thanks," instead.

I look over to the one lantern that isn't lit anymore. Its glass globe has a spider web cracked into it. The bulb is shattered. Guess that's where the bullet went after it zinged past my ear. I hold my hand up to my ear and touch it. It's wet. I check my palm. Still neon green. Still paint. Still no blood.

"You okay, ma'am?" Ceepak is back, kneeling in front of Olivia.

She's crying.

I'm not used to seeing Olivia cry. She's always been "tougher than the rest," to copy Ceepak and borrow a line from a Springsteen song. Now she's tugging at her soppy blouse, looking at where the exploding paint balloon tore open a middle button and exposed her bra. Ceepak takes off his blazer and drapes it backwards over her like a blanket.

"Thank you," Olivia whispers.

"Danny? Preliminary injury assessment?"

My man cuts through the crap. I guess this is the no-nonsense battlefield talk you use when your buddies are getting blown up all around you in Fallujah.

"I'm okay. Ribs hurt. That's the worst of it."

"Hang in there, partner."

"Roger," I say. "Wilco." I think that means I will cooperate with his request. I will hang in there.

Ceepak duckwalks to the shattered lamp.

"Possible seven-six-two millimeter special ball," he mutters to himself when he sees the shatter pattern in the glass light fixture. The bullet hole in the center of the cracked web isn't very big; in fact, it sort of looks like a hole you'd punch into the top of a mayonnaise jar if you were collecting fireflies.

"Ceepak? We should probably move Olivia inside."

"Roger that. Can you walk?"

"Yeah. But I'd rather run." Now she sounds more like herself.

"Stay low. I've got your back."

They move to Morgan's front door, hunched over, Ceepak covering her back. When they reach the door, he kicks it open so they never miss a stride. As it swings in, I can see that ancient hostess Norma with her hand over her chest like she might need CPR and paddles from the first ambulance to arrive on the scene. There's a whole crowd up near the hostess station. The bartender. A couple of waiters. People clutching doggie bags.

I see Rita. T. J.'s standing next to her. I guess it wasn't him shooting at us this time, not unless he's like The Flash instead of The Phantom and ran real fast from the water tower and got back into the restaurant before anybody even noticed he was gone.

The door glides shut.

"I found this taped to the base of the water tower."

Ceepak holds out what looks like a plastic-laminated Marvel Comics cover, only it's the size of a baseball card. On the card, in blocky orange-fading-to-yellow lettering I can read the word "Avengers." The covergirl is a superhero with flaming red hair and a tight-fitting leotard that makes her boobs look like falling bombshells. Her white-gloved hands are splayed out, like she just lost her grip on the trapeze or she's grabbing for something. Her face indicates that she's pissed.

Ceepak tucks the card inside his shirt pocket after first feeling instinctively for his cargo pants hip pouch, which his dress slacks don't have.

I turn around and see a cop car with twirling roof lights swing into the parking lot off Ocean Avenue. Sea Haven's finest have arrived.

"We need to secure this site," Ceepak says to Mark Malloy and Adam Kiger, the first cops on the scene.

"You got it," Kiger says.

"Roll out the tape," Malloy says. "I'll work the crowd inside."

He heads into the restaurant. Kiger opens the trunk of their cruiser to dig out a roll of yellow "Police Line Do Not Cross" tape.

"More units are on their way," he says. "Chief Baines, too."

I hear our dispatcher squawking from the radio inside the car.

"All available units. Ten twenty-four. Morgan's Surf and Turf."

10-24. Assault.

"This lamp," Ceepak says, pointing to the shattered light fixture. "Lock it down. We might find our bullet."

"Bullet?"

"Affirmative."

Malloy lets that register for a second.

"I'm on it," he says.

"Thanks, Mark." Ceepak turns to me. "Danny?"

"Yes, sir?"

"We need to move you indoors."

"I'm okay. We should go across the street, check out those houses."

"Did you see something in either location, Danny? Barrel flash? Shadow movement?"

"No . . . it's just that . . . I want . . . I mean I have to . . ."

Ceepak looks at me. I see something in his eyes, like he understands. Bad people hiding in the shadows have shot at his friends, too.

"We'll get him, Danny. You have my word." He turns around. "Mark?"

"Yeah?" Malloy stops unrolling yellow tape.

"We need units there and there." He does this three-finger air chop pointing at the two corner houses. "ASAP. I'm taking Danny inside."

I hear sirens, see two more cop cars swing into the lot.

"Come on, Danny. Inside."

"Yeah. Okay."

I clutch my chest. It hurts more than I let Ceepak know, but not as much as seeing my friend Olivia crying like that.

I guess this is what they mean in all those cop movies:

Now it's personal.

TWELVE

Was this a bias incident? A hate crime?" The one asking the question is Penny Jennings. She writes for the *Sea Haven Sandpaper*, our weekly newspaper and fish-wrapper.

Chief Baines doesn't answer. He's busy pacing and rubbing his mustache. Two hours after the incident, we've set up a command center in one of the function rooms Morgan's rents out to private parties. It's where the Rotary Club meets on Mondays—there's a small podium with their Golden Gear seal taped to its front lying in a corner near a stack of booster chairs.

Baines has called in Penny and several of the town's top citizens in an effort to stop any hysteria about "this unfortunate incident" before it gets started.

"If we link the attack tonight to the earlier incident at The Pig's Commitment," our reporter continues, "does that mean our shooter is some sort of white supremacist?"

"You mean because the waitress tonight and Grace Porter are both Negroes?" says Mr. Weese, my mortgage broker buddy. Weese, I've just learned, is chairman of the Chamber of Commerce's Labor Day Celebration Committee, though he seems unlikely to be the one who came up with that Boogaloo BBQ idea. Anyhow, I can tell he wants all this stuff that's not listed in the official program to go away. "That's patently preposterous!"

There are six distinguished citizens here, including Mayor Sinclair, who's dressed in his usual uniform of khakis, polo shirt, and sunglasses draped around his neck with a red Croakie string, even though it's almost midnight. Ceepak, me, and a couple of other boys in blue are here, too—just waiting for the chief to give us our marching orders. Morgan's will provide all the free coffee we want. It figures to be a long night.

Olivia is at the hospital. She wasn't hurt all that badly but Ceepak insisted she go get checked out. She didn't need an ambulance. I called Jess on his cell, and he came and drove her over to Mainland Medical. He'll stay with her all night if they keep her.

"What about the FBI? Should we call them?" Mr. O'Malley asks. Skipper's dad.

Baines ponders this. Paces.

"Can we wait until Tuesday?" Now it's Bruno Mazzilli. He owns half the buildings on the boardwalk. "I've got a shitload of money tied up in this damn MTV thing."

"We all do," says O'Malley.

"Yeah, but I'm talking perishables," says Mazzilli. "Ribs. Chicken. Burgers. Not to mention fifty-gallon drums of cole slaw, baked beans, and potato salad. We call off the damn beach party, I'm not gonna be too happy."

"Get it through your heads," the mayor says, suddenly smelling the twenty-ton gorilla in the room, the giant ape they've all been tiptoeing around. "We *cannot* call the FBI! Not again. Not twice in one summer." Our mayor is also the proud proprietor of a couple of motels, a car wash, and two ice cream shops. He doesn't want G-men scaring people away from his cash registers again the same way they did back in July. "Jesus. This could kill us!" He swipes his finger across his throat to help paint the picture. "We'd never recover!"

The chief stops pacing. He holds up both his hands, palms out.

"Okay. Take it easy, folks. Sea Haven will remain safe, secure, and serene. This is something we can handle ourselves."

The chief is acting like the stalwart sea captain in a bad storm. Everybody else is freaking out, scrambling for lifeboats, and he's keeping his hand steady on the tiller.

The business people nod their heads when they hear what they wanted to hear. They need to believe, so they do. Everything is going to be okay.

Ceepak stands up.

"Ladies and gentlemen," he says, "a rifle was fired at two off-duty police officers and a female civilian this evening." As he recites these cold facts, you can see it send a fresh chill through the assembled dignitaries.

"No need to be melodramatic, Officer Ceepak," says Mr. Weese, the way he probably says it to his wife when she squeals after seeing a bug skitter near her open-toed shoe.

Mazzilli agrees. "You sure it wasn't one of those paintballs or whatever? You sure it was a bullet?"

"I am," I say. "I heard it."

"What? A bullet sounds special?" Mazzilli flaps his hand at me. "How does this kid know it was a bullet? What does Danny Boyle know from bullets?"

"Our officers working the scene have retrieved the slug," Ceepak corrects him flatly. "It's a seven-six-two millimeter special ball cartridge."

"So? What's that supposed to mean?" Mazzilli leans back in his chair and drapes his arms across his gut. "What's this seven-six-two special ball crap?"

"Means it's the same cartridge the United States Army issues to its snipers."

Skipper's dad moans. "The army?"

"So the kid borrowed his dad's hunting rifle and stole some ammo from the army." Bruno waves the air in front of his face like it's all no big deal. "Besides, if you already got the bullet, it's a cinch to catch the guy. I see it on TV all the time. You use your ballistics. It's like a science. So just do the damn ballistics and haul the kid in." He wipes his hands together to signify that's all there is to it.

"Are we sure it's a kid?" A new voice is now heard. Keith Barent Johnson—or KBJ, like it says on the monogrammed hanky he's dabbing across his damp forehead. Mr. Johnson owns a slew of motels, most of which probably have their No Vacancy signs lit up for Labor Day weekend. I know he'd hate to have to flip off that first glowing word.

"Of course it's a kid, you schmuck!" Mazzilli practically screams. "Who else leaves a comic book as his calling card?"

"All right." Chief Baines has heard enough debate. "Here's what we're going to do."

The mayor raises his hand. "You're not gonna call the FBI are you, Buzz?"

Baines shoots an exasperated glance at him. The mayor raises both hands as if to say, "Sorry—I'll shut up now."

Baines turns to Ceepak.

"John?"

"Yes, sir?"

"I want you to intensify your investigation. Make sure you've got something besides circumstantial evidence. We either catch him red-handed or else you need to build a rock-solid case."

"Yes, sir."

"Meanwhile, Santucci and I take charge of securing the boardwalk for the Labor Day event. If you need additional resources, ask."

"I need Boyle."

"He's your partner. If you need him for this, you've got him."

"Yes, sir."

Now the chief turns his attention to me.

"Did you sustain any injuries in the assault?"

"I'm good to go," is all I say.

Fortunately, I was able to clean myself up in Morgan's restroom before the meeting started. I washed most of the paint gunk out of my hair and Rita gave me a souvenir Morgan's Surf and Turf T-shirt with a goofy-looking cow and crab dancing together on the back. When I changed shirts, I noticed I was a little bruised, but nothing serious. The worst part was drying my hair underneath the hot-air hand blower in the bathroom. I had to duck down, punch the button, and let the thing whirr on my scalp about seven different times.

The chief leans on the table, props himself up with his fists.

"Run this thing down, John. I'm counting on you."

"I'd like to call in Dr. McDaniels. State CSI."

Ceepak worked with McDaniels back in July. She's tops in her field—practically wrote the book on forensic investigation techniques. In fact, she did write one. A standard textbook. Ceepak showed it to me. He keeps a copy in the patrol car's glove compartment and another on his nightstand. Variations in blood-splatter patterns make for soothing bedtime reading.

"Call her," the chief says, "but not officially, is all. Understood?"

"Yes, sir."

I think this means Dr. McDaniels can help but only if nobody catches on that she is. Keep it local, keep it quiet. That's the message.

Baines now clears his throat, makes sure he still has everybody's attention. "We need to put a stop to whoever's doing this. Simultaneously, we need to throw a publicity blanket over our efforts. We must not engender panic. We will tell anyone who asks that tonight's incident was the reckless act of juvenile delinquents, the tragic consequence of underage drinking. Penny?" He turns to the local reporter. "Will you work with me on this?"

Since *The Sandpaper* mostly runs front-page stories about walkathons and unicyclists, the closest Penny Jennings has ever come to muckraking was this three-part series on "Cable TV Lineup Under Scrutiny." She'll play along.

"People witnessed the attack," she reminds him.

"Well, keep it vague, then. Just a prank that got out of hand. That kind of thing. No bullets or snipers, okay?"

"Are you issuing a gag order?" she asks.

"No. More like a gag request." He gives her a special smile.

"Well, in that case . . ."

"Thank you. John?"

"Yes, sir?"

"Speedy results are what I'm looking for. Anything you need, call."

"Roger that. Danny?"

Ceepak motions for me to follow him out of the dining room.

"Do that ballistics shit," Mazzilli screams after us. "Works all the time."

We hit the hallway.

"Where to?" I ask.

"Let's swing by my apartment. I need my kit."

His evidence kit. His crime scene tools. His cargo pants.

"Then we need to hit the beach."

"Which one?"

"I believe you called it Tangerine."

THIRTEEN

The Qwick Pick Mini Mart on Ocean Avenue is a cop's paradise. They have a dozen different pots of coffee going at once, everything from Decaf Ginger Espresso to Chocolate Macadamia. They also have Krispy Kreme doughnuts that are supposedly fresh, even at one in the morning, which is what it is now. There's nothing like a chocolate-iced-glazed-with-sprinkles and a cup of hazelnut to jolt you into your second or third wind, especially if you also grab a Mountain Dew from up front, the ice barrel that looks like a big Pepsi can.

We came here after stopping at Ceepak's apartment because I need Advil. My ribs ache. I walk past the aisles filled with Combos and Chex Mix and Taystee Cakes to the one where the individual-serving-size medicine packets dangle on metal pegs. Heartburn, headache, hangover: they've got all the pain bases pretty well covered. I notice Ceepak over in Beach Needs rummaging around in the inflatable balls and sand buckets until he finds a spool of kite string.

At his apartment, he ran upstairs to grab his gear. Five minutes later, he hustled back down the steps in his cargo pants lugging an aluminum attaché case and his Surfmaster II metal detector.

This is what he does on his days off. He takes his metal detector down to the beach and hunts for buried treasure. You know: loose change, Rolexes, pirate booty.

"It helps me sharpen my forensic skills," he says. "I unearth metal objects and attempt to construct a plausible history for them. Every found item has its own story. I try to decipher it."

I hand a twenty to the cashier, get my change, then tear open two packets of Advil, swigging the caplets down with some cold, caffeine-rich Dew.

"All set?" Ceepak asks, paying for his string.

"Yeah. You?"

"Roger that. Let's hit the beach."

We head out the door.

On the way over to Ceepak's, we stopped by the house and left my minivan in the parking lot, taking the Ford Explorer we normally patrol in on the job. We also heard from Kiger and Malloy. They had talked to the folks in both residences on either side of the water tower. Nobody had heard anything. Nobody saw anything. Our guys found nothing. No spent cartridges, no fingerprints, no more trading cards. Our shooter is holding on to his Phantom status.

"You think there's any significance to the comics he's choosing?" I ask as we pull off Ocean onto Tangerine.

"Certainly."

"What?"

"Perhaps he sees himself as some sort of avenger. A mystery man lurking in the shadows, righting past wrongs."

"Not your typical Sea Haven hobby."

"Or"—Ceepak ignores me—"he could just be a kid with too many trading cards he can't sell on eBay. It's too early to connect all the dots."

"So, what are we looking for down on the beach?"

"More dots."

I park at the end of Tangerine where it dead-ends against the dunes. We walk up the sandy slope, past the bench, down to where we had our little bonfire Wednesday night. I carry our digital camera and the aluminum attaché case. Ceepak has his metal detector, the kite string, and whatever else he tucked into his multiple pockets tonight.

"Are we looking for anything in particular?" I ask.

"Thus far, we have three paintball incidents. Here, The Pig's Commitment, Morgan's. Crime scenes one and three are linked by the shooter's calling cards. Hits one and three took place at night and involved glow-in-the-dark paintballs."

"You think there might be more links? Between one and three?"

"Yes. I do."

Ceepak slips on these earmuff-style headphones and flicks on his metal detector. He walks in an expanding circle around the small pit where my crew toasted marshmallows Wednesday night. He widens out with every sweep. I get a little dizzy, watching him march around and around, increasing his circle's diameter in measured increments each time he repeats the sweep. Then, on the thirteenth or fourteenth circle, he finds something. Ceepak switches off the metal detector, kneels on the sand.

"Danny?"

"Yeah?"

"In my attaché case, you'll find a photographer's squeeze-bulb brush. Could you please bring it over here?"

"Sure." I open the case. I quickly see what I think he's looking for. I pull it out of its little foam nook and hustle over to Ceepak.

"Careful," he cautions me.

"Sorry." He's digging a hole in the sand like a kid starting the moat for his castle.

"Do you have your Maglite?"

In fact, no. But I pull out my keyring. I have this tiny Bud Light flashlight hanging off it. I squeeze it and aim its dim beam into Ceepak's pit while he brushes and blows away some sand.

"There it is," he says.

I see the glint of metal. Gold. Copper. The butt end of a bullet.

Ceepak takes the digital camera and snaps some photos. Then, reaching into his hip pocket, he pulls out a pair of tweezers and a paper evidence envelope.

"Seven-six-two millimeter special ball," Ceepak says after examining the bullet. Because it landed in the sand, the tip isn't bent or crushed. It's pointy. Like a pencil or maybe a lipstick. "Note the gliding metal jacket. It is, as you see, boat-tailed."

Okay. Fine. If he says so. I have no idea what boat-tailed means. But I'm sure I'll find out.

"See how the rear is tapered for a tight, targeted flight? This is the preferred cartridge for the army-issue M-14 series as well as the M-21 and M-24 SWS's."

Sniper Weapon Systems.

"You think our shooter's an army guy?"

"It's one possibility." Ceepak marks the spot where he extracted the bullet with this little plastic putt-marker he had stowed in his knee pocket. He looks up toward the road.

"Interesting." Ceepak moves toward the oil drum trash barrel. He leans over and looks inside it.

"Danny? Your flashlight."

I hand him my keyring.

"You squeeze it to make it glow," I explain.

He gets it working and shines it around inside the trash can. Thankfully, there's not much in it besides some empty soda bottles and one disposable diaper.

"Obviously it's been emptied and moved since Wednesday night."

"Yeah," I say. "I think they empty it every day."

"They should. They should also recycle these plastic bottles."

I'm sure Ceepak recycles. I'm sure he separates his number ones and number twos—doesn't let his liquid detergent bottles mingle with his milk jugs.

He flashes my little keychain gizmo against the inside of the barrel. From the outside, I see a pinprick of white. He swings it to the other side; I see another light hole, a little lower.

"Help me here, Danny." Ceepak pulls out the kite string. "Rotate the barrel."

We twist the can so the side with the lower hole is facing Ceepak's putt-marker. Then, he threads the kite string through that hole and out the other.

"Hold that. Right against the hole."

"Okay."

Ceepak lets out a little more kite string and walks backwards. Kneeling down, he pulls the string taut and places it on top of the putt-marker.

"Rotate the can. Two degrees north."

I do.

"A little more."

I comply.

"Excellent. Slide the can toward the street two inches."

"Right."

"Hold the string."

Ceepak tugs. The kite string goes taut. We have a straight line.

"Now, step aside. Good." Ceepak pulls out some kind of chubby ballpoint pen. He lies down on the sand. "Look toward the street, Danny." I turn. "See it?"

There's a small red dot on the back of the bench, right near the edge of the top board. Ceepak's using a laser pointer to recreate the bullet's trajectory. It shoots up from the sand, through the two holes in the trashcan, hits the back of the bench. I'll bet he learned how to do this on one of his TV shows. Anyway, we just more or less confirmed where the sniper was Wednesday night.

"Of course, we can't be certain as to the exact location," Ceepak says. "A lot depends on where the trash can was previously positioned."

"That's pretty close to where it was Wednesday," I say.

"Danny?"

"Yes, sir?"

"Pretty close is never very precise."

"Yeah."

"However, we can confirm the approximate positioning of our shooter."

We have also confirmed that a bullet was fired here Wednesday night. A seven-six-two millimeter special ball cartridge. The same pointy little number I heard whiz past my ear tonight.

"Pop, snap, pop," I mumble.

"Come again?"

"Wednesday night. There were all these pops and then a different sound. More like a snap."

"Was there a long pause between the pops and the snap?"

I feel like a Rice Krispies commercial.

"Maybe. Yeah." I say it mainly because I think that's the answer Ceepak wants to hear. "Yeah, a pause. A slight one. And then the pops started up again."

Ceepak nods.

"The pops and the pause present a new puzzle. Are we dealing with two shooters or a single sniper switching weapon systems?"

"Is that possible? To change rifles that fast?"

"If you're set up to do so. If you're good."

"You could do it? Couldn't you?"

He nods.

I look at the tiny hole the bullet ripped through the trash can, see how it splayed jagged sheet metal edges inward. It's no wonder we didn't see it before. You could fit six on top of a quarter. I can only imagine what would have happened if that same small hole was in my chest. My ribs would probably hurt even worse, but I wouldn't need Extra Strength Advil because I'd also be dead.

"Now what?"

"Tomorrow, we'll have Dr. McDaniels work her magic, confirm the two bullets were fired from the same weapon. I need to call some old friends. Request all potentially useful information regarding sniper training—including known sharpshooters discharged in this area, with a special focus on those who washed out."

That's pretty heavy-duty, I think, but I don't say anything.

"We also need to talk to young T. J. See if he'll confess to the incident at The Pig."

"You don't think he did this?"

"No. I think the paintballing of Grace Porter's sign was a random act of juvenile vandalism."

I just listen. He's not done yet.

"Here and at the restaurant we see a pattern." Ceepak starts enumerating: "Night attacks. Glow-in-the-dark paint balls, the sniper bullets."

"Yeah." I scrape up a chuckle. It's one of those nervous little ones you only produce when you're starting to get totally freaked out with fear. Why do I have a hunch I know where Ceepak's going? I'm not in any hurry to go there with him.

"I believe our shooter fired the glow balls to light up his targets. Make them easier to spot. Then he switched weapons or his accomplice opened fire."

"Yeah."

Ceepak looks at me. His lips are a straight line, his eyes narrow. I'm pretty sure I know what he's going to say next.

"There's one more thing," he says.

"Yeah?" I try to sound like I'm surprised even though I'm not. "Another link? Besides the trading cards?"

"Yes, Danny." He pauses again.

Oh, let's get it over with.

"The target in both episodes," he says. "That's what we're talking about."

"Yeah," I say. "I know."

Me and my friends.

FOURTEEN

Remember how I said the Mad Mouse roller coaster on the boardwalk is so much fun because it makes you feel like you're gonna die every time the little car zips around one of those tight curves?

I take that back.

Thinking you're going to die, thinking it could happen any second, having your life become an out-of-control Mad Mouse isn't that much fun, especially when some of your best friends are crammed into the roller-coaster car with you and you don't know who's manning the controls.

The shooter wants me. Or my friends. Or both.

Why?

You tell me.

"We need to discern motive," Ceepak says as we trudge through the sand and make our way back to Tangerine Street.

"We sure as hell do," I say, not sounding nearly as professional as maybe I should.

"You know, Danny . . ." Ceepak stops walking and looks at me with sincere concern. "I'd understand if you asked to be relieved of this duty. To be temporarily reassigned. Even if you went out on disability with PTSD. Posttraumatic stress disorder."

"You mean it?"

"Certainly."

"You wouldn't think I was a coward if I went home and hid under my bed?"

"Of course not."

"Would *you* do it?"

He doesn't need to answer. I know he wouldn't run away from danger because he didn't, especially not when his buddies needed him most.

I've heard stories about some of the stuff Ceepak did over in Iraq. How he risked his own life to run up an alley under heavy fire and drag a guy to safety—some artillery gunner he didn't even know. That was back in Sadr City, the slummy section of Baghdad where they still liked Saddam. Ceepak saved that soldier's life because to him his duty is about doing more than his duty, if you catch my drift. The army gave Ceepak one of its biggest medals for that one. The Bronze Star, awarded for "heroic service" in combat.

Ceepak never wears any of his medals, of course. He never even talks about them. When he first joined the force here back in the spring, the guys all thought he was kind of a joke on account of his Code. I heard Sergeant Santucci even called Ceepak a special kind of MP—not Military Police, but a "Missy Prissy."

Then some of the guys called their buddies in the army and National Guard. Asked around. They heard the stories. About that rescue in the alley. And the time Ceepak single-handedly held off this ambush out-side Fallujah. Or the one about the unconscious, dehydrated Iraqi kid on a stretcher Ceepak saved with IV fluids because he was the only one who could tell the boy was suffering from heat stroke.

When the guys at the house heard all this stuff, they quit calling Ceepak "Dudley Do-Right" and "Goody Two-Shoes," which is one of those expressions I never understood, since everybody I know, good or bad, usually wears two shoes.

Anyhow, I know what Ceepak does when his buddies are in danger. He does not run away. He does not hide under his bed.

"What I might do in your situation is irrelevant, Danny," Ceepak now says, offering me some wiggle room.

As you may have already guessed, I've never won any medals. Not even at camp. Not even for Popsicle-stick hot-plate making—and I was pretty good at it. I don't have much practice being heroic, acting brave. Bravery for me used to mean chugging a yard of beer on a stomach full of chicken wings while my buddies chanted, "Go, go, go!"

I have to admit, the thought of someone out there who has my pals and me in his sights makes me think maybe I was too quick to dismiss that telemarketing gig with the mortgage broker. But then I'd have to call people during dinnertime, and I guess you have to be pretty brave to do that, too.

I look at Ceepak.

"I might know something that'll help us catch this guy," I say. "And I might be the only one who could possibly know it."

"You might also get yourself killed." He says it grimly. "You're putting yourself in harm's way."

"Hey, that kind of comes with the job, right?"

Ceepak nods.

"Do I get a little sermon about my life being on the line Tuesday during orientation?"

Ceepak smiles.

"Probably not," he says. "Mostly, it's W-2s and medical forms."

"Does our insurance cover bullet wounds?"

"Definitely."

"Then, I'm good to go. Besides, I can't hide under my bed. It's a mess down there. Dust bunnies. Dirty underwear. Dirty magazines."

Ceepak doesn't blink. So I do.

"Come on," I say, leading the way. "We need to get busy."

I figure there's no better way to start my new career. Someone wants to hurt my friends, they have to answer to me.

FIFTEEN

When we reach the street, a guy is standing near our cop car. It's the same one who came out when the ambulance arrived Wednesday night—the potential witness we never interviewed because it was so late. Well, it's almost one A.M. now, here he is, up and walking around.

"More trouble?" he asks.

"No, sir," Ceepak answers. "You live around here?"

The guy gestures over his shoulder to the three-story house on the corner, the one closest to the beach and, therefore, probably the most expensive rental on the block.

"We rent. Two weeks every summer. Always the same place. We have four kids. There's satellite TV."

I can't quite make the connection between the number of kids and the number of digital channels at his disposal.

"I'm a night owl," he says. "When the kids call it quits and the wife sacks out, I watch old movies."

"Yes, sir," Ceepak says. "We didn't stop by Wednesday night because your house was dark."

"Blackout blinds."

"Excuse me?"

"The TV room has blackout blinds. Makes the picture sharper. Room's soundproof, too. Nice in there. Like a movie theater."

Our friend's probably late thirties, early forties. Short. Ferret-faced. He's wearing a T-shirt so I can see he has a wooly patch of hair growing up his back and extremely fuzzy forearms. In fact, he has hair everywhere except, of course, on the top of his head. Up there he's got only a few thin wisps trying desperately to crawl across a vast desert of shiny skin. I peg him to be an accountant.

"Is this a good time to ask you a few questions?"

He checks his watch.

"Sure. *Dirty Harry* doesn't start till one thirty."

"Wednesday night." Ceepak pulls out his notepad.

"The Dirty Dozen."

"Pardon?"

"It was on Turner Classic Movies. Wednesday. You like *The Dirty Dozen*?"

"Sure."

"Hey, what guy doesn't, am I right?"

"On Wednesday—"

"Wednesday was *Beach Blanket Bingo. Animal House*."

"I thought you said it was *The Dirty Dozen*."

"No. I mean those kids down on the beach having some kind of beer blast. I could hear them. Laughing. Listening to loud music."

"You heard them? I thought your television room was soundproof."

"Had to hit the head. Put the movie on pause. We have TiVo, too."

"So why don't you catch these late-night movies during the day?" I ask. I know TiVo. Wish I had it. Watch what you want when you want to watch it. For instance, I could watch *The Simpsons* all day long.

The guy looks my way. "You don't have any kids, am I right?"

"No, sir."

"Just wait. You'll see. They change everything. Kids show up. Your life is basically over. Anyhow, I was on my way to take a whiz and I heard all this rap music. That's illegal, isn't it?"

Ceepak looks confused. "Rap music?"

"No. Beer parties on the beach."

"Yes, sir. Consumption of alcoholic beverages is against posted beach regulations." Ceepak says this without giving me a dirty look. But that doesn't mean he's forgotten it. He's already given me a ticket for that illegal left turn. He probably has a few blank citations left in his pad. Then again, I'm not the guy going around town shooting at people with two rifles. Maybe he'll let me off with a warning.

"Did you notice anything else?" he asks the man.

"You mean when the ambulance came?"

"Or before."

"No. Just that the kids making all the noise parked over there." He points to the spot right in front of the wooden walkway. "That's also illegal. See?" Now he points at the No Parking sign. "I wasn't going to make any big stink about it. It was late."

"When did you see this vehicle?"

"When I went into the kitchen to make more popcorn."

"Did you notice the time?"

"Around midnight."

"You sure about the time?"

"Positive."

"You checked your watch?"

"No. The microwave. It has one of those automatic popcorn buttons but I prefer to enter the time manually to insure proper poppage."

"Because microwave oven temperatures may vary." Ceepak understands. Of course he does. He also follows the instructions—the rules—plainly written on the side of every Orville Redenbacher box.

"Exactly. I can see this no-parking zone from the kitchen window. I guess I should've called you guys. Told you to bring your tow truck. People shouldn't park in no-parking zones."

"Sir, do you happen remember the type of vehicle you saw parked out here?"

"Wednesday?"

"Yes, sir."

"Because people park there all the time even though they're not supposed to. Maybe you guys need a bigger sign or more tow trucks."

"What sort of vehicle was parked there Wednesday night?"

"One of those minivans. I don't know the make or model. They all look pretty much the same to me."

I agree. Try finding one in a mall parking lot. Try finding mine. I never can.

"Do you remember the color?"

"White."

Just like mine. Just like half the vans in Sea Haven.

"Anything else?"

"No. Not really."

"There's one thing," I say.

They turn to look at me, surprised.

"I didn't park there."

"You drive a minivan?" The guy stares at me like I've got a big "L" pasted on my forehead.

"That wasn't your van?" says Ceepak.

"Couldn't be."

"You're certain, Danny?"

"Hey—I'm a cop. I saw the sign. You think I'd do something illegal? Besides, I couldn't afford another ticket."

SIXTEEN

A white minivan?" The chief shakes his head. "Well, that certainly narrows things down, now doesn't it?"

It's close to two A.M. We've set up a war room at the house. It's actually the interrogation room in the back part of the police station, but since we don't have any suspects to chat with right now we're using it as our situation workroom. Ceepak has stuck these big paper sheets on the walls, keeping track of what we know or suspect.

I cringe every time I see "Danny Boyle + Friends = Targets?" scribbled up there in one of the columns.

The chief and Santucci were already here when we came back. They're pulling an all-nighter, going over their Labor Day security plans for about the ten millionth time. I think they even have helicopters flying down for the day. And they're borrowing the airplanes that usually buzz the beach towing banners advertising the New Jersey State Lotto.

"We can't put out an APB for white minivans," the chief says. "They're like seagulls. Too many to count."

"Roger that," says Ceepak. Then he places the plastic sheets holding the shooter's two different "calling cards" on the table in the center of the room. The two recovered bullets are sitting on the table in labeled evidence envelopes next to folders lined with digital photographs detailing the site of each slug. I've never seen so many close-ups of a shattered lamp or a hole in the sand. Some of the photos have black lines and angles drawn on them, like they've been used for geometry homework.

"Did you reach Dr. McDaniels?" the chief asks.

"She'll be here at noon tomorrow to help us make positive matches on the slugs and determine more exact trajectories."

"Nothing official?"

"She understands. I'm also hoping she can give me her opinion on these."

"What about them?" The chief leans down to study the two trading cards.

"They're similar, but different." Ceepak points to the Phantom card. "Here we have a photograph. An actor or model costumed like the comic book hero posing with this woman."

"Is that Lois Lane?" the chief asks.

"No, sir. Lois Lane is a character from the Superman stories. This is the Phantom."

"Well, she's got that Lois Lane look, you know?"

"Note also how she is standing behind the Phantom, peering over his shoulder," says Ceepak. "I wonder if that is psychologically significant."

"Could be," the chief says. "You never know with these nutballs."

So much for sophisticated psychological analysis.

"This second card," Ceepak says, "has a more traditional comic-book look. It appears to be a cover illustration."

The chief peers at it.

"Why is one card an illustration, the other a photograph?" Ceepak asks rhetorically. "I'm hoping Dr. McDaniels might offer a theory."

"Fine. Maybe she can lift some prints off those things, too."

"Possible. But doubtful."

"Yeah. This guy hasn't made a lot of mistakes, has he?"

"They all make mistakes, sir. For instance, he parked in a no-parking zone. But the biggest mistake thus far committed is the violence he and/or his accomplice have perpetrated against our citizens and their property."

"You really think there could be two shooters?"

"It's a possibility."

"Yeah."

It's one of the questions Ceepak listed on the Post-it sheet labeled "Unknowns." We also don't know what kind of sniper rifle he or they used: an M14, M21, M24, or M40A1. The army has a lot of M's."

"So, Boyle," the chief says, "we know who your friends are. Some of them, at least. Now we need to think about your enemies. Who hates you enough to try to kill you?"

It's weird to hear him say it out loud like that, even though I've been asking myself the same question.

"I didn't know I had any enemies." I'm not kidding. I really didn't.

"Anybody spring to mind?" Baines sits down. "Anybody at all?"

Nobody leaps out.

Until yesterday, I thought I had only friends. Lots of them. I grew up in Sea Haven. Lived here my whole life. I've always been kind of laid-back, never too ambitious, never a claw-your-way-to-the-top type. Springsteen tells us, "Everybody wants to be the man at the top." Not me. I'm happy in the middle. That's where the crowd is. And where there's a crowd, there's usually a party.

"Anybody at all?" Baines asks again.

"Well, there was this crazy guy on the boardwalk," I say. "Remember him, Ceepak? The skinny dude in the desert-camo?"

"I remember him."

"Remember how he said he could take us down? Take *me* down? Then there were these college guys at Schooner's Landing."

"What about them?" The chief sounds excited, thinks maybe I'm onto something.

"They were playing rough with this kid in a wheelchair. I intervened. Remember, Ceepak?"

"Yes, Danny. I recall the incident. Thursday afternoon."

"Yeah. Ceepak came by. These guys, and they were huge, like football players, like the whole front line, they told me to watch my back."

"They did?"

Ceepak nods.

Of course, those five New Jersey Giants don't know who I am. They also don't seem to be the sort with attention spans long enough to remember I pissed them off. This sort of logic doesn't slow the chief down. He's happy to finally have a list of possible suspects. He's jotting notes on a legal pad. Whole paragraphs—with circles and arrows.

"These football players. Are they locals? Visitors?"

"I'm not sure. Never saw them before."

"Well we need to find them."

"Then there's the ring toss guy. T. J.'s boss. And Bones—the skinny dude. He was *there*, too. At the Lord of the Rings Toss. He flipped me the finger."

"Slow down." The chief starts scribbling on a second sheet of paper.

"Danny?" Ceepak says it in a soft way that makes the chief look up from his notes.

Ceepak shakes his head.

The chief lays down his pen. "What?"

"The incident on Tangerine Beach took place Wednesday—before we met up with any of these individuals."

"Oh. Yeah."

He's right. I've got nothing.

"Well," the chief says, thinking a moment. "What if crimes one and three aren't linked?"

"They are," I say.

I glance at the two pointy bullets. They look like identical twins, only one's a little more smushed—the one that hit the lamp instead of sand.

"Ceepak's right. It's got to be somebody else."

The chief sighs. Rubs his eyes. "I'm not sure you should remain active on this investigation, Officer Boyle."

"I feel he's safe until tomorrow night," Ceepak says. "Danny's the key to identifying motive, which will, I'm certain, eventually lead us to our perpetrator."

The chief looks me in the eye. "You okay with this, Boyle?"

"Yes, sir."

He checks his watch. "What's your plan for tomorrow, John?"

"It's falling into place, sir. Do my sniper background checks. Work ballistics with Dr. McDaniels. Swing by the boardwalk. Get T. J. to own up to the Pig incident so we can take it off the board. See who else might stick out in the paintball crowd as a sharpshooter-level player. Ask if anyone's been spending an inordinate amount of time at the range honing their skill set. I'd also like to run these trading cards by an expert. Find out where they come from, who sells them, who buys them. I might need logistical support for some of this legwork. There are a lot of questions to ask of quite a few people."

"I'd like to see Katie tomorrow morning," I blurt out.

"Miss Landry?" The chief knows her last name because it's on the Possible Targets list. Danny Boyle. Becca Adkinson. Olivia Chibbs. Jess Garrett. Harley Mook. Katie Landry.

"I think I should warn her."

"No," the chief says. "You can't do that."

"Sir?" It's Ceepak.

"I'm sorry." The chief stands up. "We have to play this thing by the book. No leaks. No dissemination of unsubstantiated information, even perceived threats."

"You want me to pretend like I don't know what's going on?" I ask.

"No. I want you to act in a professional manner, Officer Boyle. We never discuss ongoing investigations except through officially sanctioned channels."

"I think Danny has a duty to tell her the truth," Ceepak says, his back getting stiffer. "She may be in serious danger."

The chief's spine goes ramrod straight, too. "We don't know what the truth is, John. Not yet. We have some evidence. Maybe a theory or two about a military sniper. But what we really have are merely half-truths. Half-truths encourage rumors, rumors incite public panic.

Besides, if your shooter or shooters get wind of what we suspect, he or they may simply skip town in something other than a white minivan."

"We could be putting Danny's friends, all of whom are innocent civilians, in jeopardy." Ceepak refuses to back down. "We should encourage all four individuals to leave town or at least take precautionary measures."

"No. If we blow our chance at catching our perp, we're not really protecting Danny's friends or anybody else, are we?"

What's going on here? Is the chief really doing what's best for the investigation, or is he more concerned about protecting Sea Haven's public image for the Chamber of Commerce types who sign his paycheck?

I can't tell.

"Sir, I'm sorry," Ceepak says, "but this makes no sense to me."

"Listen, I'm simply telling you and Officer Boyle to follow established protocol, as well as the proper chain of command. Am I not making myself clear enough?"

Ceepak takes a minute, then finds his answer.

"Yes, sir."

"Good. Boyle? Talk to Miss Landry in the morning. Let her know you're okay."

"Yes, sir."

"But if you two had any plans for tomorrow night—cancel them."

SEVENTEEN

It's two thirty in the morning when Ceepak tells me to go home.

"Get some sleep. We both need it."

He's right. We won't be much good stumbling around town zombiefied.

"I'll meet you at Schooner's Landing," he says. "When will you be seeing Miss Landry?"

"I guess around eight. She has to open everything up because her boss is taking the day off."

"Then I'll see you around eight thirty. I'd like to talk to T. J. on the early side."

"Too bad you didn't get her number."

"Whose number?"

"His mom. Rita. You don't even know her last name, do you?"

"Lapczynski. She's never been married. Works days at a bank, nights at Morgan's. They live in Avondale."

"On the mainland?"

"The Wilcox Court Apartment complex. Eleven-oh-five Wilcox Boulevard."

"When did you . . . ?"

"While you were in the men's room."

"You old dog."

"See you tomorrow, Danny."

I drive south on Ocean Avenue. My apartment is pretty far from the center of Sea Haven. I guess that's why I can afford it. It's actually an old motel they converted to an apartment complex when the owners realized they wouldn't have to work so hard if their tenants paid by the month instead of the week. Of course, it's not my fantasy version of living in a motel. At the Sea Village apartment complex, we have no ice machine, no cellophane-wrapped toothpaste cups, no free HBO, no nothing. They even filled in the swimming pool and planted shrubs in the hole, most of which have already died. Too much chlorine in the soil, I guess.

There's a twenty-four-hour diner on Ocean Avenue on the way to my place. It's an old-fashioned railroad car set up in a parking lot near Tidewater Street. We're way past the streets named after trees. Down here they just sort of named them after whatever sounded watery.

Anyhow, I'm not really hungry when I reach the diner, but I see Mook's car parked out front. He drives this flashy Mazda Miata, a tight little red convertible with an intercooled turbocharger. I only know this because he tells me. All the time.

His Miata is parked next to a white minivan.

I pull into the otherwise empty parking lot. If I start freaking out every time I see a white minivan, I'll go nutzoid before noon tomorrow. But I figure I should stop because I haven't seen Mook since he flipped me off back on the boardwalk. I know I can't warn him—that would be against the chief's rules. But I can make sure he's okay. He may be an asshole now, but he was my friend first.

The Shore Liner Diner is all silver and chrome outside. Inside, it's done up in about fifty different shades of blue. The booths have blue vinyl seats, the counter stools are baby blue, and the blue walls are covered with bad art—oil paintings by some local artist, with price tags taped to driftwood frames. Still-lifes of pink seashells. Panoramic views of make-believe lighthouses on cliffs near foamy surf. Sickly pastel seaside cottages like the ones that guy Kincaid sells at the mall, only these are even worse. Sometimes, all three artistic ideas are combined and you get pink seashells near a cozy cottage with a lighthouse on the far horizon. I think the painter is related to the Shore Liner's owner. Actually, it might be his wife.

The only people in the diner are Mook and his buddies. I see them crammed into a booth near the back. Six of them. All guys. All laughing and rattling ice cubes around in their big blue Pepsi cups. Mook is the center of attention. I call them his college buddies because most of them are wearing different versions of Mook's business school T-shirt.

Except this one. He's tall and looks strong and has on a gray T-shirt with ARMY printed in block letters across the chest. Ceepak has the same shirt, and this guy is showing the same kind of muscles Ceepak shows when he wears it. I think they all buy the shirt two sizes too small on purpose.

The ARMY guy looks a little older than the rest of Mook's crew, as if he did his hitch, got out, and went to grad school. But he's kept the scary military buzz cut: shaved sides ringing a thick patch on the top of his skull.

"Hey, Mook!"

"Detective Danny!"

When he says that? The other guys get real quiet. Nobody's laughing anymore. They just rattle ice or jab french fries into ketchup pools on their plates. ARMY sizes me up with squinty eyes.

"Where'd you get that dorky shirt?" Mook asks.

I forgot. I'm still wearing the Morgan's Surf and Turf tee Rita gave me when my blue oxford got splattered.

"Morgan's," I say.

"Morgan's? You actually eat there, dude?"

"Tonight I did."

"Jesus, dude. How were the canned green beans?"

"Limp and salty. How you doing?"

"Bored shitless." Mook jiggles his knee up and down like he's had way too much Pepsi. "We're blowing this piece-of-crap tourist trap. Heading south."

"Really?"

"Yeah. Hitting the big A.C."

Atlantic City, about fifty miles south, has legalized gambling and glitzy casinos to do it in.

"I'm definitely up for a little blackjack action," says Mook.

"And some primo pussy," adds one of his pals. "The skanks up here are colder than shit, bro."

"Totally." ARMY agrees.

"A.C. is the place for me," Mook chants, and the guys all knock knuckles, do finger-shakes, and basically run down a hand-flapping ritual I've never seen before. Not that you'd ever catch me doing one.

I'm happy to hear Mook plans to head out of town. That way I won't have to worry about him.

"Well, have fun," I say. "It was cool hanging with you again." Oh, if Ceepak could hear me lying like that, he'd wash my mouth out with Scrubby Bubbles toilet bowl cleanser. "See you next summer."

"What you doin' up so late?" Mook asks.

"Working."

"Fuck, Danny Boy. Here we are, coming up on the real deal. Labor Day weekend. An official, government-approved holiday. Means you don't work."

"Yeah. Well, I gotta run."

"Hey, hang with us. Have a Pepsi."

Mook's knee shakes so much under the table, it rattles the dirty plates and silverware. I wonder how many he's already had tonight, and, in fact, if Pepsi's all he's on. It would be no big news if he and his crew had scored some other stimulants. My guess would be speed— methamphetamine. It's cheaper than Ecstasy, and Mook has always been a little on the tight side.

"No, thanks," I say. "Gotta head home, grab some z's."

"Hey, I saw your boy shoot."

"My boy?"

MAD MOUSE

"Cedric. Sixpack. What the fuck is his name?"

"Ceepak?"

"Yeah. I was tailing you guys. Saw him line up those paintball shots and nail Saddam on the nose. Boom! Boom! Boom!"

"Yeah. He's awesome."

"He's okay. But, my boy?" He nods toward ARMY. "He's better. Hey, tell you what—we can set up a little competition. They could do paintballs or those BB guns where you shoot out the star—hell, we could even do water pistols in clown mouths and pop balloons. What-ever. I'll give you two-to-one odds."

"Maybe next time you guys are in town."

"No. Shit. We should do this thing. It would be better than Atlantic City. This, after all, is a sure thing. I win all your money!"

"I don't think Ceepak—"

"What? Is he like afraid of some serious competition?"

"No. He just doesn't like to show off."

"Oh." Mook leans back in the booth. "Oh. You're saying he's better than my man Rick?"

"Bring it on, dickweed," Rick says, the naked scalp surrounding his little hair carpet burning purple. "Bring it on."

He doesn't know it, but the last thing I want is for Mook to hang around town.

"I'll see you guys later."

I turn to leave.

"Hey, Danny." Mook slides out of the booth to follow me. He drapes his arm around my shoulder like we're still fifteen, still best buddies, which I don't think we ever really were, even back then.

"Walk this way." Mook does that crouching, loping Igor-the-hunchback bit from *Young Frankenstein* like he always does. I let him lead me to this empty table near the front door.

"Why are you so fucking uptight, man? That paintball deal on the beach? That shook you up bad, huh?"

"Some." I hope it's what he wants to hear and that once he hears it he'll leave me alone.

"Look, Detective Danny, maybe somebody was just yanking your crank. Having a little fun."

"Is that right?"

"Sure. If they really wanted to nail you? They would have nailed you, bro. I think they were just, you know—helping you celebrate your new career choice, welcoming you to the wacky world of weaponry or whatever."

"You've got to be kidding."

"Nah, bro. I know a lot of guys who'd think it was pretty funny. Plastering you like that."

"You didn't think it was so funny."

"Hell, they ruined my hat! But, I got over it. Took a chill pill." He mimes popping a tiny tablet in his mouth. "Don't be so skeered, okay, bro?"

"Thanks for the tip, Mook."

"It's all maple syrup."

"What?"

"It's all good. Hey, I've got a line on some awesome shit that'll totally mellow you out, mon." Now he's doing his Jamaican reggae act. "Primo ganga weed."

"I gotta go."

Mook looks insulted.

"So you and Katie?" Mook leans back in his chair, rocks it back on its legs. "Never thought you'd jack my girl, bro."

"Katie Landry?"

"We used to date."

"When?"

"That summer we all met? Katie was with me."

"No, she wasn't."

"Oh yes she was."

"Bullshit."

"Word. Katie is my woman. Always has been. Always will be. She's my forever girl."

"I see. And does Katie know any of this?"

"Oh man, Boyle. That's cold. That's nipply cold."

"Have fun down in Atlantic City." I turn and walk away.

I want to punch Mook. I want to drag him outside and kick him in the ribs. Instead, I take a deep breath. I figure it's what Ceepak would do.

I head out to the parking lot. I swing around the back of the other white van to check out the bumper stickers, to see if I can, indeed, cool down by doing a little impromptu profiling.

The van has to belong to one of Mook's college buddies, since they're the only people in the diner other than the staff, who park out back.

The guy's got a few choice slogans pasted here.

"Screw the Planet, Save Yourself."

"Pave the Rain Forest."

And this other one. Black on gray. All it says is "ARMY."

EIGHTEEN

I go home and try to fall asleep while thinking paranoid thoughts.

What if Mook is behind all this? What if this whole thing is just one of his stupid gags? Some big practical joke that, like all his pranks, isn't funny at all. Did he and his gang orchestrate the hit on the beach? Did they pull the stunt outside Morgan's? Did ARMY miss us with the real bullets on purpose?

Add in the jealousy angle, the fact that Mook believes he once had some romantic claim on Katie, and everything almost fits. He might've been trying to confess, telling me that I didn't need to be "skeered" anymore because he was all done punking me.

Add in the Mountain Dews from the Qwick Pick and Morgan's Mississippi Mud Pie, on top of the prime rib and the beer, plus the fact that it's nearly dawn, and I don't sleep very well.

Which isn't such a big deal since I have to get up less than four hours after crawling into bed.

Seven thirty A.M. Time to go see Katie.

I think of calling Ceepak, letting him know about Mook's ARMY friend, the sharpshooter with the white van.

I strap on my watch.

I'm meeting him in an hour. Ceepak can hear it then.

• • •

A little before eight, the public parking lot next to Schooner's Landing looks full even though the shops don't open for another hour or two. Since it's a long holiday weekend, most of the rental houses and bay-side condos are crammed with extra guests bunked down on floors, flopped on sofas. Unfortunately, cars can't sleep on couches, so the extra ones come here.

I see a lot of white minivans in the lot—at least ten. No surprise there. I see one last parking space. It's a good one. Near the sidewalk. You can see the front door of Salt Water Tammy's from that spot. I want that spot.

So does the woman in the silver Lexus. Her tires screech when she jams on the accelerator to get there a nanosecond before I do.

She smiles. You know, the "Oh, were you planning on parking here, too?" smile.

I wave. The old "No, go ahead, pull in—you beat me fair and square" wave.

I shift into reverse. The great spot was also the last one in the whole lot. Now I'll have to go park around back, near the loading docks, Dumpsters, and service entrances. Maybe I can park behind the candy shop in Salt Water Tammy's spot. After all, Tammy's not coming in to work today. That's why Katie and I are meeting so early in the first place.

I guess Katie came to the same realization. She's already taken her boss's spot.

I see her Toyota parked in the space that says "Reserved." I admit defeat. I go park over at the condo construction site. I find a spot near a bulldozer and start walking the half mile back to where I just was.

Katie Landry is worth it. Every inch. Some people may wonder what I see in Katie—besides, of course, her flaming red hair and hot bod. Well, for one thing, she's sweeter than fifty packets of raw sugar, which is something I know because I did the sugar bit once when I was a busboy. Another guy and I had a contest. He won but we both bused our tables a whole lot faster that day.

Katie also has this playful little bounce in her step, like she can't wait to see what's up ahead, what's next. She's someone to ride the Mad Mouse with, that's for sure. I'll bet she'd just giggle every time that car jigged and jagged her around some scary new curve. I'll bet she'd smile and say let's ride it again.

She's also got that Irish Catholic sense of duty (or guilt) that turns a bunch of us into cops and firemen and teachers and nurses. Katie tells me her best days are when some kindergartner quits crying because she helped him figure out how to stack his blocks so they don't fall down. Her kids call her Miss Katie, and if she ever gets married I'm sure she'll invite her whole class to the wedding. She'll probably serve juice boxes and cookies with the champagne and cake, too.

I reach the parking lot where I wanted to park in the first place. The early morning breeze is flapping the sails on the schooner that gives the mall its name. Manicured shrubs and flower beds glisten in the sun. It's not dappled dew or anything poetic. It's just what's left after the sprinklers spritz the plants first thing every morning. To keep green things alive in our sandy soil you need to hose them down on a regular basis. That's why most of the homes down here have lawns made out of pebbles and rock chips.

Through windows, I see a shopkeeper folding T-shirts, another dusting off his wall of sand-dollar clocks. One lady comes out to hang a banner in front of her shop, those flags people in suburbia fly in front of their McMansions. You know, the leprechaun for St. Patrick's Day, the scarecrow for Halloween, the martini glass for any general-purpose party. The lady finishes unfurling a brown bear banner and sips coffee from a cardboard cup with one of those too-hot-to-handle wrapper things around it. The Sun Coast Coffee Company. Upstairs. Top floor. Coffee is my friend. And Sun Coast is obviously open.

I'll go up there, grab a couple of cups, maybe even a soy latte for Katie, then hustle down to Candyland.

I have a plan.

I must be waking up.

The hike has done me and my foggy brain good.

Now if I can only pull off telling Katie to get the hell out of town without letting her know why.

NINETEEN

Halfway up the first ramp, my cell phone rings. It's Jess.

"How's Olivia?" I ask.

"Holding her own. But the bruises won't be going away for a while."

"Great." I have one, too. It changed colors this morning.

"The doctors say she can go home."

"Awesome."

"You guys catch him?"

"The paintballer?"

"The total jerk who did this."

"We're working on it."

"What does that mean?"

"Our investigation is ongoing."

"What?"

Yeah. I didn't like the way it sounded either. I try again.

"We're still, you know, following up on some leads and stuff."

"So the answer is no?"

"Yeah."

"Was it just another paintball?"

"What?"

"Olivia thought she heard glass shatter. She told me there might have been a bullet or something."

"Like I said, our investigation—"

"Jesus fucking Christ, Danny. How long have we known each other?"

"Long time."

"Jesus fucking Christ, man."

Jess has never talked to me like this before. Then again, one of our friends—the one I think he's falling in love with—was never shot at before either. And, back in the good old days, like last week, I could tell Jess just about anything. Now it's different. The chief says I have to be professional.

"I'm sorry, Jess."

"Tell you what, Danny. If you find whoever did this, call my cell. We're staying on the mainland."

Great! I want to scream. *Stay there! Stay until it's safe.*

"That might be best."

"Yeah."

"I'll call you when we catch him, Jess. I promise. As soon as I know anything definite."

Jess doesn't say anything. I think he hung up before I even said his name.

The phone call carried me up to the top deck. I clip my cell back onto my belt and round the corner.

I freeze.

Harley Mook is sitting at a table downing a tiny cup of espresso under a green umbrella.

"Hey, Detective Danny!"

He's holding his cell phone with one hand and yammering away to someone. With the other hand he's waving like a lunatic to me. Like I won't see him even though he's the only person sitting outside sipping coffee.

"Love the uniform, dude!" Mook's conversation is over just as I

reach his table. I'm wearing my summer cop getup: khaki cargo
shorts, blue polo shirt, and baseball cap with POLICE stitched across
the crown. "Where's your weapon?"

"I'm not authorized to carry a sidearm."

Mook leans back. Surprised to hear me talk like such a cop. I'm
only doing it to help me remember I'm in uniform and, therefore, can't
punch him in his big fat face for insinuating he and Katie were ever a
hot item.

I look at his eyes. They're red-rimmed, bloodshot. It's still last
night to him, but I think his meth has worn off. He must hope a
double espresso can jumpstart his heart.

"Why aren't you on your way to Atlantic City?" I ask.

"Where?"

"You guys said you were going down to A.C. The casinos?"

"Did we?" He yawns. "Oh, you mean at the diner? Yeah. We
thought about it. But, the motel already has my credit card, and they'll
charge me for the whole weekend if I check out."

Mook. Cheap as always.

"So, we decided to stick around. Thought I'd hang with some of my
old school buds."

"I'm busy today."

"Not you, pal. Nothing personal, but you're not that much fun anymore. You've been hanging out with Seedpack too much."

I know he mispronounced Ceepak's name on purpose. I let him.

"Enjoy your coffee," I say and start for the door into Sun Coast.

"You here to see Katie?"

I stop.

"Maybe."

"She works downstairs, right?"

"So?"

Man, we even sound like we're fifteen again. At least I don't add a
"What's it to ya?"

Mook smiles. He knows he's annoying me and he's loving every
second of it.

"Say 'hey' for me." He looks at his watch. "I'm meeting up with this guy from back in the day. Tell you the truth, I never really liked him, but hey . . ."

Maybe the feeling was mutual.

"Sort of a doofus, you know? But he called out of the blue yesterday, said he had that weed I was telling you about. Primo ganga. Jamaican. You ever do Jamaican?"

"Just Red Stripe."

"The beer?"

"Yeah."

"Beer just gives you a gut," says Mook. "Weed? Completely non-fattening. Except for the munchies, of course."

Marijuana. Like the T-shirt says, it's a special kind of stupid.

"Never pictured this dude for a dealer," Mook says. "Wheezer was always more like a loser."

"Enjoy." I head for the door. "See you next summer."

I go inside to order some coffee. For sure I'll see Mook sooner than next August. I'll be seeing him when "Seedpack" and I go ask him a few questions about his ARMY buddy's minivan.

"For me?" Katie unlocks the door and sees the tray with three cups of coffee jammed into the cardboard circles.

"One for you, two for me."

"Great. Let me lock the door." She leans in to twist the key.

"Something smells good." I sniff her hair.

"That's chocolate, Danny. The store is full of it."

"No. Your hair. Smells great."

She laughs and her green eyes sparkle. I take another deep whiff of her hair.

"Rosemary and chamomile organic conditioning," she says. "Enjoy it while you can. In another hour, it'll reek of candy apples."

"Yum."

"Help yourself." She points to a tray where shiny red apples are lined up on a sheet of wax paper. It looks like some kind of Apple Day parade and the flat-bottomed balls are carrying sticks for flags they forgot to sew.

"Maybe later," I say.

"So? How was the big dinner?"

"Did you talk to Olivia?"

"Nope. Was she working last night?"

"Yeah."

"Did you guys get one of her tables?"

"No. Katie . . ."

"What?"

I'm not ready. So, I change the subject. "Hey—were you and Mook ever a couple?"

"Uh, *no.*" She does this funny little puff of air out one side of her lips that sends her bangs floating up above her face like wisps of cotton candy. "I think we played spin the bottle once. In fifth grade or something. I think I had to kiss him."

"You lost, huh?"

"Exactly."

"So you two never . . ."

"Never what?"

"You weren't ever a couple?"

"Me and Mook?"

"What about that summer we all met?"

"Nope. I was hanging with Becca and I think she knew Mook. Maybe *they* were dating. I forget. Becca dated a lot of guys."

"Still does."

"And then we met Olivia in the dressing room at—"

"Teeny's Bikinis!" I know this because it's one of my favorite stories—probably because it involves three topless girls giggling at each other when one of them forgot to slip the little hook in the eye on the half door and the three of them ended up sharing a changing booth. I always figured they became friends because they had nothing left to hide from each other.

"And you knew Jess, who I knew already because he was a

lifeguard." Katie giggles. "Remember how all the girls used to hang out around Jess's chair?"

"Yep. It's why I hung out there, too."

She smiles and goes behind the counter to empty a bag of jelly beans into their Plexiglas bin.

"You want some help?"

"Sure. Thanks"

I move behind the counter and get the gist of it pretty quick. You open a cardboard box, pull out the five-pound plastic bag of whatever, find its bin, pour it in. If the cop thing doesn't work out, here's a possibility.

"Hey, Katie . . ."

"Yeah?"

"Last night . . ."

"It's okay you didn't call."

"Hmmm?"

"I figured you'd call and tell me all about your big night. What happened? Did you and Ceepak hang afterwards, celebrate some more? Is that why you need *two* cups of coffee this morning?"

"No." Moment of truth. "The thing is, we were shot at again last night."

"WHAT?"

Remember—keep it simple.

"Just another . . . you know . . . kid with a paintball gun. Maybe the same guy . . . from the beach."

"Are you okay?"

"Yeah. I'm fine. Just a bruise. Olivia was a little less lucky, though."

"What do you mean? Olivia?"

"She was in the parking lot with me and Ceepak. She took a shot in the ribs."

"Ohmigod."

"Don't worry. Jess took her to the hospital. Mainland Medical."

"Is she okay?"

"Jess says so. Treated and released."

"I should call her."

"Yeah."

"Do you guys know who's doing this stuff?"

"We're working on it but, you see—I'm not supposed to talk about it too much."

"Sure. I understand."

"You do?"

"Yeah. Grab that box there."

"The Junior Mints?"

"Yeah."

Before I bend over, Katie frowns.

"You've got to catch this guy, Danny."

"I know."

"No matter what. I mean it. It's not funny. People shouldn't get their kicks like that, hurting other people."

I try to make her smile.

"We should all play nice." I put it in kindergarten terms.

"Yes. We should."

"Don't worry. We'll get him."

"Good." She surprises me with a kiss on the lips. Mook may have kissed her first, back in the fifth grade, but I doubt little Katie Landry lingered on his lips like big Katie's lingering on mine. It's the sweetest kiss of my whole life, in fact, and not because we're in this candy shop and there's chocolate fumes and sugar dust in the air.

When we're done, Katie looks into my eyes.

"Do your job, okay, Danny?"

"Yes, ma'am."

"I mean it!"

"I will."

"Good." She checks her watch. "Eight twenty-five. I better hustle."

"Okay. Ceepak's meeting me here in, like, five minutes."

She moves some rainbow-colored suckers around on the top of the counter. I rip open another cardboard box.

"Where do these go?"

egenstein

"Second shelf."

I bend down, lift out the plastic bag.

I hear a crack. Cinnamon hearts start to trickle down to the floor behind me. I see their Plexiglas bin has a tiny hole bored in its bottom so it's paying off like a slot machine, raining down a steady stream of red beads.

I look to my left.

Katie's on her back on the floor.

There's a small circle of red seeping through her white blouse like a leaky pocket pen.

"Katie . . ."

I cradle her head.

"Daaa." she can only croak out half my name, the gurgling in her chest cuts off the rest. Her eyes go swimming before they roll up white and flutter shut.

"Hang on, Katie."

I can barely say it.

"Hang on."

TWENTY

I hear knocking on the glass door.

Ceepak. I raise my head above the counter and scream. "Call nine-one-one! Call nine-one-one!"

Ceepak reads my lips and slams his palm against the lock above the doorknob. When the lock won't pop, he slams the door's steel frame with his shoulder. He bounces back and does it again, putting his bulk behind it. I see him wince at the impact but the door flies open.

"She's hit!" I call out.

Ceepak punches the shoulder mic to his walkie-talkie.

"This is Officer Ceepak. Urgently request Medevac helicopter. Schooner's Landing. Saltwater Tammy's. Gunshot wound." He peers over the counter and sees Katie sprawled on the floor, her head cradled in my lap. "Severe chest trauma. Send the helicopter now. Over."

"Ten-four," I hear our dispatcher say. "I'll check with the chief and—"

"Now! Do I make myself clear, over?"

"Roger. But Medevac is state and—"

"Do it. On my say-so. Over."

"Roger. But—"

"Send the chopper, Helen. Send it now."

"Roger. Wilco."

When you ask Ceepak to call 9-1-1, he calls *9-1-1*. He crouches behind the counter, looks at Katie's chest.

"A,B,C,D, Danny," he says. "Make sure her Airway is open." He scoops some pinkish foam and chunky vomit out of Katie's mouth. "Second, monitor Breathing." He bends down to listen to her nose and mouth. "Shallow but steady. Check Circulation." He grabs her wrist and flicks over his watch so he can monitor her pulse. "Weak. Check for any Disability."

"Disability? He fucking shot her!"

"Danny? Focus."

I hear sucking sounds echoing Katie's short, hollow breaths. Every time her chest expands, I hear a gurgling wheeze, like someone's Hoovering the bottom of a milkshake.

"Is there any Saran Wrap in the shop?" Ceepak asks. "Perhaps a plastic bag?" Ceepak tears open Katie's blouse. I see blood has seeped into and stained the bottom of her left bra cup. The one over her heart. "Danny? We need a sheet of plastic. ASAP."

Ceepak pumps Katie's chest.

"Any plastic will do."

I pull the half-empty bag of Junior Mints out of its box, dump the chocolates on the floor, hand Ceepak the plastic bag.

"That'll work. See if you can secure some tape."

"Tape."

"Roger that." He keeps pressing down on Katie's chest at regular, rhythmic intervals. In between pumps, he spreads and smooths the plastic bag over her chest wound.

I head for where I see a stack of foldable white boxes near a candy scale. There's a roll of "Saltwater Tammy's" cellophane sealing tape.

"Exhale, Katie." Ceepak waits for her to expel a breath. "That a girl." He stretches the plastic sheet taut over the bullet hole. "Tape. Three long pieces." He extends his right hand like a surgeon calling for a scalpel. My hands shake but I'm able to rip three pieces off the roll using my teeth. Ceepak tapes down three sides of the bag. "We need to leave one corner open to create a makeshift flutter valve," he says after securing the plastic to Katie's bloody chest. "We don't want air becoming trapped in the chest cavity."

He leans in close to Katie's ear.

"Help is on the way," he says, lightly stroking damp hair out of Katie's eyes. "Help is on the way."

I sink back on my haunches. Scared. But I know: help has already arrived.

A helicopter landing at the entrance to Schooner's Landing wasn't listed on the schedule of "Special Labor Day Weekend Events," so the noisy arrival of the whirlybird draws a crowd when it touches down. Paper cups and napkins and newspaper sheets scatter like grass clippings in the wake of an enormous leaf blower.

Ceepak and I run beside the gurney as they wheel Katie out. We move into the air wash under the blades. The EMTs have strapped an oxygen mask over her nose and mouth. IV bags dangle off poles welded onto the sides of the rolling stretcher. The helicopter is thumping and whumping so I can't hear everything Ceepak's saying to the paramedics, but it sounds like he's giving them a rundown of Katie's vital signs. They give Ceepak the thumbs up and slide Katie into the chopper.

"Danny? Go!" Ceepak tilts his head to tell me to climb in and ride in the helicopter with Katie.

But I remember what Katie said: *"Do your job."*

"No," I yell to Ceepak. "I can do more here."

Ceepak slaps the side of the chopper.

"Go!" he yells to the pilot and, hunched over, we trot away as the helicopter lifts off, swoops south, banks west, and zooms across the bay.

"She'll be at Mainland Medical in under five," Ceepak says. "The trauma team is standing by at the ER and will be fully briefed by the incoming EMTs."

"Good. Thanks."

"We need to notify her family."

"She . . . doesn't have any. Her parents are both dead."

Ceepak nods.

"She's strong, Danny."

"Yeah."

"Real strong."

"Yeah."

"John?" It's Chief Baines. "Inside." He does a quick head tilt toward the candy shop. "Now!"

TWENTY-ONE

I thought you said this guy only attacked at night?"

"Yes, sir. Until this morning."

The chief looks flustered. Ceepak looks like his mind is twirling as fast as those helicopter blades. The shooter just changed the rules of the game. Ceepak needs to adjust. Anticipate the next move.

"And why the hell did you call in the chopper? The state police are going to start asking questions. Medevac is state!"

"I assessed field conditions and determined the airlift to be the most prudent course of action given the severity of the situation."

"Jesus, John. You could've called an ambulance. Or isn't an ambulance dramatic enough for you?"

"Drama did not enter into the equation, sir."

"Well, what the hell *were* you thinking?"

"Sir, holiday weekend traffic patterns suggest the causeway will be gridlocked at this time on a Saturday morning. Even with an ambulance's siren, flashing lights, and a bridge full of cooperative motorists, the land route would have taken too long. We are in what search-and-rescue teams call 'the golden hour.' How quickly Ms. Landry receives thorough medical attention will determine her chances for survival."

Jesus. *Survival?*

"I see," Baines says, sucking in a deep breath. "Okay. Okay. Good call, John. Good call."

I hear brakes squeal outside and see the police department's flatbed truck pull up in front of Tammy's. It's the truck we use to haul parade barricades and detour signs and stuff like that around town. There are six guys in the back with a tall stack of full plywood sheets. The guys lower the tailgate and slide off the first twelve-foot panel. I see the cop in charge pointing to Saltwater Tammy's plate-glass windows, one of which now sports two bullet holes. One for me. One for Katie. The guys outside will seal off the scene of the crime. Hide it from public view. Keep what happened in here a big, fat secret.

"We need to keep the evidence chain clean for Dr. McDaniels," Chief Baines explains to Ceepak when the crew leans the first sheet of plywood against the plate glass windows. "Need to discourage the looky-lous from congregating outside, contaminating the crime scene."

"Right," Ceepak says. I don't think he's even listening to the chief. I think he's thinking, working the mission. I also think Chief Baines may have his own mission. He wants to stop anybody from guessing what really happened in here before he has a chance to spin the story the way he wants it to go.

"The shooter has undoubtedly fled the scene," Ceepak says. "We need to immediately canvass all potential sniper sites." He does his three-finger hand-chop in the direction of all the possible locations.

Tammy's is situated in a valley shadowed by the shopping center's three-tiered boardwalk, the fake lighthouse up on the third floor, and the crow's nest atop that schooner's mast. Plus, there's a water slide across the street and about a hundred balconies being built onto condos across the parking lot at that construction site. Potential sniper sites, all.

"You think he left another calling card?" the chief now asks.

"Yes, sir. Unless he's changed that part of his M.O., too."

"Mook was upstairs," I say.

"Come again?" Ceepak says.

"Who the hell is Mook?" The chief is a step or two behind.

"Mook did this." I have everybody's attention now. "Him and his friends. He was upstairs at the coffee shop. He has a buddy who's ex-army with a white minivan. A sharpshooter."

The chief jams his hands against his hips. "How do you—?"

"Last night," I interrupt the chief. I'm probably not supposed to do that but I'm new on the job. "I ran into Harley Mook at the diner. He's someone I know. He said his friend was a better shot than Ceepak. Mr. Mook also gave some indication he was jealous about the nature of my relationship with Ms. Landry." I'm trying my best to say it like Ceepak would say it.

"Where did you see him, Danny?" Ceepak asks. "Where was he this morning?"

"Sun Coast Coffee. Upstairs."

I point out the front window. I never had any reason before to notice that you can see the tops of Sun Coast's caf, umbrellas from down here, that Saltwater Tammy's was a stone's throw away from the coffee shop upstairs.

A stone or a bullet—take your pick.

Ceepak and I walk purposefully up the boardwalk ramps to the third level. Other cops are scouting all the other possible sniper locations. We're only walking when we'd rather run because the chief specifically ordered us not to run, not to draw any "undue attention" to ourselves.

"Where was he?" Ceepak asks.

"Over there. That table. Closest to the door."

I notice Ceepak's eyes scanning the horizon. I do the same. Mook is long gone.

"Was the other one here?" Ceepak asks. "His soldier friend?"

"No. Not that I saw."

We reach the café table and do a quick visual survey of the scene. No plastic-wrapped trading cards. Ceepak feels around underneath the table.

Stops.

"What's wrong?"

"I forgot to put on my gloves."

Ceepak pulls his hands out from under the table, reaches into his cargo pants, pulls out a pair of white evidence gloves, slips them over his hands, and goes back to work, patting under the bottom of the circular table.

He finds something, drops to his knees, fishes out his tweezers. He peels whatever it is from the underside of the table.

"Baseball card." Ceepak shows me his tweezered treasure. "Derek Jeter. New York Yankees."

"Excuse me? Officers?"

We look over. It's this guy wearing a chef's apron and bow tie. He has colorful buttons pinned up and down his apron straps. I recognize the costume. It's what the waiters wear at The Chowder Pot. I check out their outdoor dining deck. If you kneeled behind the wooden railing, you'd have another clean shot down at Saltwater Tammy's windows.

"I was setting up tables on the deck, and I think somebody might've lost this. Sorry it's wet. The sprinklers must've hit it this morning." He holds another baseball card with water beads dotting its plastic sleeve. "It's Jeter's rookie card. 1996. Could be pretty valuable. Figure I better turn it in."

"Thank you, sir." Ceepak uses his tweezers to take it from him. "Thank you for doing the right thing. This card might prove very valuable, indeed."

TWENTY-TWO

Thirty minutes later, the municipal brain trust from the Sea Haven Chamber of Commerce and the mayor's office is assembled inside Saltwater Tammy's.

Good thing the candy shop has bright fluorescent bulbs. Because the plywood walls the police crew propped against the windows have totally blocked out any natural light. Two cops are posted in front of the makeshift door—a sheet of plywood that wasn't screwgunned into place with all the others. Tammy won't be very happy when she sees what we've done with her place.

Mazzilli is behind the counter. He helps himself to free malted milk balls. Mayor Sinclair is next to him nibbling nervously on a foot-long gummi worm, taking it in a centimeter at a time, like Bugs Bunny working his way down a carrot. I'd write them both up for shoplifting, but we're kind of busy.

"I still feel we can safely assume no immediate threat to the general population," Baines says, mostly to hear himself say it.

"You're right," Mazzilli says and pops another malted milk ball in his mouth. "It's some kind of vendetta against one young man and his friends." He points at me. There's melted chocolate smeared all over his fingers.

"He's right," says Mr. Weese, the mortgage broker. "We can't risk everything we've worked for all year long to protect one individual. Sorry, son."

Yeah, as long as your kids and grandkids are safe, who cares about everybody else?

"Boyle here is a professional," Chief Baines says. "He understands that this town cannot and will not be held hostage by terrorists."

Baines is strutting again. His flop sweat is gone. Somebody must've brought him a fresh shirt from the office. It also looks like he nipped into Tammy's washroom and slicked down his hair after a refreshing head dunk in the sink.

"Officer Ceepak and his team will continue their investigation. Right, John?" Baines doesn't give Ceepak time to answer. "Meanwhile, we'll tell anybody who asks that what happened here this morning was the work of intoxicated college students armed with BB guns."

BB guns, my ass.

We found another one of those special ball cartridges buried in the cinnamon-hearts tub. It had been meant for me, but I'd just happened to duck down to open a crate of candy when it whizzed past. The good news? Ceepak says the hole in the window coupled with the hole in the Plexiglas Red Hots tub will enable us to calculate a pretty precise trajectory. Two points make a straight line, he reminded me.

Dr. McDaniels is also on her way. She'll probably point out something we don't see, probably something that's right under our noses.

Ceepak has been working his phone. I told him what Mook told me this morning: that he'd been paying for his Sea Haven stay with a credit card. Ceepak just asked our computer people back at the house to track Mook's recent transactions and tell us which motel.

Other calls are also going out from headquarters to sporting goods stores and eBay on account of all the Derek Jeter baseball cards. So far, we have seven, one Jeter taped in almost every possible sniper location. Upstairs at the coffee shop and The Chowder Pot, across the street at the water slide, on top of the schooner mast—the Derek

Jeters were everywhere. The ones near any kind of shrubbery were wet, spritzed by sprinklers.

"Our doer placed them prior to six A.M.," Ceepak concludes. He's talked to some maintenance people and found out when Schooner's Landing automatically flips on the waterworks every morning. "The hydration moves across the mall in a series of contiguous zones. Each zone is sprayed for an interval of ten to twelve minutes. The timers initiate the spraying cycle at five A.M., complete it at six-oh-two."

The wet cards were in place before 6:02 A.M. Mook must've pulled an all-nighter.

And all of the Derek Jeter cards are from his first year with the New York Yankees, 1996.

"This one's worth twenty-five, thirty bucks," Mazzilli tells us when he sees the card the waiter found at The Chowder Pot. It shows Jeter, his eyes squinting in the Bronx sun, chasing some kind of pop fly. "That's a Select Certified Blue."

Bruno knows his "memorabilia." In his shops up and down the board-walk he peddles postcards, collectible foam beer Koozies, fake street signs that say stuff like "Parking For Italian Americans Only," and T-shirts featuring "The Man," with an arrow pointing up at your face, and "The Legend," with another arrow pointing down at your pants.

He also sells this one totally creepy tin sign I just now remembered. It's printed to look bullet-dinged, like a highway sign on some rural road where farmers take target practice. It says: "If you can read this, you're in range."

Sort of sums up my whole weekend.

I'm thinking about this stuff so I'll stop thinking about Katie and the preliminary reports from the hospital.

They say the bullet tore through her left lung, tumbled, then per-forated some kind of pulmonary vein and broke a rib when it exited out the back of her chest. It might've nicked her spinal cord on the way out, too.

They don't know if she'll make it.

Katie might die.

BB guns, my ass.

We found her bullet buried in the shelf behind where she was standing when we kissed. It was the same kind of bullet as mine, like some kind of "his and her" matching ammo set. An M-118 7.62 millimeter special ball cartridge. The same as all of them. The kind of bullet the army gives its snipers, guys like Mook's pal Rick, guys who drive white minivans with ARMY stickers plastered on their bumpers.

Ceepak puts his hand on my shoulder.

"Denise thinks she'll have a credit card hit in under five."

Denise Diego is our top computer geek back at headquarters. She's awesome. Works in the dimly lit room next to Dispatch, hovers over her keyboard, fries her eyes staring at the flat screen until she finds what she's searching for. She's a super cybersleuth, an excellent indoor detective. She'll find Mook's motel.

Ceepak goes back to the baseball cards.

"What do you make of all the Jeters?" I ask.

"The shooter is playing with us, Danny. Having fun. He knows we now know his M.O., so he placed the baseball cards in every conceivable sniper location prior to actually targeting you at eight twenty-six hours."

"Why Jeter? Why a baseball player? What about the Phantom and the Avenger? Why not more comic book stuff?"

"I'm not certain at this juncture."

My sense is he's angry with himself for not knowing the answer.

"I saw Mook real early this morning at the diner," I say. "Two or two-thirty A.M."

"He could've placed the cards any time before six A.M. Even before you saw him at the diner."

"Yeah. And playing with us? Rubbing our noses in how brilliant he is?"

"Yes?"

"That's Mook. He's a first-class smart-ass."

"Folks?" Chief Baines wants everybody's attention. "I'm heading out front to talk to the tourists." He exhales, straightens his jacket, and eyeballs the mayor. "You people hang back here. I don't want a big crowd. Don't want them seeing you, Mr. Mayor."

"I'm good in here," Mayor Sinclair says. He's found the Jelly Bellys.

Chief Baines tugs down on the brim of his dress-white hat. He looks like the skipper on *Gilligan's Island*. He slides outside to talk to the tourists.

I walk over to the windows and stare at the grain pattern in the plywood. There's nothing to see, but I have to hear this.

"Folks? How is everybody doing this morning? Another beautiful day, huh?" I can't see him, but I know Baines is flashing his shark-white teeth, probably blinding someone. "As you might've heard, we had an incident here this morning. Couple college kids with a BB gun thought it might be fun to shoot out some store windows. An employee was injured."

Her name is Katie!

"She's been airlifted to the hospital. She's going to be fine. But say a prayer for her, okay? She'd appreciate it. So would I."

The crowd murmurs some. They'll all pray. Right after they finish eating their cinnamon buns and bear claws.

"Folks, what we have here is a prime example of what can happen when we ignore the rampant problem of underage drinking—which, in my short tenure, I've already identified as Sea Haven's public enemy number one."

Unless, of course, you count the sniper.

"Some intoxicated teens stumbled over here this morning on their way home from an all-night keg party and took a couple pot shots with their pellet pistols. Don't worry, we'll catch them, you have my word. Meanwhile, we're cracking down. I call on all beverage distributors to ID everyone under the age of thirty. If you won't do it, guess what? We will. We'll give any unlawful drinkers we catch a prize: a free ride in a police car!"

The crowd chuckles.

"This weekend, we are putting plainclothes officers in package stores up and down the island. We're patrolling the popular bars and nightclubs. We'll be working the beach. We can and must put an end to this problem and keep Sea Haven safe for wholesome family fun!"

The crowd applauds.

Buzz Baines is good. He has turned my near-death experience and Katie's critical-condition chest wound into a pep rally against the evils of teen drinking. He does it so well, I almost believe him, even though I know he's lying every time his mustache wiggles up and down. That's the thing about a lie—you make it big enough, say it loud enough, repeat it over and over, it starts sounding like the truth. Hell, by now, Baines probably even believes it. He may really think some freshman with a six-pack also scored M118 special ball cartridges with his fake ID at Fritzie's Package Store and jammed them into his BB gun. Undoubtedly Fritzie's sells the bullets right next to the Slim Jims, or maybe over in the racks with the pork rinds, beer nuts, and rocket-propelled grenades.

Baines can get away with this because his bosses, the Concerned Citizens who run Sea Haven, are mostly concerned with their bottom lines, about making enough money this summer to make it through to another one next year. The one reporter who knows the truth, our resident journalist, won't tell anybody what she knows because her newspaper sold a ton of ads for its special Labor Day Weekend Edition. Huge ads. Some restaurants even bought two and three full pages to run their entire menus, to lure Labor Day visitors with the promise of Early Bird Specials and two dozen choices starting at $7.99.

I guess I wouldn't be so upset by all this chicanery and skullduggery—two words I learned from Ceepak—except that I just found the gift Katie planned to surprise me with so we could celebrate my new job.

It's in a square white box tucked on the shelf right underneath the cash register. I see my name written with pink marker on the outside. Katie's loopy handwriting. She drew a cartoon cop car on one side of the box, a sheriff's star on another.

I open the box.

She had somebody in the candy kitchen mold me a chocolate baseball cap and write POLICE on front with curly white icing.

My cop cap. Wow.

Katie was so proud I got the job, that I was becoming a cop, that I was willing to put my life on the line to protect people like wheelchair Jimmy from the bullies, that I'd be out there every day trying to do what was right.

"Danny?"

Ceepak taps me on the shoulder.

"What's up?" I ask.

Ceepak smiles.

"Denise got him. Smuggler's Cove Motel. Mr. Mook used his MasterCard."

TWENTY-THREE

I t's a five-block run from Schooner's Landing to Smuggler's Cove.

I see a sheet rolling out of the little dot-matrix printer we have up front in the patrol car. We now have a hard copy of Mook's driver's license and his plate number. I hear officers radioing in with possible white van sightings. The guys out here on the street? They're working the case. They're not hiding behind plywood walls covering their asses.

Ceepak is driving real slow because he doesn't want to draw any undue attention to our approach—not because the chief said so but because he doesn't want Mook to hear us coming. So he's doing the posted 25 mph.

The speed limit signs are new on Bayside Boulevard and say stuff like "25 mph: Yes, Your Car Can Actually Go That Slow." The new signs were Buzz Baines's idea. Tough but friendly. Like a barroom bouncer who still remembers to smile at kittens and puppies when they pop by for a brewski.

Mook's motel, Smuggler's Cove, is one of Sea Haven's seedier establishments. It's tucked off Bayside Boulevard on a side street. Typically, they rent out the same bed several times a day, if you catch my drift. Sometimes they even change the sheets. If you like those *Girls Gone Wild* videos, they sell them in the Smuggler's Cove gift shop. (Everybody has a gift shop in Sea Haven, even our low-rent rendezvous motel.)

"Do you see his car?" Ceepak asks.

"No."

The motel parking lot is one of those pothole-filled numbers with heaving humps of cracked asphalt creating random speed bumps every two feet.

"This is twelve," Ceepak says into the radio microphone. "We're ten-eighty-four." He means we're on the scene. I climb out of the car, realizing I have at least eighty-three more 10-codes to memorize by Tuesday.

Ceepak and I step into the filthy lobby and squint because it's so dark, what with the pink scarves draped over all the lamps to help set the mood. The place reeks of incense, the kind they sell on sidewalks. A string of little bells jangles when the door glides shut.

"Be right with you," says a woman from somewhere behind the check-in counter. I hear her groan, like she's having a hard time standing up. "Hang on!" Now she grunts.

The lobby walls are decorated with porn posters. *Debbie Does Dallas. The Devil in Miss Jones. Candy Stripers.* The classics.

"Danny!"

Emerging behind the front desk is Donna Pazzarini, my friend Tony's big sister. By big, I mean older as well as huge. She weighs at least three hundred pounds so, all of a sudden, the grunting and groaning I heard make sense. Donna's the kind of girl who typically needs a forklift to help her up out of her chair.

"How you doin', Donna?"

"Good, good. You?"

"Can't complain."

"Good, good." She's dusting doughnut sugar off her enormous chest and eyeing Ceepak. "Well, hello handsome." She tugs up on one of her black bra straps and tucks it back under her sleeveless blouse. "What can I do for you boys?"

"We're looking for someone," I say.

"They're usually here—the ones people are lookin' for. You're with the cops now, right, Danny?"

"Yeah."

"That's what Tony says. I said, 'Good for Danny,' you know what I'm saying?"

"We need to inquire about one of your guests," Ceepak says.

"Short-term or long-term?" Donna lets loose with this rumbling laugh—part belly shaker, part smoker's cough. "We have a lot of 'guests' who don't stick around for the free breakfast buffet, you know what I'm saying?" She gestures to a sour-smelling Mr. Coffee machine on the windowsill next to a half-empty box of Dunkin' Donuts.

"His name is Harley Mook," I say.

"Sure, sure. Mook. He was here. But he checked out."

Donna wobbles back around to the other side of the counter, taps the keyboard. I figure she's calling up room records. Instead, I see her slide a King around on a solitaire spread. I guess she was playing with one hand, juggling a doughnut with the other.

"When?" Ceepak asks. "When did Mr. Mook vacate these premises?"

"Little while ago," says Donna. "Around nine thirty. Seemed like he was in a big hurry all of a sudden. Acting all antsy, you know what I mean?"

"What room was he in?"

Donna squints at her computer screen. I can tell she doesn't like the idea of closing her card game to open whatever program tells her who was in what room.

"Usually, we don't mind when our guests check out early," she says, clicking and sliding more cards around the screen. "But seeing how this is a holiday weekend I told Mook he had to pay for tonight even if he didn't stay. He gave me a little attitude but, like I said, he seemed eager to leave. Had ants in his pants."

Ceepak drums his fingers on the counter. "What room?"

"The maid hasn't cleaned it yet. I've been kind of busy." She rumbles out another laugh. Her upper arms jiggle.

"Ma'am?"

"Give me a second." She finishes her final pile. Smiles at her tidy row of kings. "Okay. Here we go." She taps a couple of keys and calls up her room records. "Mook was in two-oh-seven. Upstairs."

"You got a passkey?" I ask.

"Why? You guys want to search his room or something?"

"Yes, ma'am," says Ceepak. "We surely do."

"Wait a sec." Donna crosses her arms over her chest. "Isn't that like against the law? You need a warrant, am I right?"

"No, ma'am," says Ceepak. "Since Mr. Harley Mook has checked out, any property, record, or information he may have left behind is considered abandoned and, therefore, not subject to the Fourth Amendment protections provided by the Constitution."

Donna purses out her lower lip. Nods. She's impressed. "Interesting. You go to night school or something?"

"The key?"

"Sure, sure." Donna reaches under her tiny desk and finds a miniature baseball bat with a key dangling off the handle.

Ceepak takes it. "Upstairs?"

"Yeah. Two-oh-seven. Second floor. Seventh door down."

"Thanks, Donna."

"Any time, Danny."

We hustle toward the door.

We pass the ratty Coke machine, reach the staircase, clank up the rusty metal steps, and hurry down the crackled concrete landing to 207.

Ceepak works the passkey into the lock. The door squeaks open and we're hit with a wall of recirculated air that stinks of cigarettes mixed with mildew. The air conditioner is rattling away underneath a window darkened by thick, plastic-based drapes. The room is a mess. The sheets and flabby pillows are clumped in a tangled bundle in the middle of the bed. Back in the bathroom, I can see a pile of soppy towels lying in a puddle near the shower stall. There's a Domino's pizza box feeding flies on top ot the TV. Judging by the color of what used to be cheese, I'd say the pie's been sitting there since at least Thursday.

Ceepak spies a pink slip of paper wedged under a half-empty beer bottle on a small table with a wrinkled walnut veneer. The pink beer coaster is actually one of those "While You Were Out" phone message deals.

"Apparently," says Ceepak, "someone named Wheezer called Mr. Mook at eight forty-five A.M. The woman downstairs must've given him this message when he returned from Schooner's Landing this morning. Prior to his decision to check out."

"Wheezer is Mook's local drug connection," I say. "The guy with the 'good ganga.' "

"The front desk did not record the caller's number. However, there is a note: 'He'll call your cell.' "

Ceepak secures the pink slip in an evidence envelope and moves toward the rumpled bed. He tilts his head to study a notepad near the telephone on the bedside table. Now he reaches into his cargo pants and pulls out a stubby carpenter's pencil. Okay, even I know this one: he's going to rub the pencil on the empty sheet of paper and see if he can pick up whatever was written on the sheet that used to be on top.

"Wheezer, again," Ceepak says after he's done dusting the pad with pencil lead. "Noon. Circled. I suspect twelve P.M. is the time Mook and Wheezer agreed to meet in some undisclosed location for the drug buy. Mook will most likely drive there."

"In his little red Miata."

"Roger that," Ceepak says. "Red Miatas are much easier to spot than white minivans." He tucks the small sheet of motel notepad paper into a second evidence envelope. "We'll definitely nab him."

"Great."

We're going to catch the creep. Just like I promised Katie.

"Danny?"

"Yeah?"

"Since we seem to have some time . . ."

Ceepak has this look on his face.

"What's on your mind?" I ask.

"The lady downstairs. She's a friend, I take it?"

"Donna Pazzarini? Yeah. Well, I mean I know her on account of her brother. Tony. We worked together at a gas station one summer."

"I'd like to offer an observation."

"Sure."

"Everywhere we go, you know people. In fact, you have more friends than anyone I've ever met."

"Maybe. Of course, I grew up here. Plus, I'm just, you know, sociable, I guess. Friendly."

"Here then is my question: with all these friends, why is our shooter only singling out certain individuals? Why not Ms. Pazzarini downstairs? Why not her brother or your former colleagues at the Pancake Palace? Why not that girl you know over at the ice cream shop? Why is the sniper only targeting the people you were with Wednesday night?"

I wonder.

Why Becca, Katie, Olivia, Jess, and me? Especially if the bad guy is Mook. What'd we ever do to him?

"Good question," I say to Ceepak.

"It's *the* question, Danny. The only one we really need to answer."

"Okay. Let me think about it."

"Think hard, Danny. Think fast."

I nod. "You want to search the room?"

"No. We'll ask Kiger and Malloy to swing by." He checks his watch. "I want us mobile prior to noon. I suspect someone will spot Mook's Miata before he connects with his dealer. In the meantime, let's stop by the house, pick up the Phantom and Avenger cards. Dr. McDaniels will definitely want to see those."

I'm about to follow Ceepak out the door when he takes a detour to the window air-conditioner unit. Using the eraser end of his pencil, he pushes down on the button to turn the humming monster off.

"You should always set the thermostat to seventy-five or higher when out of your residence for an extended period of time. Especially during peak hours of consumption."

Right.

It's suddenly quiet, now that the sour-air recirculator is shut down. I hear a vehicle bump and crunch its bottom across the blacktop humps down in the parking lot. I step out on the crappy veranda to see if it's Mook's Miata.

It's a white minivan.

I guess the driver sees us, too—sees we're cops.

He's peeling wheels in reverse, burning rubber and taking off like maybe he just did something really, really bad.

TWENTY-FOUR

The white van is out of the parking lot before I can spot its bumper sticker display, see if there's an ARMY plastered back there.

"Male driver," Ceepak announces as he dashes down the balcony toward the stairs.

"What else?" I ask, running behind him. "Did it look like an army guy?"

"Couldn't tell. Sun glare."

Ceepak grabs one of the railings and slide-flies down the steps. I try to do the same thing. Rust chunks scrape my palms.

"He's at the corner," Ceepak says. "Turning onto Sunshine, direction Ocean."

"Great. That gives us a chance!" Traffic. You want to stay off Ocean Avenue on any summer Saturday because it's basically bumper-to-bumper from nine A.M. on.

We leap into the Explorer. Ceepak snatches the radio mic.

"This is Unit Twelve. Request all available backup. Ten-eighty. White van. We are in pursuit."

Those asphalt humps in the Smuggler's Cove parking lot feel more like moguls on a ski slope the way Ceepak blasts over them, slamming pedal to rubber floorpad. When we first started working together, Ceepak didn't drive on account of this horrible thing that happened in his Hummer back in Iraq. Now I see the man has driving skills, like the army sent him to Aggressive Driving School or he studied with the stunt guys who drove the Mini Coopers in that movie *The Italian Job*. We're barreling down this quiet residential street nobody's ever barreled down before and I see the minivan screech into a right turn. We do the same thing.

"This is Twelve," Ceepak says into the mic. "We are southbound on Sunshine, approaching Oak."

Make that Pine. We're moving fast and the streets are just clipping along.

"Unit Twelve, this is Six. We're approaching on Spruce."

Ceepak flicks on the lightbar and sirens. No way the white van doesn't see us coming up behind him, no way he doesn't hear us, no way he can't tell we're the Police and he should slow down, pull over, and stop—*now*.

But he doesn't, he keeps racing down the road, pushing his soccer-mom van to do 70 mph. If nothing else, he's earning himself a speeding ticket today.

And one for reckless driving, too, because he just hung an incredible tilting Louie—both his right-side tires lift off the pavement. Ours do the same thing when Ceepak mirrors the move and hangs a hard left.

"This is Twelve. Suspect vehicle is now *east* on Quince heading toward Ocean."

There's a stop sign at Ocean Avenue.

Mr. White Van doesn't stop, earning him traffic ticket number three.

Tires squeal. Cars rock. The van shoots across the intersection. At least he gets everybody on Ocean Avenue to stop for us. We reach Ocean and zoom across because nobody's blocking our path.

Except this one little girl on the other side of the intersection.

Ceepak slams on the brakes.

Maybe she's deaf. Didn't hear the police siren. Maybe she's blind.

Didn't see the swirling lights. Whatever. Right now, this seven-year-old sweetie-pie in a pink sundress is in the crosswalk standing behind her baby doll stroller.

Her parents run into the street and grab her. Boy, does the kid give us a dirty look—like we should know that when the sign says "WALK," she and her dolly have the right-of-way.

Ceepak nods, smiles, and gestures for the little girl to proceed.

"She has the light," he says.

"He's getting away," I say while we wait.

Up ahead, I see the white van making another left turn, this time on Shore Drive, which will take him north, back toward town.

"Ceepak? He's going to get away!"

"No he's not, Danny." Ceepak slams our Ford into reverse. The tires whine and spin and I smell fried rubber. We might need retreads before the morning's over. We whip backwards onto Ocean Avenue.

"This is Twelve," he says to the radio. "Suspect has turned north on Shore. We will attempt to cut him off at Ocean and Maple."

Okay. Now I get it. Ceepak's been studying his Sea Haven street maps. He knows Shore Drive dead-ends when it hits Maple because that's where Sunnyside Playland is and they're spread out for two blocks from Ocean Avenue down to the Beach. You can't go very far on Shore before you have to head back up to Ocean.

"We've got Maple blocked on the other side of Ocean," says a voice I don't recognize over the radio.

"This is Six. We are continuing down Spruce to Shore and will block his retreat."

"Ten-four," Ceepak says. He's got the radio mic in one hand and the other one is twisting back and forth on the steering wheel as we wiggle our way up Ocean Avenue, snaking around cars, zigzagging past RVs, generally having a grand old time putting the Explorer through its paces like we're in one of those TV commercials talking about rack-and-pinion steering, which, I hope, is something that comes standard on Fords, especially the ones that leave Detroit and grow up to become police cars.

We near the corner of Ocean and Maple. I hear what I think is a foghorn until I look over and see there's this fire truck straddling the far side of Maple, blocking the street. Guess that's who radioed in earlier. The fire department must've been mobile when all the radio chatter started and dropped by to help. They're blaring their air horn and making so much noise that most vehicles on Ocean Avenue have pulled over to the shoulder of the road so the drivers can cover their ears and cringe. This gives Ceepak and me our own express lane right up the center yellow line.

The minivan shoots up Maple, slams on its brakes when it sees the fire truck blocking its path, and skids into a sharp right turn in front of us.

I can see the bumper very clearly now.

"No ARMY sticker," I shout. "It's not my guy."

"Roger that."

So, naturally, I expect our little chase scene to be over.

I, of course, am wrong.

Ceepak presses down harder on the gas, and now we're, I swear, two inches from the van in front of us. I can read his window decals. Somebody apparently went to Dartmouth. They have a parking permit for a garage. The tiny little decal says they're number 3246. Like I said, we're that close.

Whump.

We're closer.

Ceepak thumps the guy's bumper.

Mr. White Minivan must not have felt our little love tap. He doesn't slow down or pull over.

I make out two people in the minivan. The driver, who looks to be somebody's dad, mid-forties or early fifties. And the passenger. Female. Younger. A mop of wiry, curly hair bouncing up and down.

Whump.

I guess this is why they call them bumpers. We bump the van again, nudging it forward, sending me bouncing.

"Seat belt?" *Now* Ceepak asks.

"Ten-four." I strapped myself in back at Smuggler's Cove. It's instinct when Ceepak's behind the wheel.

"Hang on."

He's done with the love taps. He eases up on the gas for a second. When the space between bumpers widens, he jams back down on the accelerator, twists the steering wheel. We slam into the van's rear end at a slight angle and send the vehicle spinning into a spiraling skid.

Of course the road ahead of the van is clear. Ceepak wouldn't have made his move if it wasn't.

Now the van makes *its* move—sliding off the road, scooting backwards, careering into the parking lot of Barnacle Bob's Beach Bikes, this hut of a shop where they rent all kinds of bikes and have about a hundred of them lined up in their parking lot. The white van slams into one end! The whole row dominoes down in a rippling wave. One hundred beach bikes lay wounded on their sides, sparkling in the sun.

The van has finally stopped.

"Call in our location." Ceepak tosses me the radio mic.

He's out the door, gun drawn.

"This is Twelve," I say. "Our twenty is Barnacle Bob's Beach Bikes. Ocean and Jacaranda. Uh, possible ten . . . ten . . . uh—I think we might need an ambulance."

I *really* gotta memorize those 10-codes by Tuesday.

I hop out in time to see a girl stumble out of the van. She's wearing some kind of Victoria's Secret swimsuit. She's basically naked except for her stiletto heel sandals. One stiletto must've snapped off because she's limping. Her face is hidden, covered with a tangle of wild curly hair.

Ceepak gets the driver to spread-eagle on the ground. White hair. Fancy Rolex watch. Maybe he's the girl's father.

"Hands behind your back," Ceepak barks. "Now."

"You could've killed me," the guy whimpers into the hot blacktop.

"Now!" Ceepak orders.

"You drive like a fucking maniac!"

"Only when forced to do so, sir." Ceepak slips a pair of plastic cuffs on the guy's hands. He tugs them snug but not nearly as snug as I would after some idiot almost made me run over a little kid in a crosswalk pushing her dolly's stroller. I do a quick visual inspection of the minivan interior. I see juice boxes and sippy cups on the floor. Scattered Disney DVDs. The idiot kissing asphalt is somebody's dad. I don't think the woman who stumbled out the side door is his wife. I think we caught them sneaking off to Smuggler's Cove—and not just to buy videos in the gift shop.

"Danny?" It's the female. Of course she recognizes me. Like Ceepak said, I know just about everybody on the island.

"Marny?"

"Hey." She pulls the curls out of her eyes and tries to smile and fluff her hair. She can't do it with her usual flip and flair because some stray hair strands are glued to her lip with blood.

"You okay?"

"I think so." She tugs on a bikini strap and looks down at her cocoa-brown breasts to see if anything got punctured or jostled out of alignment.

"Who's your friend?"

"Stan. Stan Something."

"Okay."

"I swear I didn't know he was mental . . . driving like that."

"Unh-hunh."

"He's from out of town. We kind of hooked up last night and this morning . . . you know . . ."

"Right."

"Hey, Danny? Guess what?"

Marny does this little finger wiggle suggesting I come closer so she can whisper her big secret in my ear. She does this, I know, so I will be forced to stare directly at her gravity-defying breasts and, therefore, be much more likely to believe anything she tells me.

"What?"

"He's rich," she gushes, her breath reeking of orange juice and champagne. "Really, really, really rich."

"Cool." I try not to be too judgmental. Especially since Marny has that bloody lip.

She leans on my arm for balance so she can slide her broken-heeled sandal back on her left foot. "I think he might be married, too." She holds her finger to her lips to shush me because she thinks it's a big secret.

"You okay?" I ask again.

"Yeah. I think I bit my lip." She shivers, and goosebumps pop up all over her body.

"Hang on, Marny. I've got a jacket in the car. Some Band-Aids, too."

"Thanks, Danny." She gives up on her sandal and sits down on the pavement.

I go to the car to get my navy blue windbreaker. Ceepak is stuffing the driver into our back seat. The guy looks scared. Yeah. His life and wife are flashing in front of his eyes.

"He's not Mook's buddy," I say. "He's not the guy."

"Oh, yes, he is," Ceepak says. "He's the guy who needlessly endangered several lives by attempting to evade a police officer."

Yeah. Okay. He's *that* guy.

"Ceepak?" I don't recognize the voice now squawking across our radio. "Ceepak? Come in. Am I pushing the right button?"

"Danny? Can you handle that?"

"Ten-four." I say, repeating the one code I know I know.

I reach for the radio. The lady keeps squawking. "Listen," she says, not using any kind of code, "when you boys get done playing Smokey and the Bandit, we have some bullet holes we should talk about. Over."

"Tell her we're on our way," Ceepak says.

I'm confused. "Okay. Who is it?"

"Dr. McDaniels. Who else?"

TWENTY-FIVE

The state's top crime scene investigator, Dr. Sandra McDaniels, is waiting for us back at Saltwater Tammy's, so we hand Marny off to the paramedics.

They seem happy to have caught this call instead of making another run to a motel bathtub to help a grandmother who's fallen and can't get up. When we left, I noticed that one of the EMTs was kindly helping Marny reexamine her bikini'd breasts in the back of the ambulance. He was holding his flashlight. She was searching for silicone leaks.

We dumped Stan, the white minivan man, back at the house. The desk sergeant, Gus Davis, said he'd handle the paper work and "book the cheap, cheating bastard." Gus says stuff like that. He's old. He's grumpy. He's spent too much time in the sun.

We park on the walkway outside Saltwater Tammy's plywood-covered windows. The chief pulls me aside to give me an update: Katie's still unconscious, still on the operating table. He says they're sewing her back up. Closing up the bullet hole in her chest and the exit wound out her back.

When he tells me the news, I don't think about punctured lungs and nicked spinal cords.

I think about freckles.

The ones splattered across Katie's chest. In the summer, in the sun, her freckles blossom and creep across her skin like clover flowers popping up in a weedy field. I used to tease her about them. One game was to connect a few with my finger and make freckle constellations. The dog. The cat. The guy with the bow and arrow and six-pack. The Greeks never saw that one. I saw it right below her collarbone, right above where her halter top usually stopped.

Katie always giggled when I connected her dots. Partly because my fingertip tickled. Partly because she thought my made-up myth about the Greek hunter hoisting his six-pack to appease the gods of beer and pretzels was funny.

After the chief gives me the update, he gives me a bulletproof vest. Actually, as Ceepak reminds me, it's a bullet-*resistant* vest. Ceepak also tells me that the vests don't help much with rifle rounds.

"So why wear it?" I ask, when I feel how heavy it is.

"Let's take what precautions we can," Ceepak suggests. "The layers of Kevlar could catch the bullet and spread its momentum over a larger portion of your body, deforming the round and, hopefully, bringing it to a stop before it can penetrate your skin."

Before it can rip a hole in my lung and nick my spine.

"Put on the vest, Boyle," the chief says, smiling over my shoulder at the small cluster of shoppers surprised to see cop cars parked outside the boarded-over candy shop. "Put it on, or I'm putting you on administrative leave." He says all this through a huge smile, in case any tourists are looking our way.

I start peeling off my polo shirt.

"Inside!" the chief says before I finish working the shirt up over my head. "Inside."

Through the knit holes in my shirt I see his smile go so wide and toothy he might split his cheeks. He pushes me into the store. Since we're telling everybody in town that Katie had been "injured" by a BB gun fired by a rowdy gang of underage drinkers, I can't be seen in public putting on a flak jacket. You don't slip on a bulletproof vest because you're afraid of BBs.

Inside, with my shirt up over my head, I hear this little voice.

"You need to do more crunches," she says. "Need to tighten up those abs, Mr. Boyle. You're looking a little flabby."

It's Dr. McDaniels, the CSI whiz, examining my physical evidence.

"Dr. McDaniels," I hear Ceepak say. "Good to see you again."

"You can't see me," she says. "I'm not officially here, remember?"

"Yes, ma'am."

Dr. McDaniels is pushing sixty and doesn't take guff from anybody. She probably thinks the whole "keep-it-a-secret" deal is stupid. And she'd be right, too.

"I can't wait until we actually work together," she says to Ceepak.

"Me, too."

"Don't tell my husband I snuck down to meet you. Let's make that another one of our little secrets."

"Yes, ma'am."

"Dr. McDaniels?" says Chief Baines. "Thank you so much for coming down on such short notice. We need you to wrap this thing up ASAP."

Wrap it up? ASAP?

He acts like we're in total control of the situation here, that if we work a little harder, move a little faster, we should have the case cracked before the first rack of ribs hits the barbecue pit Monday morning.

"And John?"

"Yes, sir?"

"I need *you* to start using your brain. I do not need you racing up and down the street chasing the wrong minivan, scaring pedestrians, and endangering motorists!"

Ouch. That's gotta hurt. Ceepak doesn't say anything. Neither does the chief or anybody else for a couple of seconds.

"Okay, John?"

"Yes, sir."

"Good. I'm heading back to the house. Sandy, if you need anything, give me a holler. Pleasure to meet you."

"Pleasure to meet you, too," says Dr. McDaniels.

She says it, but I can tell she doesn't mean it. McDaniels and Ceepak worked together back in July when she helped us on the Tilt-A-Whirl case. I don't think she's keen on anybody suggesting Ceepak's not doing his job the way it should be done.

"Santucci? Let's roll." The chief and his sidekick leave.

I finally yank the shirt off my head. I almost take my nose and ears off with it.

"Here we go, Danny." Ceepak holds out the bulletproof, I mean bullet-*resistant*, vest. He drapes the Kevlar shield over my head and shoulders and works the Velcro side straps into place. I feel like a horse being saddled. The vest is hot, the day humid. Maybe I'll sweat my beer gut away. Maybe I can go on late-night TV with an infomercial and hawk my new Sauna Suit: "Lose the pounds, not your life!"

"Sorry about your lady friend," McDaniels says when I'm all bundled up. This I can tell she means. She has the map of Ireland written on her face just like Katie, only Dr. McD's map has more roads wrinkled into it. "Hang in there, kiddo."

She moves over to the glass display case filled with chocolates and candy.

"We've worked out the trajectory." McDaniels gestures to some bright-yellow yarn strung between the plate-glass windows and the bullet holes behind the counter. "Two points make a straight line," she says, echoing what Ceepak said earlier. "Works every time."

McDaniels is a tiny woman. Spry. She flits around like Tinkerbell. She's wearing cargo shorts that show off her matchstick-skinny legs and knobby knees. She's also wearing a Hawaiian-style shirt with Tabasco bottles printed all over it.

"For precision, we concentrated on the bullet that missed Mr. Boyle." She points to the hole in the cinnamon hearts tub. "We matched it to the corresponding hole in the window. This, of course, gave us an uninterrupted firing line."

Uninterrupted. My bullet didn't get knocked off course, didn't tumble around inside my chest the way Katie's did.

I see McDaniels has brought along two associates, two state CSI technicians who came in on Saturday, maybe their day off, because Sandy McDaniels asked them to. Both guys are wearing shorts and T-shirts. Tabasco sauce T-shirts. I guess it's a Casual Saturday theme with the state CSI team, the Tabasco collection. I wonder if they own the hot-pepper boxer shorts. I do, but I didn't wear mine today. I didn't get the memo about Casual Saturday.

Ceepak does one of this three-finger points toward the window. "Have you run the line outside?"

"Your chief wouldn't let us," McDaniels says. "He was afraid we might invite unwanted scrutiny and questions."

"I see." Ceepak sounds disappointed.

"So we used the laser," one of the CSI guys says.

"That'll work." Ceepak's happy again. "Find anything?"

"Not much," McDaniels says. "The line took us to an empty parking spot. The only one in the whole lot. Section D."

"Near the Dolphin sign," says the taller CSI guy.

They mark the parking lot here with alphabetical signs to help you find your car. You know: Alligator, Blowfish, Clown Fish, Dolphin, Eel. I think they stole the idea from Disney World.

"The parking lot?" Ceepak's ruminating again. "Fascinating."

"Of course, the line continued."

"Yeah," the other CSI guy says, "all the way to nothing—an empty patch of sky between the condos and the water slide."

"So, we figure it was a park and shoot," McDaniels says. "And the guy was tidy. No shell casings."

The parking lot.

I would have figured the sniper took aim from one of the elevated locations surrounding Saltwater Tammy's. Some place high like where we found all the baseball cards.

"That scenario also seems to fit with your prior crime scenes," McDaniels says. "The first attack on the beach."

"Roger," says Ceepak. "We suspect those shots came from the street."

"Where the cars park," I add.

"Crime scene number two." McDaniels opens a bin and carefully helps herself to a single Jelly Belly. "Morgan's Surf and Turf restaurant."

"Outside," Ceepak says. "The parking lot."

"Either there or across the street—beneath that water tower or in the driveway of one of those houses. I think he likes to park, then squeeze off his shots." She pops the Jelly Belly into her mouth. "Hmm. Fascinating."

"What?" Ceepak asks.

"It really does taste like Dr Pepper. How do they do that?"

"Chemicals?" I suggest.

"Forget I asked." She pops another Jelly Belly.

"I suspect the weapon is an army-issue M-24," Ceepak says.

McDaniels nods her head. "Also sold as the Remington 700 hunting rifle."

"Accurate to eight hundred meters."

"Bolt action."

These two could sing duets.

"Uses the M118 special ball cartridge."

"Calculating the angle of the line coming out the window, projecting it across the parking space, I put the shooter at approximately six and a half to seven feet off the ground," McDaniels says.

"He's a tall guy?" I ask.

"Or he props his rifle on top of something that tall," McDaniels says.

"Six and a half feet," Ceepak says. "The height of a standard minivan."

"Right." McDaniels rubs her spiky white hair. "I suspect the shooter parks, waits, props his bipod on the vehicle's roof to steady his shot, squeezes off his rounds. Same with the paintball weapon."

"If he's getting out of his minivan with a rifle or two, why didn't somebody see him?" I ask.

"Maybe somebody did," McDaniels says.

"Doubtful," Ceepak says. "Two hits were at night. The other first thing this morning."

McDaniels agrees. "He could pop off his two shots, open the hatchback, toss in the weapon, and look like he got here early for hot 'n' fresh cinnamon buns."

"The night shoots were more complicated," Ceepak says. "Might be a team of snipers. One man on the glow-in-the-dark paintballs, another on the M-24."

I speak up. "I saw about ten white vans in the parking lot this morning."

"And," McDaniels says, with that leprechaun twinkle in her eye again, "Chief Baines tells me you two just ran down another one."

"Wrong vehicle," Ceepak says.

"So why'd the driver take you on such a merry little ride?"

I field this one. "The girl in the van young enough to be the driver's daughter?"

Dr. McDaniels frowns. "Let me guess—she wasn't?"

"Yeah."

"Figures. Men. You just can't handle us more mature gals, can you?" McDaniels's eyes twinkle. "Come on." She gestures to her two guys to scoop up the seven Derek Jeter baseball cards. "I need to see the rest of your card collection. I hear it's a doozy."

TWENTY-SIX

Sea Haven has been steadily filling up.

Every motel we pass on the way to police headquarters has the "NO" neon lit up next to the "VACANCY."

It's a little after 11:30 A.M. We know Mook is meeting his dealer at noon. We don't know where, but you can bet every cop car, fire truck, street sweeper, and meter maid is on the lookout for his little red convertible.

Ceepak flipped on the radio when we climbed into the car. Not the police radio. The radio radio. Sometimes the music helps him think.

They're playing an obscure Springsteen song that happens to be one of my favorites. I just didn't want to hear it today: *Red Headed Woman*. Mrs. Springsteen? She's a redhead like Katie.

> *Tight skirt, strawberry hair*
> *Tell me what you've got baby, waiting under there*
> *Big green eyes that look like, son*
> *They can see every cheap thing that you ever done*

The part about the eyes? That's Katie.

Well I don't care how many girls you've dated, man,
But you ain't lived till you've had your tires rotated
By a red headed woman

I'm smiling. Not about getting my tires rotated. It's because The Boss adds:

Well brunettes are fine, and blondes are fun,
But when it comes to getting the dirty job done,
I'll take a red headed woman.

Me, too. They're feisty, those redheads. They don't give up easy. Katie will pull through. I know it. So does The Boss.

"That's Bruce Springsteen," the deejay chatters when the song ends. It's my buddy Cliff—The Skeeter. He plays the sound of this annoying mosquito whine whenever he says his name. Skeeter. *"Hey—maybe The Boss will bop by the boardwalk on Monday—"*

Ceepak snaps off the FM box.

"Let's hope Bruce will decide not to join us," Ceepak says.

"Yeah. Then we'd have *two* million people on the beach instead of just one."

"Actually, given the presence of MTV, the chief estimates attendance might reach fifty thousand."

"Wow."

Ceepak shakes his head. I know what he's thinking: fifty thousand folks clumped together on the beach and boardwalk unless the chief shuts down the big show.

Fifty thousand targets.

We pull into the parking lot outside the police station. Dr. McDaniels and the two CSI guys are behind us in a government-issue Taurus.

"The evidence is inside," Ceepak says when everybody crawls out of the sedan.

"Good," McDaniels says, squinting in the white-hot sun. "If you stored it out here, it would melt."

We head into the house.

In the lobby, above the gumball machine, we have this bulletin board. There are a couple of FBI wanted posters stapled to it, just in case any international terrorists decide to drop by Sea Haven for a little R&R. There's also this "Summer Safety Tips" poster with a fish riding a bicycle and wearing his helmet.

My favorite item on the board? This thank-you note from the kids in Miss Simmons's second grade class. According to the letter, which is scrawled with red crayon on blue-lined paper, the best part of their recent tour was getting locked inside our jail cell.

My favorite part of the letter?

The school the kids go to: Holy Innocents—just like everybody who's ever set foot inside one of our jail cells. They all swear they're innocent.

I grew up Catholic and did time at Holy Innocents Elementary myself. All in all, it was a great school. But I remember we had one of the world's oldest nuns come teach us religion on Wednesday afternoons. I think she was retired in a rest home on the island and the school let her drop by now and then to lend a hand. I also think she might have been senile. I know for certain she was crazy scary. First, she wore the old-fashioned black-on-white habit you don't see much any more. And she wore it in September when the thermometer was still hitting 80 and 90.

One time, when we were studying our Catechism for First Holy Communion, she told us this story about our souls and how they were big jugs of milk and every time we sinned it was like dribbling black ink drops into white milk. When we went to Confession, said our Act Of Contrition, and were absolved of our sins by the priest in the booth, most of the black ink would be washed away.

Most of it, but never all.

Since we had sinned, our soul would never be as good as new, no matter how much Good Works Brand Bleach we poured in, no matter how many Hail Marys we said. Our milk jugs were forever stained like gym socks your mom can't make come clean.

We walk past grumpy Gus Davis at the front counter and troop into the interrogation room, currently known as our command center.

Dr. McDaniels moves to the wall and studies the two trading cards pinned there in plastic sleeves. The Phantom. The Avengers.

She taps the comic book cover card with her pen.

"These things are huge."

She's studying the superhero lady's chest. I guess everybody's eyes go there first.

She moves down the wall to the Phantom card.

"I remember that movie," she says.

"Excuse me?" Ceepak is interested. "A movie?"

"Yeah. That's Billy Zane. He played the Phantom. The girl behind him? She's, you know, that actress. What's-her-name."

"Interesting," Ceepak says.

"Yeah. It was pretty good. As a boy, the Phantom sees these pirates murder his father, and then he falls overboard and washes up on this beach near the jungle and swears an oath of vengeance to fight pirates and injustice . . . you know . . . the usual."

"Interesting," Ceepak says again and moves closer to the wall so he can stare at the two cards. "Then the Phantom is tied to The Avengers by the common theme of Revenge."

"Maybe so. Very powerful motive, revenge." McDaniels looks at me. "Were you ever a pirate, Mr. Boyle?"

"No."

"Didn't think so. These things are never that easy. The two cards have another common link: the lead characters are wearing tights. Leotards. Doesn't necessarily mean our shooter is a ballerina."

"What about all the Derek Jeter cards?" I ask. "What's up with that?"

"That's the key," McDaniels says. "The Jeters will help us decipher these first two cards. It's why the guy left seven of them."

"Does he want to get caught?"

"No. Usually, they just like to show off. Let us see how damn clever they can be."

One of the CSI guys lays the seven baseball cards out on the table. Different poses. Different card makers. All Derek Jeter.

Ceepak sees something.

"Dr. McDaniels—when did this movie debut?"

"*The Phantom*? I forget. It was in the summer. You know, they always bring out the superheroes in the summer."

"Do you remember the year?"

"No. Back in the nineties, I guess."

"I suspect it was nineteen ninety-six."

"You do?" She curls her lip and nods. She's impressed by whatever logic train Ceepak is riding on. "How come?"

"These baseball cards? They're all different yet the same. They're all from Jeter's rookie year with the New York Yankees."

"Nineteen ninety-six?"

"Yes, ma'am."

"What about the other card? The Avengers?"

"I have a hunch. Come on."

We follow Ceepak out the door and down the hall.

We're off to see Denise Diego, Sea Haven PD's resident computer nerd.

TWENTY-SEVEN

Diego has a plastic Legolas Greenleaf action figure taped to the top of her terminal.

That's the character Orlando Bloom played in *Lord of the Rings*. The hunky elf with the arrows. As I said: Diego rules when it comes to computer research. And, like all her cybergeek brethren, she's got a pretty heavy thing for LOTR.

"You think this guy is sending you a message?" she asks as she taps some keys. Her fingers dance across the keyboard like she could type a hundred words a minute on an accordion if she wanted to. "Is this some kind of code?"

"It's a possibility," Ceepak says.

"Awesome. Yesterday, I downloaded a Zip file of a program package that can crack most monoalphabetic substitution ciphers." She's tapping keys the whole time she's talking except when she grabs a Nacho Cheese Dorito out of the vending machine bag she's having for a late breakfast along with her Mountain Dew.

She's Googling "Marvel Masterpiece Trading Cards." She recognized the Avengers card as coming from the Masterpiece series. I guess she knows people who collect these kinds of cards—guys she meets at *Lord of the Rings* fanfests.

Google now sends us off to some comic book Web site.

"Crystal," Diego mumbles.

"I beg your pardon?" Ceepak asks.

"I think the red-haired chick on the card is called Crystal." She clicks on a link. "She hangs out with all the other Avengers."

The screen switches and there she is. Red hair. White leotard. Extra-strength cleavage.

"It comes from the nineteen ninety-six Marvel Masterpiece trading card set made by Fleer," Diego reads us the information she and Google dug up. "They also have the Human Torch, Invisible Woman. I'm curious . . ." She clicks the Invisible Woman link. "Thought so. She's wearing blue tights. Why does she need to wear anything if she's supposed to be invisible?"

Diego clicks her back button and we're with Crystal again.

"Nineteen ninety-six," Ceepak says.

"Yes, sir. I can print this out if you want it."

"That'll work. Be good to know the mythology surrounding this Crystal character."

"I think she used to date the Human Torch. They were hot and heavy."

She doesn't know she's making a joke. I think she thinks this comic book stuff is actually true. That Crystal really did date the Torch.

"Then she moved to the moon and married this mutant named Quicksilver. They had a baby. Luna."

I'm beginning to wonder whether Diego spends too much time alone in this darkened room, staring at her screen, talking to the little plastic elf.

"What about this movie," Ceepak says. *The Phantom?*"

Diego taps a few more keys and hits return a couple times. Once again, Google comes through.

"Release date: June seventh, nineteen ninety-six."

"Nineteen ninety-six."

"Hmmm."

"What?"

Diego points to something on her screen.

"Catherine Zeta-Jones was in it. Must've been before she was, you know, *Catherine Zeta-Jones*."

"Yeah," I say. "Nineteen ninety-six."

It's dark in here, but my eyes have slowly adjusted. I can see Ceepak staring at me. McDaniels is staring, too. I figure they both want to ask the same question.

Ceepak goes first.

"Danny—what happened in nineteen ninety-six?"

"Think, Mr. Boyle." McDaniels moves in closer. "Nineteen ninety-six."

"You mean like in history?"

"No," Ceepak says. "In your life."

"I dunno. Nineteen ninety-six. I was, what? Fifteen."

"What about in the summer?"

McDaniels takes another step forward. "We've got Derek Jeter, one of baseball's 'boys of summer.' We have *The Phantom*, a summer movie."

It hits me.

Duh.

"Nineteen ninety-six is the summer we all met. The summer we started hanging out."

"Who?" McDaniels doesn't know about National Toasted Marshmallow Day.

"Me, Jess, Katie, Becca, Olivia, and Mook."

"Our primary targets," says Ceepak. "And our possible shooter."

"Okay," McDaniels rubs her tiny hands together. "We're getting someplace."

"Officer Ceepak?" A young cop from the radio room is at the door. "Yes?"

"Are you guys still looking for a Harley Mook?"

"Roger that," Ceepak says.

I glance at the clock. Twelve ten P.M.

"Has he been spotted?" Ceepak's ready to roll.

"No. He just called in."

"Excuse me?"

"He just called nine-one-one."

TWENTY-EIGHT

Sea Haven's cellular service is pretty technologically advanced. We have something called E911 for Enhanced 9-1-1. That means our cell towers can tell our 911 operators where you're calling from, thanks to some sort of GPS technology Ceepak probably understands but I never will.

It's the only way we have to find Mook. He never told the operator his location. No address, no landmarks. According to the transcript, the call went something like this:

> OPERATOR: *This is nine-one-one. What is the nature of your emergency?*
> CALLER: *He fucking shot me.*

That's it.

The call stayed connected but Mook didn't say anything more, which isn't like Mook at all. Usually, the guy never shuts up. Not when we were fifteen, not now. They know it was Mook on the line because the caller ID system at 9-1-1 told them that, too.

E911 is sending us to Oak Street near Beach Lane. Probably a house. It's close to the public beach where Jess had his lifeguard chair in '96, the beach where I used to hang out with my best bud and casually bump into the bathing beauties who were always there because Jess looked like one of those tanned weight lifters in red gym shorts from *Baywatch*. Jess was only one man, so there was no way he could flirt with all his fans. I took care of any spillover.

We're almost there. Couple more blocks.

The operator added a note to the transcript:

While the line remained open, I heard a faint pop in the background. Possible gunshot.

Makes me think somebody "fucking shot" Mook twice.

We swing off Ocean Avenue and head down Oak Street. No sirens, no lights. Mook called *us* so he's not going to run away—especially if he's wounded. If the shooter is still in the vicinity, we don't want him to know we're coming.

The state CSI crew is close behind us. Malloy and Kiger will come up Beach Lane to provide backup. An ambulance is on the way, too, because we figure Mook is going to need one. Now all we need to do is find exactly where on Oak Street near Beach Lane he is.

I squinch my eyes and look for a little red sports car. It's not parked in the street, and, for the first time since this thing started, I don't see any white minivans, either. The people on Oak prefer SUVs. Range Rovers. Expeditions. GMCs. Even one of those civilian Hummers. This single block would suck a gas station dry if they all hit empty at the same time.

"There," Ceepak says.

He does his three-finger point to a million-dollar reconstruction job. The rich people who own the houses closest to the beach are always tearing them down and starting over. That's what we see at number 2 Oak Street. A huge, three-story beach house with Tyvek-wrapped walls ready for the vinyl siding neatly stacked in the gutted front yard. Some of the windows upstairs aren't in yet; the ones that are have Anderson stickers covering the panes. The house is sort of built on stilts—concrete piers that form a shaded carport underneath.

That's where Mook parked his Miata.

Ceepak coasts up to the curb. I check my bulletproof vest to make sure it's snug in case the shooter is still in the neighborhood, waiting for me to make my big entrance.

"Hang back," Ceepak says.

This is an order.

He won't let me out of the car until he determines whether or not it's a sniper trap. He's probably thinking what I'm thinking: this Wheezer character lured Mook here with the promise of primo weed, then took a potshot at him. He might want to do the same to me. Mook could be the bait the sniper's using to pull me into his trap.

McDaniels and her crew park behind us. Ceepak hops out, stays low, and hugs the side of our car for cover. He flips up the palm of his hand at the CSI guys. Nobody is allowed out except him. I check the rearview mirror. McDaniels nods her head. She's okay to wait until Ceepak says it's safe to come out and do her job.

Ceepak pulls his pistol out of its holster, lets the gun hang loose at his side, does this crouching dash to the carport. He moves in a zigzag pattern, ducks behind piles of cinder blocks, then a cement-mixing drum. No straight lines, nothing to give anybody an easy shot. If you want to take down John Ceepak this afternoon, he's going to make you work for it.

He reaches the Miata. Squats. Duck walks around to the driver side. Looks inside.

He reholsters his weapon. Shakes his head. He's not in a hurry anymore.

Poor Mook. He must be dead.

TWENTY-NINE

It's one P.M.

Malloy and Kiger and about six other cops have swept the surrounding area, searching for possible perps. They must all think the shooter fled the scene, because Ceepak finally gestures that it's okay for me to crawl out of our car. I feel like a little kid, like the adults had to make sure it was safe before I was allowed to go outside and play. I'm also extremely glad they did so.

I start the long walk up the newly poured driveway. Dr. McDaniels and her crew run yellow yarn through a hole in the sports car's windshield. One CSI guy has a plastic protractor, like we had in seventh grade geometry class, even though I can't remember what we did with them. Something about angles. Triangles. Now he's pointing across the street and McDaniels is nodding her head. I look over my shoulder. There's another huge house on the other side of Oak Street with a Realtor's "For Rent" sign posted in the front yard beyond the white PVC picket fence. That house also has three stories, and a garage underneath. There are decks on all three floors and another one of those widow's walks up on the roof.

Deer stands.

It's like the architects design these beach houses for hunters and snipers. Give them lots of levels to work with. You can prop your rifle on any of the porch railings and nail your neighbor across the way if his dog barks too much.

Some kids hang out in the street to watch the crime scene action. Junior looky-lous. There's a crowd of them in bathing suits, wrapped up in beach towels. All ages, six to twenty-six. They dragged their boogie boards up from the beach and bumped into cop cars and an ambulance and wondered what all the excitement was about.

Word must be spreading. Behind the kids, I start seeing adults in swimsuits, moms with gauzy flowered sarongs wrapped around their bottoms. The grownups came up to rubberneck because this is better than anything down on the beach or over at the boardwalk; this is something to talk about when people at the office ask you what you did on your summer vacation.

"He's dead," Ceepak whispers when I reach the carport.

I look into the driver seat.

Mook's head has fallen backwards. There's a bloody bullet hole in his right shoulder. Another in the center of his forehead. His cell phone lies open in his lap, like he dropped it when the second shot hit him in the skull. He had his convertible top down, made himself an easier target. Behind Mook, there are gray spongy chunks spattered across folded roof fabric, blood is splashed on the roll bar. I think the second shot made his brain explode.

My stomach lurches. I've never seen a dead person my own age before, never someone I used to hang out with, someone who used to be my friend back when we spent all day on the beach doing nothing. Even if I wanted to kill him, myself, yesterday.

"You okay, Danny?"

I swallow hard. I haven't eaten much today. There's nothing in my stomach so maybe nothing will come up. I let the wave of nausea roll over me and wash away. This job is teaching me a whole new kind of surfing.

I look at Mook's face. His lips are purple.

"Jesus. How long has he been dead?"

"Approximately fifty-two minutes," McDaniels says. "The call came in at twelve-oh-eight. He had already sustained the shoulder shot at that time, precipitating his call."

These professional people who poke around dead bodies all day long? They use words like "sustained" and "precipitating" to give them what they call "emotional distance." I need to learn how to do that trick. Need to learn it quick.

"He was able to speed dial nine-one-one with his thumb," she continues. "When he brought the phone up to his ear, he alerted the shooter that the first shot wasn't fatal. 'He fucking shot me,' the victim stated, and the shooter fired a second round. Given the nature of the second shot, the cranial impact, the bullet path entering the frontal cortex, exiting the striate, I suspect death was instantaneous."

He fucking shot me. The famous last words of Harley Mook, the class clown who always had to get in the last word. *He fucking shot me.* Not your best line, Mook. In fact, it's not funny at all. Nobody here is laughing.

"Why are his lips so purple?" I am totally fixated on the purple lips. Maybe it's my own emotional distancing technique, dwell on the weirdest thing in the scene. Don't look at the whole bloody picture, just the lips. I know lips turn blue when you die from lack of oxygen. But purple?

"Grape soda," Ceepak says and points to the car's cup holder.

Mook has a twenty-four-ounce bottle of Fanta grape squeezed into it. Grape soda. Purple lips. Purple tongue. Mook must've been sitting here, sipping his favorite summertime soda, waiting for Wheezer to show up. Now that I see the bottle, I realize the whole car reeks of gumball grape, the mouth-puckering kind of grape you only taste in grape soda and grape gum, never in any real grapes they sell at the grocery store. Mook loved his artificially flavored grape soda. Fanta. Nehi. Welch's. Some summers, he was the only one on the whole beach drinking the stuff.

"We think the shooter positioned himself over there." Ceepak gestures with a quick nod to the house across the street. He's not pointing, not chopping the air with his arm, because he knows several dozen civilians are currently watching our every move.

"We need to secure the scene," McDaniels says to her crew. "Come on, guys. Let's lock it down."

The CSI team trots across the street.

Dr. McDaniels points at the corners of the lot, and her two guys start stringing POLICE LINE DO NOT CROSS tape all around the house.

Kiger and Malloy hustle up Oak Street to knock on doors, canvass for witnesses.

Ceepak moves around the car, searching for clues. He peers into the cockpit of the convertible. I try not to look at Mook, who's frozen in place like he's leaning back to snore through a real long nap but kept his eyes wide open.

Ceepak freezes. He just saw something, I can tell.

"Dr. McDaniels?" He shouts across the street.

She looks over.

Ceepak waves for her to come back over to our side of the street. She steps into the street. He digs into his cargo pockets to pull out a pair of forceps.

"What is it?" McDaniels is a little winded. I think she never usually moves that quickly.

"Not sure."

Ceepak leans into the car. The center console seems to be his target. There are two air-conditioning vents up top, the climate-control knobs below those, a CD slot under that.

"It's cardboard."

I see it now. A straight edge of gray sticking out like somebody jammed in a card where the CDs usually go.

"Gentle," McDaniels says.

"Roger that."

Ceepak clips the edge with his forceps and slowly, carefully tugs out the piece of cardboard.

It's another trading card. The man in purple. Another still frame from that movie. *The Phantom.*

"Guess they're cheaper by the dozen," McDaniels cracks.

Ceepak turns the card over.

"Fascinating."

"Something on the back?" McDaniels reaches into her cargo shorts, pulls out her reading glasses.

"Yes, ma'am. He left us a note."

"What's it say?"

" 'You'll never remember. I'll never forget.' "

THIRTY

Square one.

I figure that's where we basically are. Back at the starting line, inside one of those tiny wooden boxes they squeeze the horses into at the Kentucky Derby.

We're nowhere.

Maybe Mook's ARMY buddy turned on him. Maybe he was done having fun when they wounded Katie, but maybe his ARMY buddy couldn't stop. Maybe Rick, I remember that was his name, maybe Rick is a killing machine without an "off" switch.

"Richard Westerfield," Ceepak says. His friends in the army just faxed us a list of discharged snipers known to have recently returned to college. "Pfc. Westerfield never saw action. He was honorably discharged before the initiation of Operation Iraqi Freedom."

So Mook's college buddy learned all this sniper stuff but never got to use it, never hunted a human. Maybe, after shooting at us a couple of times and missing, he wanted more, wanted to see the pink mist when his bullet made a skull explode. Wanted to go for the kill when Mook wanted to move on to the next joke. Maybe Richard Westerfield took out party pooper Harley Mook.

CHRIS GRABENSTEIN

That's my best guess right now.

Ceepak and I sit in the front seats of the Explorer. He's on his cell phone to someone back at the house.

"You have Westerfield's plate number?"

Ceepak nods so I guess they do.

"Able Baker four-nine-four Charlie seven. Got it." Ceepak writes the number in his little spiral notebook. "Excellent. Thanks, Denise." It's Diego. The woman puts in a full day. "This will help. Have Gus issue an APB. Suspect has been seen in the area but could be mobile, could be . . ." he looks at his watch, does some mental math, "anywhere in a radius of a hundred and fifty miles from our current position. Right. Thanks."

Ceepak closes up his cell and clips it back on his utility belt. He has so much gear dangling off that thing he could pass as a plumber.

"You think it's Mook's new buddy?"

"It's one possibility."

"Right."

When we're working a case, all things are possible with Ceepak until they have been proven otherwise. Or something like that. I forget sometimes, especially when people are shooting at my friends and me.

"This drug dealer Wheezer? What do we know about him?"

"Not much. Just what Mook told me."

Ceepak waits.

"Focus, Danny."

I try. But my eyes and mind drift over to the small crowd of civilians clustered around Chief Buzz Baines and Mayor Sinclair. The bosses have arrived on Oak Street and are giving the curious citizens some sort of impromptu press conference. They're quite the dynamic duo: the tall, handsome police chief and the sandy-haired, boyish mayor. They're smiling, then frowning, then smiling again, then shaking their heads in dismay, telling everybody that Mook's murder was "the tragic consequence" of a "drug deal gone bad." The chief says the good people of Sea Haven have nothing to fear, unless, of course, they have plans to purchase illegal narcotics in the near future.

The crowd chuckles.

I hear Baines wind up: "Unfortunately, this is where underage drinking ultimately leads. There's an express lane that takes teenagers from beer blasts on the beach to marijuana binges to crack houses and heroin addiction. That express lane dead-ends right here." He hangs his head like a graveside preacher, and everybody knows what he means: Harley Mook got shot in a carport by drug thugs because he bought beer with a fake ID when he was fifteen.

Buzz Baines has done it again. He's linked Mook's murder to his favorite boogeyman—underage drinking.

"Danny?" Ceepak must sense that I'm floating along like a stringy clump of seaweed. "Wheezer?"

I need to focus. Work the evidence. Chief Baines can tell the people out in the street anything he wants. It's up to us to find out the truth.

"Yeah. Okay. What Mook said was that Wheezer was a guy 'from back in the day.' "

"A school friend?"

"I don't know. He wasn't specific. Just 'back in the day.' "

"Go on."

"Mook said he never really liked the guy but that Wheezer had this primo ganga. That's—"

"Marijuana. Was Wheezer Mook's usual dealer?"

"I doubt it. But I really don't know. Mook was just in town for a week or two. Summer break from grad school. He was here having fun, seeing old friends. Wheezer sounded like someone Mook accidentally reconnected with, or bumped into at a bar. Not like a guy he went looking for. He also said he never 'pictured the dude for a dealer.' "

"Is that so?"

"Yeah. Said Wheezer was more like a loser."

"Interesting. Do you remember this Wheezer?"

"No."

Ceepak nods. "He didn't think you would."

"What do you mean?"

"The note."

You'll never remember, I'll never forget.

If only I hadn't done so much underage drinking. All that beer, Boone's Farm and those Icees laced with Bacardi, which is how we used to enjoy rum and Coke without buying cocktail glasses or ice.

"You think he left that note for me?"

"Yes, Danny, I do." Ceepak fixes me with an odd look. "I think he intended the note to be read by you and your friends from, as you say, 'back in the day.' The beach crew from nineteen ninety-six."

"The six targets."

"Five, Danny. Five."

Yeah. Mook was just scratched off the list. One down, five to go. Unless, of course, Katie doesn't pull through. Then, there's only four little Indians left.

"Don't worry, Danny. We'll nail the guy."

"Yeah."

The chief and mayor march over to our car. The crowd has now dispersed. I guess they bought the chief's act. Now that he's not on, I can see Baines looks worried. Angry. I wouldn't want to be his mustache right now. He's in a plucking mood.

Ceepak and I climb out of the car. We stand in front of the chief.

"Noon tomorrow," Baines says in this real tight whisper. "If you don't catch this kook, we're calling the other thing off."

"Yes, sir," Ceepak says.

"Call it off?" Mayor Sinclair pushes his Ray-Bans up his nose. "We can't just 'call it off,' Buzz —"

Baines cuts the mayor off in midbabble. "Noon tomorrow, John. That's it. Catch this creep, or we tell everybody to go home. We shut this island down."

Good for Chief Baines. He'd rather lose his big new job than see anybody else lose a life.

"Buzz?" Mayor Sinclair doesn't give up easy. "Come on. Don't be rash. What about MTV? Kids all across America are counting on us! This is *their* beach party, too! And what about Bruno Mazzilli? He just unloaded ten tons of raw pork ribs off a refrigerated truck down by the boardwalk. You ever smell what happens to pork after it sits in the sun? It's worse than fish, Buzz. Worse than fish!"

Baines turns his back on the mayor and walks away.

"Buzz? Hold up. Wait a second." Sinclair chases the chief up the street.

The chief climbs into his SUV and slams its heavy black door in the mayor's face. Sinclair, being a politician, is used to people slamming doors in his face. He's like one of those Jehovah's Witness ladies with the free magazines. He doesn't take it personally, he just runs over to his own car, hops in, and races after the chief so he'll be poised and ready to knock on his door again wherever the chief stops.

"What's our situation?" Dr. McDaniels comes over for an update.

"We have a deadline," Ceepak says.

"Interesting choice of words."

"Noon tomorrow."

"Fine."

"You found something?"

"Maybe."

"Shell casings?"

"No. Our shooter is still quite tidy. However, he needs to watch where he walks. There was an oil stain on the garage floor across the street."

"He stepped in it?"

"You can say that again. Size twelve. Converse All-Stars. Looks like he went for a little walk."

"Where to?"

"Around the front of the vehicle, over to the passenger side. Reached the rear tires, stopped, turned around, walked back to the driver-side door."

"You think he had a flat rear tire?" Ceepak asks.

"One possibility."

"We should alert the service stations."

"Yep. You really should." McDaniels smiles happily. This could qualify as a break. If the sniper had tire trouble, he might've gone to a gas station after shooting Mook. We might be able to track this guy down, maybe even before noon tomorrow.

Ceepak radios Gus Davis back at the house and tells the desk sergeant to coordinate the service station sweep. Phone calls from police headquarters start going out the second Ceepak signs off. He turns to McDaniels, eager for more.

"Any tire tracks?"

"Oh, yeah. Whoever owns that house? They must have one hell of a leaky Mercedes. Puddles everywhere. Oil. Transmission fluid. We picked up several tire tread patterns that look similar."

Ceepak nods. "The homeowner's vehicle."

"Right. And one set that doesn't match any of the others. Very fresh."

"Minivan?"

"That'd be my first guess. Need to run it by the lab. But they look like all-season radials. Maybe Bridgestone BT70s, which are pretty common on minivans."

"You know your treads," I say.

McDaniels shrugs off the compliment. "American, Japanese, German, and Italian. I need to bone up on my Chinese. Anyhow, I'd bet serious money it's our minivan."

I'm thinking about Rick again, the trained sharpshooter with the white van.

"I'll ride to the morgue with the body," McDaniels says, seeing the EMTs zip Mook up inside a black vinyl bag. "See if the late Mr. Mook can tell us anything else. You boys heading back to the house?"

"Negative," Ceepak says. "Danny and I will remain in the field. We need to talk to some people. Fast. We have less than twenty-four hours now to grab our shooter. The clock is ticking."

"Okay." She waves to her team across the street. McDaniels climbs into the back of the ambulance with Mook's body bag. When she thinks no one is looking, I see her make a sign of the cross and say a quick prayer.

The ambulance and CSI car pull away from the scene. It looks like a very small funeral.

Adam Kiger, one of the cops who went up the street to hunt for witnesses, jogs down toward us.

"Ceepak?" he says. "I think we found somebody."

THIRTY-ONE

I f Kiger and Malloy have found a witness to go with our foot and
tire prints, things are definitely starting to look up. Which is good.
We need to catch our killer or else summer ends early this year in
Sea Haven and may never reopen again.

Mark Malloy, another of our guys, is about ten yards behind Kiger.
He walks alongside this very tan thirtysomething guy in khaki shorts
and a King Putt T-shirt. King Putt is one of the many miniature golf
courses on the island. They have the best logo: a pharaoh who looks
pretty authentic until you see the putter in his hands where the staff
of Ra should be.

"This is Mr. Goldstein," Malloy says to Ceepak. "He and his family
are renting for two weeks at Fifteen Oak. Sir, could you please tell
Officer Ceepak what you told my partner and I?"

"Now? I have to be on a conference call with a very important
client in, like, five minutes."

"I'd like to hear your story," Ceepak says. He towers over the witness. Six-two to five-two. I think the very important client can wait.

"Okay, okay." The guy sighs like we're ruining his day. Murder
will do that. "Like I told these two officers already, my boys and I

went down to the beach this morning, came back early for lunch. Around eleven thirty. Anyhow, I saw a car parked over there." He points to the garage where the CSI team has just wrapped things up. "Figured it was the Realtor, stopping by to check up on the place. The house has been empty all summer I hear. Guess they're asking too much. Overpriced it."

"What sort of vehicle was it?" Ceepak asks.

"Minivan," Goldstein says. "White. They pulled in backwards."

"Excuse me?"

"They backed into the garage. The door was up and I could see the front end pointing forward. I remember thinking that was weird. You ever try to back up into a garage? Tough to do. You gotta work the side mirrors so you don't scrape against the walls."

"Right."

"Or you can back in too far. Bump into the wall, crush your golf bag, knock over your weedwacker."

"Right."

"I did it once. Backed into my garage. Put this big scratch down the whole side of my truck. Dinged the bumper. Of course, my truck is a lot wider and longer than a minivan. That's it up there. See it? The silver Lexus? The LX 470?" He points and takes a self-satisfied moment to give us enough time to admire his shiny boy toy and calculate his net worth. "It lists for sixty-five but I added some options. We left the Porsche at home this year." He gives us another minute so we can try to guess how much the options and Porsche must've cost.

When he has decided we're sufficiently impressed, he starts up again. "I remember thinking, why would you go through all that trouble to park your van butt in, nose out? It's easier just to pull in and back out, you know?"

"Yes, sir. Was anyone in the minivan?"

"No. Not that I saw. Could have been, but I didn't see anybody. Of course, I wasn't really looking for anyone, since I was heading home for lunch."

"Was this red sports car parked where it is now?"

"No. Not when the boys and I came up from the beach."

"And that was approximately eleven thirty?"

"Eleven thirty-two. I have one of those Atomic watches—syncs with the clock out in Boulder?" He waits for us to be impressed again. "They sell it at Hammacher Schlemmer?" Another pause. I just hope the watch didn't cost sixty-five thousand like the SUV.

"I remember checking the time right after I looked at the minivan," he continues. "I phoned my wife from the beach, told her the boys and I would be home at eleven thirty-five. We were right on schedule. Anyhow, at eleven thirty-two, all I saw was the minivan and, like I said, I figured it was the real estate agent or maybe a maid brigade dropping by to dust off the furniture."

"Why'd you think it was the Realtor?"

"The license plate was local. You know, one of those 'Shore To Please' jobs with the lighthouse."

New Jersey sells 'Shore To Please' license plates to people who tick a box and donate a few bucks toward saving our seacoast from pollution. Most people here in town buy them. But, then again, so do a lot of other people all over the state who like visiting clean beaches for a week or two every summer and not worrying about stepping on hypodermic needles the tide dragged in.

"And," our witness continues, "the van had a resident beach sticker on the bumper. You know, the green jobs? Little square with 'Sea Haven' written in that boring typeface? Helvetica. That's the lettering they use in airports."

"Yes, sir." Ceepak is smiling. I think he can't believe how lucky we are to have found a witness who actually saw and then remembered so many minute details. Most people don't see diddly or squat. This guy remembers typefaces. And don't forget, he has that atomic watch so he knows precisely when he saw them.

"Tell me, sir," Ceepak asks, "do you work in the graphic arts?"

"Yeah. I'm an art director. Advertising. You know that commercial with the people standing on top of the yellow mountain and they all have arthritis?"

"Sorry. I don't watch much TV."

"I'm sure you've seen it. It's a national spot. The field of yellow flowers? People dancing? They're wearing yellow gaucho hats?"

"Sorry."

"The pill looks like the sun with yellow sunbeams glowing out the sides? Everybody feels better at the end and they play Frisbee with the yellow Labrador retriever? The Frisbee's yellow, too."

"Sorry."

"It's on the news every night. Usually right after the one for hemorrhoid cream. I did not do *that* one."

"I'm going to look for it."

"It's good. Very visual. Very yellow. Very sunny."

"The hemorrhoid cream?" I ask.

"No. Mine. It's for Zolflam. The dawn of a new arthritis pain relief day. We bought that classic song *Lemon Tree*. I wanted *Yellow Submarine* or *Mellow Yellow*, but the price tags were too steep. Anyhow, the whole spot works like a mnemonic device for the warmth and comfort of this little yellow pill."

"I see," Ceepak nods like he knows what a mnemonic device is, which maybe he does. To me, it sounds like a jackhammer or something you fix sewer pipes with. "We have your contact information, Mr. Goldstein? In case we need to talk again?"

"Yeah. I gave it to Officer Kiger."

"That'll work. Thank you. If—"

Ceepak stops.

Behind Goldstein, he sees what I see: a white minivan cruising slowly down the street, heading right for us.

License plate: AB494C7.

THIRTY-TWO

Danny? Get in the car."

"It's Mook's ARMY buddy!"

"In the car."

Ceepak nods at Adam Kiger.

"Mr. Goldstein?" Kiger says to our witness. "If you'll come with me." Kiger practically drags the guy in the King Putt T-shirt down to the end of the street.

"That's not the van . . ."

That's all I hear Mr. Mnemonic say as he is hauled out of harm's way. Kiger has his arm wrapped around the dude's waist and is carrying him on his hip like a grocery sack stacked with six-packs.

"Officer Boyle?" His partner, Malloy, has his hand on my shoulder. "You heard Ceepak. Into the car. Now."

I move toward the Ford, walking backwards so I can see what Ceepak is going to do, moving fast so I don't get hauled away like Goldstein.

"Move it, Danny." Malloy puts his body between the minivan and me—and I'm the one wearing the bulletproof vest. "Hustle, kid. Into the car."

I do what he says. I don't want Malloy babysitting me when he could be out there helping Ceepak.

I see the guys on our team reach for their weapons. Ceepak. Malloy. I look in the rearview mirror. Kiger has his semiautomatic out, too. He has Goldstein stuffed behind a beach bench and is kneeling in the sand at the end of the street, taking aim at the minivan's tires.

Everybody on this job has a gun except, of course, me. I just have a big bull's-eye pasted somewhere on my forehead.

I check the van's front bumper: no green "Sea Haven" sticker. So, I figure, it's not the one Mr. Goldstein saw at eleven thirty-two A.M. Ceepak, however, isn't taking any chances. His gun is out and aimed at the driver's head.

"Stop!" he says.

The van stops. Funny how a gun works. Even better than a stop sign.

This big, burly guy tumbles out of the passenger side door with his hands up over his head. He has a 7-Eleven Big Gulp cup in one of his hands so soda sloshes over the top when he hoists it up over his head.

Rick steps down from the driver's side, arms raised.

"We're cool," he says. "We're cool."

Two other passengers fall out of the sliding side door, like they had trouble jimmying up on the handle and lost their balance. All four now have their hands up over their heads. I recognize their faces from this morning with Mook in the diner. Rick, the ARMY guy, has on a new T-shirt: black with a sparkling gold front. It shows the bust of Julius Caesar, only he's wearing sunglasses. It's from a casino down in Atlantic City: Caesar's.

"On the ground," Ceepak barks. "All of you. Now."

The college guys do as they're told even if it means spilling the rest of their Big Gulps.

"Kiss the asphalt!" Malloy barks.

Ceepak kind of looks at Malloy, like he wonders where he learned that line. My guess? One of those Vin Diesel movies or some cop show that comes on when Ceepak's busy watching *Forensic Files*.

Since all the potential bad guys are lying in the street, I figure it's safe for me to step out of our cop car. I make my way up to the minivan.

"Danny?" Ceepak hears me coming up behind him. "Do you recognize these gentlemen?"

Kind of a funny question to ask right now, since all of them are sprawled facedown on the hot blacktop. But I saw them earlier when they tumbled out of the van like drunken clowns at the circus.

"Yeah. They're Mook's friends."

"That's right," the lanky one says, lifting his head, pushing his sunglasses back into place.

"Kiss it!" Malloy snarls. Lanky's mouth goes back to the blacktop.

"Mark?" Ceepak says.

"Yes, sir?"

"I think we can let them up."

"Should I cuff them?"

"No need," says Ceepak, holstering his pistol. "Am I right, gentlemen?"

"No need . . . we're cool." The four of them mumble their agreement into the tarmac.

"Stand up. All of you." It's Malloy. He likes giving orders.

Mook's pals haul themselves up off the asphalt, which is hot, and brush themselves off. I move around to the back of the van.

The bumper stickers are all still there plus a new one: I SCORED ROYALLY AT CAESAR'S!

"Where's Mook?" I hear one of them ask.

"Are you gentlemen looking for him?" Ceepak asks.

"Duh," the guy says, maybe forgetting what it felt like back on the asphalt.

"He called us," Rick, the ARMY guy, says. "From his cell phone. Said to meet him here. Oak and Beach. Said he'd just heard about this awesome party in Philly tonight but first he was going to score us some . . ." The guy remembers we're cops, decides to change the subject. "We drove up from Atlantic City."

"Is that so?" Malloy moves in closer. He still has his weapon aimed at their heads. He flicks from one to another and back again, like he wants to make sure, should it become necessary, that he can personally mow all of them down with as few bullets as possible, like he's working out his shooting angles.

"It is," says Ceepak. "They went to Caesar's."

"Just because he has on the T-shirt?" Malloy sounds itchy, like he wants to shoot somebody soon. "You can buy those at the Qwick Pick, at the gas station."

"They parked in deck four." Ceepak taps on the minivan's slanting front windshield. Behind it, on the dashboard, is a small orange stub. A receipt from the Caesar's parking garage. Ceepak saw it from fifteen paces.

"Is Mook here?" Rick asks.

"No," Ceepak says sort of softly.

"He told us he had this great parking spot. Free. Right near the beach."

"He did." Ceepak points to the empty red sports car tucked under the big house being built at the corner. "Real good spot."

"Is Mook okay?" another friend asks.

"Did something happen?"

They suddenly sound sad, maybe scared. They also seem as if Mook really was their buddy, like he really used to be mine.

"Gentlemen, Mr. Harley Mook was murdered this morning."

"Jesus," the tall guy says. "Murdered?"

"Sniper," I say, looking at Rick.

"Fuck." He kind of gasps it. "Fuck, man." He sounds truly upset.

Now I'm certain: Rick has never shot anybody in his life. Never wanted to either. He just went into the army to pay for college and see the world. He's not our guy.

"Fuck, fuck, fuck."

Ceepak nods his head like he agrees with Rick's assessment of the situation: it is totally fucked.

"Officer Malloy?"

"Yes, sir?"

"Please escort these gentlemen back to headquarters. We need detailed statements." Then Ceepak turns to the guys standing in the street, their hands stuffed in the front pockets of their shorts, shaking their heads, trying to figure out what the hell happened here this morning.

"Thank you for your cooperation," Ceepak says. "I'm certain it will assist in our apprehension of Mr. Mook's killer."

Then he turns to me.

"Wheezer, Danny. We need to find Wheezer."

THIRTY-THREE

So now we know we definitely don't know who did this.

We also know we're looking for a minivan, maybe one with a bum tire.

And we're looking for a local.

We have less than twenty-four hours. Unless, of course, our local sniper shoots somebody else before noon tomorrow. It was the chief who made the Sunday deadline. I don't think he consulted with the bad guy.

Ceepak and I head back to the boardwalk. He wants to talk to T. J. again. While we're doing that, about a half dozen cop cars will cruise into service stations up and down the island and ask about flat tires and minivans.

"When we finish with T. J.," Ceepak says, "we need to talk to your friends about nineteen ninety-six. All of them."

Except Mook. And Katie. He's dead. She's still unconscious.

"We'll meet them at the hospital," Ceepak says. "Mainland Medical. Sixteen hundred hours." It's a little after two P.M. He wants to meet my Marshmallow Crew at four. Jess and Olivia are still with friends on the mainland. I called and told them about Mook, asked them to think about "Wheezer." The Avondale police will escort them over to the hospital for the meet. Jess said he wanted to drive himself. I told him no, he didn't.

Next I call Becca, tell and ask her the same things. She freaks out for a second but pulls it back together pretty quick; she even volunteers to dig out her Nineteen ninety-six yearbook.

"We'll send a cop car over to drive you to Mainland Medical," I say.

"I want Ceepak to drive me," Becca says.

"He can't. We're busy."

"Then send Riggs."

"Jim Riggs?"

In the driver's seat, Ceepak smiles.

"Excellent choice," he says.

Jim Riggs is this twenty-nine-year-old cop who spends more time on the locker-room weight machines than anybody else. If we did one of those "Hot Cops of Sea Haven" calendars, I guess Riggs would be the coverboy.

We park near the boardwalk. The only reason we find a space is because, basically, we're in a cop car and can park anywhere we want. The place is packed. Twice as many half-naked bodies cruising up and down the sun-drenched planks as usual. The weekend weather is cooperating: 90 degrees with low humidity and a light breeze coming in off the ocean. The wind carries the scent of saltwater and taffy and Italian sausages and french fries. So far, not a whiff of gunpowder or hot steel. Like Ceepak says: it's all good. Good and greasy.

"Take it easy," Ceepak says with a smile.

T. J. is wolfing down this entire tub of fries. We're at a concrete picnic table in the middle of a bunch of boardwalk food stalls. Ceepak bought three orders of fresh-cut fries from this booth where they take a whole potato and slice it into thick slats with one quick pass of a razor-sharp gizmo that sort of looks like a Popeil Veg-O-Matic.

T. J. licks salt off his fingers, tries to pace himself.

"Sorry," he says. "I only get a fifteen-minute break."

We picked T. J. up at Lord of the Rings Toss, where people were throwing their money away left and right. Apparently, anybody who saw Ceepak demonstrate his "crouch-like-a-kid" technique earlier in the week has left town. All that's left now are the losers, guys spending big wads of cash in a mad scramble to win stuffed Sponge-Bobs for their heartthrobs.

T. J. whacks the bottom of his fries cup with the heel of his hand, tries to dislodge the last potato wedge stuck down there, probably glued into place by coagulating ketchup.

"Guess I was hungry," he says.

"Busy day?" Ceepak nibbles on a fry. I think he's only eaten, like, two while T. J. and I sucked our paper cups dry.

"Unbelievable," T. J. says. "Never seen the boardwalk so crowded."

T. J. and Ceepak seem to get along even though they make a pretty odd pair. Ceepak with his close-cropped military-style hair, big broad shoulders, neatly pressed uniform, and Boy Scout politeness. T. J. with his spiky blond dreads, wrist-to-elbow arm tattoo, droopy clothes, and slack-jawed whateverness.

"We won't keep you long," Ceepak says.

"Whatever. I've still got ten minutes."

"We're interested in anything unusual you might have seen or heard at Paintball Blasters."

"I heard you kicked ass."

Ceepak smiles, saying only, "I had a pretty good day."

"Totally. I haven't been shooting much lately. Not for a couple weeks."

"How come?"

"Well, like I said, I only get two fifteen-minute breaks. I usually grab something to eat on the first break and head over to Blasters on the second. Try to squeeze in ten minutes or so on the targets. It's my only chance to shoot, blow off a little steam."

"You don't have your own paintball gun?"

"No. Can't afford it. Not with rent and all."

"You pay your mother's rent?" I say.

"She doesn't charge me or anything. I just, you know, chip in."

"Admirable," Ceepak says.

T. J. shrugs.

"My dad dumped her before I was born. We try to help each other out. Besides, it's pretty easy to find work around here. Especially in the summer. I do a night gig at Burger King."

Ceepak nods his head. I think he likes this kid.

"So—you got the hots for my mom?"

Before Ceepak can say anything, T. J. plunges ahead. "My mom. Rita? Are you, you know, interested or just stringing her along?"

"Well, I'm . . . we only just met . . . the other night."

"You ought to ask her out, man. She's cool, not so totally uptight like you might think when you first meet her. You should take her on a date or whatever. She's cool."

Ceepak's ears? Redder than red. I think they call it crimson.

I step in to give him a breather.

"So," I ask, "have you noticed any unusual characters at the paint-ball place? Anybody stick out?"

"No. Just your usual weirdos. Sandman. He's this skinny dude who always wears desert camo and one of those boony hats like they had in Vietnam. Then there's these two goth chicks. They dress all in black, even in the middle of summer. Black lipstick, too. Gemmy and Jackelyn. Gemmy's the one with the dog collar. They both like to shoot at the Britney Spears target. Take turns. Oh, then there's this dork I call Asswipe. He's the main reason I haven't shot much lately."

"Who is he?" Ceepak asks.

"Asswipe? Older guy. Twentysomething. About his age." T. J. points at me. "All last week, he hogged number three."

"What's number three?"

"My favorite gun. I know how to sight it, you know what I mean?"

"Sure."

"Anyway, Asswipe likes number three, too. I tell him it's my favorite and like I only have a couple minutes, and he tells me to go fuck myself. He won't budge. Keeps hogging the rifle even when

1232

32

there's four or five other guns nobody's using. Even when the dude behind the counter, Larry, tells Asswipe to cut me some slack, Asswipe just smiles and says shit like, 'I paid, didn't I? I can use any gun I choose, can't I?' Total asswipe."

"Is there anything special about weapon number three?" Ceepak has his pad out.

"I dunno. It's just the best gun. I think the barrel is a little straighter or something. Maybe the rifle's a little newer. I know it's the one Larry uses whenever he challenges anybody to a shootout."

Ceepak smiles.

"Roger that. I was on number four."

"And he was next to you on three, am I right?"

"Right."

"Larry is so lame. And you still beat him?"

"Tell me more about this guy."

"Asswipe?"

Ceepak nods. Too bad. I wanted to hear him say "Yes, Mr. Asswipe," like that was the guy's name.

"Let's see, he's kind of tall. Has this wavy, weird hair and a bushy little beard. Wore a pair of nerd glasses."

"Nerd glasses?"

"Yeah. Old ones. Like he's had the same pair since high school or whatever. I got real tired of him pretty fast."

"How do you mean?"

"You know—him acting like he was smarter than anybody on the beach, and being all happy ruining my day, taking my favorite gun away from me and everything."

"Any distinguishing marks? A tattoo perhaps?"

"This guy? No way. He looked way too straight. Wore these color-coordinated pants and windbreaker, like his mom picked them out at Sears or wherever. I remember one day he had on this totally brown outfit. Brown pants. Brown zippered jacket. Who wears brown on the boardwalk, man?"

"Only asswipes," I say, thinking I'm being cute.

Ceepak shoots me a look. So does T. J. I guess they both think I should stick to my grown-up words.

"Have you seen this fellow lately, T. J.?"

"No, sir. Not since, like, last Wednesday."

"Was he a local?"

"No. At least I don't think so. His skin was pasty white. Like he lived under a rock someplace cold."

"Okay. Thanks." Ceepak checks his watch. "We know you have to get back to work."

"Yeah."

"You want the rest of my fries?"

"Nah. Thanks. I'm cool."

"Can I ask one last question, T. J.?"

"Shoot."

"If you don't own a paintball gun, how did you attack The Pig's Commitment?"

It's a classic Ceepak move: slip in the big question when the witness thinks you're all done.

T. J. looks embarrassed. He also looks like he's tired of telling lies, like he figures he'll do better with Ceepak if he tells the truth. He's right.

"Slingshot."

"I see."

"I borrowed paint balls from Larry."

"Borrowed?"

"I didn't steal them. Larry gave them to me. It was his idea, kind of. Thought the blue balls on the sign would be funny. Larry basically hates black people. Hates Grace. Said somebody needed to knock her down a few notches, put her in her place."

"What about you?"

"I just wanted to, you know, do it for a goof. Show him I could."

"You don't dislike Ms. Porter?"

"Nah. She's pretty cool. We talked the other day."

"You did?"

"Yeah. I went by her place to tell her I was sorry. Told my mom, too."

"Good for you. What did Ms. Porter say?"

"Said she was too damn busy to deal with me on account of the holiday weekend and I should come back Tuesday if I wanted to apologize so damn much."

Yep. That sounds like Grace Porter.

"Then she made me breakfast."

"Really?"

"Yeah. Eggs, bacon, and biscuits with gravy."

"Did you try the scrapple?" Ceepak asks.

"No way, dude. That stuff will kill you."

T. J. crumples up his fry cup.

Ceepak smiles.

"Thanks for your help, T. J. If you run into this fellow again, please give me a call." Ceepak hands T. J. one of his cards.

"No problem." T. J. stands up from the table, his eyes drift to the side. He remembers something. "This guy Asswipe?"

"Yes?"

"This one time, he gave me a card. Like a bubblegum card, you know?"

"Do you still have it?"

"Nah. I tossed it in the trash. But he gave it to me once when he wouldn't let me have gun number three. 'Here you go, kid,' he said. 'Go home and whack off to this instead.' "

"What was on the card?"

"This blond superhero chick in blue tights."

"The Invisible Woman?" I ask.

"Yeah. Maybe. It was like a comic-book cover only it was on a trading card. That was the same day he wore the gloves."

"While he was shooting?"

"Yeah. Surfer gloves. You know—black neoprene. Totally weird. Nobody wears surfer gloves around here except maybe in the winter."

THIRTY-FOUR

You ever race through traffic with a siren screaming and roof
lights spinning?

Cars pull off to the side of the road to get out of your way.
You fly across the causeway bridge. It's pretty cool. Until you
remember why you're doing it: you're a cop on your way to Mainland
Medical where one of your best friends lies unconscious after doctors
dug a bullet out of her chest, a bullet that might've been meant for you.

You remember that, and it's not so cool.

My three other Marshmallow Crew friends are meeting us at the
hospital. Ceepak thinks if we brainstorm about the summer of Nineteen ninety-six maybe one of us will remember who the hell Wheezer
is and why the hell he might want to kill us.

Meanwhile, back on the island, surf shops have been added to the
list of places to go ask questions. T. J. is right. Nobody wears rubber
surf gloves in the middle of August except maybe some rifleman who
thinks the neoprene will hide his fingerprints. And to make sure he
can still squeeze a trigger? He goes and checks himself out at the
paintball arcade.

Dr. McDaniels has called some folks over at the state Major

Crimes Unit and requested a sketch artist to sit with T. J. A town the size of Sea Haven doesn't have a police sketch artist, so we need to borrow one from the state, unless, of course, we go grab one of those guys who draw caricatures down on the boardwalk. But if we do that, our suspect will have a big bubblehead, gigantic buck teeth, and wear some kind of dopey clown hat.

Our guys have already tracked down a couple of minivans with flat tires, but none with that green beach-pass bumper sticker. The search continues.

We'll find Wheezer.

Especially if any of us can remember who the hell he might be.

Mainland Medical operates what they call the Regional Trauma Center. If you get hurt real bad while you're on vacation, this is where they'll send you.

It's about 3:45. Fifteen minutes before we're supposed to meet with Becca, Olivia, and Jess.

"Can I go see Katie?" I ask the second we park outside the emergency room entrance in a no-parking zone.

Ceepak checks his wristwatch.

"That'll work."

I hop out and notice we're parked under this covered entryway, a concrete canopy. I guess Ceepak doesn't want to make me an easy target while I dash for the door. Once I'm safely inside, I'm sure he'll go find someplace to park that's legal.

Katie has been moved to the Intensive Care Unit. They let me stand at a window and look in at her. Her red hair is tucked up underneath a pale green shower cap. A forest of metal poles with dangling drip bags surrounds her bed. A spaghetti tangle of tubes snakes down to her thin arm. I know Katie's heart is still beating because I can see her pulse playing on a TV set clamped to one of the poles. I watch the line move up and down and know she's still here even if she's gone.

I wonder if Katie remembers Wheezer.

I wonder if she'll ever wake up.

Ceepak has commandeered the visitors' room at the far end of the first floor for our brainstorming session. It's clean and tidy, filled with chalk-colored furniture. Pink. Teal. Blue. Even the carpet is a soft, soothing gray. The sofa is done up in splotchy pinks and purples that sort of match the mass-produced abstract art hanging on all the walls. The kind they sell at those Giant Art Expos at the Holiday Inn.

It's the kind of art that's supposed to calm you down after you've seen a loved one lying unconscious with tubes stuck in her arms and up her nose.

It's not working.

Becca takes a seat in a chair underneath some speckled water lilies. She's wearing sunglasses, even though the room has no windows. She still has that shiner from where the paint ball walloped her in the eye. "Where's Ceepak?"

"He went to the cafeteria to score some coffees."

Becca's chauffeur, Officer Big Jim Riggs, is guarding the door with two other cops—the guys from the Avondale PD who brought Jess and Olivia to the hospital.

"I could definitely use a coffee," says Jess. He helps Olivia creak her way down onto the sofa.

"Thanks." She moves stiffly.

"Guess I'm the only one who hasn't been shot at yet," Jess says.

"Maybe because you're the one who's shooting at us!" Becca says in a blazing leap of logic.

"What?"

"You're a painter. We were hit with *paint*balls? Hello? I don't have to be a rocket scientist to put two and two together and get, you know, four or whatever."

"Becca?" I say.

"What?"

"Jess was with us. On the beach. Remember? He got splattered by a paintball, too?"

"Oh. Yeah. Sorry."

Ceepak walks in balancing a cardboard tray jammed with six lidded cups of coffee. No doughnuts.

"Let me help." Becca is up and arranges cups on the coffee table in front of us. She does the morning breakfast buffet at her folks' motel. The girl knows how to set up a coffee service.

Everybody grabs a cup, and we all sip in silence for a second. We quickly discover it's cafeteria coffee. Thin and weak. It tastes more like warm Styrofoam soup than anything else.

Jess dumps his full cup into a plastic-lined trashcan.

"So, who's Wheezer?" he asks Ceepak.

"That," says Ceepak, "is the million-dollar question. Does the name ring a bell with any of you?"

We all look at each other. "No" seems to be the unanimous answer, judging by the headshakes.

"Sorry," says Olivia. She grimaces, holds her ribcage.

"I even checked all my old junior high and high school yearbooks," adds Becca. "No Wheezer. I found a Grabber. He signed my book with these hearts and stuff. I forget who he was."

"Was Wheezer a friend of Mook's?" asks Olivia.

"More likely an acquaintance." Ceepak gives everybody the description T. J. gave us. Tall. Nerdy glasses. Wavy hair. Bushy goatee.

Becca scrunches up her nose like she just smelled boiled cabbage. "Still doesn't sound familiar."

"Let's talk about the summer of nineteen ninety-six," says Ceepak. "That's when you all met?"

We run down the who-knew-who-first stuff until Ceepak's up to speed. The girls retell the bathing suit fitting room story. I talk about Jess's lifeguard chair. "I used to hang out there, after I worked mornings at the Pancake Palace."

"Is that the summer you were a busboy?" Olivia smiles, remembering.

"Yeah."

"And they fired you for dropping too many trays?"

"They hired me back, like, two days later."

"They were desperate," says Jess.

"Yeah." He's right. They were. I was pretty lame busing tables. Kept breaking milk glasses when I jammed dirty silverware inside them.

"No retreat, no surrender," Jess says.

"Springsteen?" Ceepak recognizes the quote.

"Yeah. That was our motto that summer, remember?"

We all nod and have to laugh as we remember how cool we thought we were. We actually had A Motto: *No retreat, no surrender.* It's off Springsteen's *Born in the U.S.A.* album. In fact, it's the same song John Kerry used during his presidential campaign. I always loved the first couple of lines:

> *We busted out of class*
> *Had to get away from those fools,*
> *We learned more from a three-minute record*
> *Than we ever learned in school.*

It's all about friends hanging out, probably in the summer, probably on the Jersey Shore, and they promise to always remember each other, swear to stick up for one another, no matter what, to be "blood brothers against the wind."

No retreat, no surrender.

"What did you guys do that summer?" Ceepak asks.

"You know, the usual," Becca says.

Olivia nods. "Work. Then hit the beach."

"Chase boys."

"Let the boys chase us."

"Sometimes we'd just cruise the boardwalk. Check out the arcades. Ride the rides."

"I ate way too much candy," Olivia says, "because Katie had this job at . . ."

She pauses, realizes it's the same place Katie was working this morning.

". . . Tammy's."

Jess shoots me a look. I nod, hoping to encourage him to say whatever is on his mind.

"Can we be like totally honest?"

Ceepak will not lie, cheat, or steal, nor tolerate those who do. Total honesty? He's down with that.

"Of course."

"You're not going to, like, retroactively arrest us or anything?"

Nervous laughter titters around the room.

Ceepak raises his right hand. "On my honor."

"Well," Olivia says, "we were only fifteen and sixteen."

"But," Becca adds, "sometimes, at night, you know, we liked to party . . . drink beer."

"And Boone's Farm."

"Nuh-uh, Olivia. You were the only one who liked Boone's Farm."

Olivia shrugs. "At the time, I thought it was wine."

"It's basically soda pop that they mix with malt liquor," Jess says, speculating on the secret Boone's Farm recipe. "And, it had that handy screw-off top."

"So," I say, "we spent our days working, hanging out on the beach. At night, we'd find somebody to help us buy a six-pack or two. Some wino who didn't mind aiding and abetting our underage drinking, especially if we gave him a few extra bucks, bought him a quart of Colt 45."

"Then, we'd just, you know, chill," Jess says. "Maybe build a little driftwood fire. Check out the stars. Listen to music."

"Make out," says Olivia. "A lot of cute boys drift through town during the summer."

Becca sighs. "Every week was like a new summer camp full of 'em."

"Other people would join us," Olivia adds. "Kids we knew from school or people we met at our jobs. Kids on vacation with their folks. And Mook? He was always our evening's entertainment. The cruise director. He always had something stupid up his sleeve. Some joke or wild idea."

The room gets quiet again. Everybody remembers Harley Mook. Before we grew up and began to change. Before he was murdered.

"I miss Mook," Becca says. A tear trickles out from behind the sunglasses. "He was funny back then, you know?"

Olivia sinks deeper into the sofa. "Yeah. He was."

"Wheezer." Jess hisses the name. "Wheezer." He's trying hard to remember. Me, too. Was Wheezer one of those guys who used to join us sometimes? Maybe just a summer renter's kid? Somebody from the Pancake Palace? Maybe a lifeguard?

"What's his real name?" Olivia asks.

"We don't know," answers Ceepak.

"Well, Mook was always giving everybody names. He called me Liver Oil."

Becca grins. "I was Betcha-Can't-Eat-Just-One. Like the potato chips. I think it was supposed to be dirty."

"I was Jess. Dude never hung a handle on me."

"Whom might he have called Wheezer?" Ceepak paces around the room. "A schoolmate? Someone he worked with? Someone he met that summer? We suspect Wheezer is a local."

On account of the bumper sticker.

"But someone who has probably since moved away."

How'd he come up with that?

"We know his complexion is currently pale. Even a local using SPF 50 would show a slight skin coloration."

Okay. I'm with him again.

"We also know Wheezer felt insignificant in your presence. In his last communication, the shooter suggested that you'd never remember him. I suspect he was something of a loner, not one of the 'cool kids.' In fact, Mook told Danny that Wheezer was a loser."

"A loser?" Becca seems surprised.

"I always thought *we* were the losers," jokes Olivia.

"We were," Becca says. "Except Jess. Jess was always cool."

"I was not."

"Dude, you were a lifeguard."

Jess shrugs, and we all rack our brains trying to remember ten summers ago and some loner or loser who drifted into our lives.

I've got nothing. I look around the room.

Nobody has anything except lost and unhappy expressions on their faces.

"Keep thinking about it," Ceepak says. He checks the time. Four thirty. I don't think he's concerned about the chief's deadline. I think he's worried about the forty-eight-hour rule. Ceepak once told me that if you don't solve your case in the first two days, chances are you never will.

The clock is ticking.

"I think it would be wise for all of you to remain in protective custody for the remainder of the weekend," Ceepak says. "We'll post police officers outside your residences. It would be best if you stayed indoors."

"Me, too?"

"Yes, Danny. I'm pulling you out of the field. I need you to focus on Wheezer. It's how you can best aid the investigation."

I nod. He's right.

A speaker up in the ceiling bongs a series of chimes.

"Code Blue. ICU. Code Blue."

The voice is incredibly calm, but I know Code Blue means there's some kind of medical emergency in the ICU. I hear people run up the hall outside our door.

They're running to the ICU.

Where Katie is.

THIRTY-FIVE

I sit on a couch and stare at a curtain.

The couch is another one of those teal and speckle jobs that are supposed to calm people down. The curtain is a thin cotton sheet pulled across the glass window into Katie's ICU room. The nurses let Ceepak and me come this far only because we have badges. The other guys had to hang back in the visitors' room.

The doctor rolled the curtain across the window because he didn't want us to see them in there pounding on Katie's chest.

Ceepak is sitting next to me on the couch. When the radio clipped to his belt squeals he turns it off. He has about five billion other things he should be doing right now. Instead, he sits with me. I have my head in my hands.

"She's strong," he says. "She'll make it. This is not her time. Today is not her day."

I know it's a string of clichés, the kind of things people say in made-for-TV movies or something. But Ceepak's seen stuff, watched his buddies being blown to bits in Iraq, seen others who pulled through. Maybe he knows what he's talking about. Maybe he can tell who'll make it, who won't.

A doctor comes into the hallway and lifts his mask.

"She's stabilizing," he says. "She lost a tremendous amount of blood and her BP became dangerously low."

"But she's gonna make it?" I ask.

"She's stabilizing." That's the best the doctor can do right now. He slides his mask back up and goes into Katie's room.

"Danny?"

It's a nurse. Someone I know (of course). Christine Lemonopoulos.

"Hey."

"How you doing?" she asks, genuinely concerned. Christine and Katie are friends. I think they go to chick flicks together, and one of them is always in charge of the Kleenex.

"I'm hanging in there," I say.

"Ma'am?" Ceepak says to Christine.

"Yes?"

"Will it be all right for Officer Boyle to remain here in the hallway?"

"No problem. Just, you know—don't get in anybody's way, okay, Danny?"

"Sure. I'll just, you know, hang here."

"Cool. Can I get you guys anything? A Coke or something?"

"No thanks," I say.

"We're good." Ceepak isn't thirsty either.

"Hang in there, Danny."

"Yeah. You, too, Christine."

"Thanks."

We're both going to try.

Five P.M. Ceepak is still on the couch next to me. The doctors pulled open the curtains when they had Katie's Code Blue situation under control. She's still unconscious but I guess she's Code Green or whatever color it is when you're doing better.

"Shouldn't you be out there looking for that minivan?" I ask. "Tracking down the surfer gloves?"

"Soon," he says. "Don't worry. Our guys are on it."

"I'm okay here," I say, trying to give him permission to hit the streets.

"Danny, did I ever tell you about the Christmas choir when I was a kid? Midnight mass?"

Okay. Now he's being totally random.

"No. I don't think . . . no."

I've only heard maybe one or two stories about Ceepak's child-hood, which I know is more than he's told most people. His past is basically unavailable for public viewing because he didn't have a very good one. His dad was a drunk who used to beat up his mom and drove Ceepak's little brother to suicide. Somehow, I doubt his Christmas tale is going to be one of those Hallmark Hall of Fame numbers where somebody discovers the true meaning of the season and saves the day for all the crippled orphans in town.

Ceepak sinks back on the couch.

"My father used to play the drums," he says.

"You're kidding? Drums?"

"He was in a rock band in high school. Played some in college. Nightclubs. Bars. Places that paid with free beer. Anyhow, my father kept his drum kit stowed in our basement. Every now and then, he'd go down there and make a racket. I could tell how much he'd been drinking by how badly he kept time, his lack of any discernible rhythm."

I can just imagine it: Old Man Ceepak, toasted out of his gourd, drumming away, smashing and crashing cymbals. I'll bet it sounded like all hell broke loose in that basement, like when a two-year-old gets a toy drum for his birthday and gives everybody a free concert and a migraine.

"Was he any good?" I ask.

"Not really. But this one Christmas, when he swore to God he was sober, when he promised my mother his drinking days were behind him, he decided he'd show her what a good man he had become by volunteering to play drums for our church's Christmas choir."

"And you were you in the choir?"

"I was nine. I believe participation was considered somewhat mandatory."

"Don't tell me: you guys did 'The Little Drummer Boy?' "

"Of course."

"And your dad? He did a drum solo?"

"Such was the plan. Christmas Eve, I helped my father haul his drums up to the choir loft. Set up the kit. It was all good. At least when we rehearsed."

"What? He'd started drinking again?"

"He never stopped, Danny. He just told my mother he had. He lied to her. Made me lie to her as well."

"No way. You lied to your own mother? On Christmas Eve?"

"At the time, I would have told you I was protecting her from the truth."

"What happened?"

"Midnight mass. Hundreds of parishioners pack the pews. All of sudden, there's this tremendous commotion up in the choir loft. Drums topple over. Cymbals crash to the floor. Microphones squeal. My father was so drunk he slid off his stool and took everything down with him."

I probably shouldn't laugh. So I just chuckle.

"It only lasted a few seconds. My father climbed back onto his stool and was able to pound out the requisite pa-rum-pum-pum-pums. After mass, my mother asked me about the noise, asked me what happened."

"What'd you tell her?"

"I told her the choir director tripped on a microphone cord."

"You lied?" I'm amazed.

"The children of drunks grow very accustomed to telling lies, Danny. It quickly becomes one's hardwired first response."

"Come on. Give yourself a break. You were just a kid."

"I know."

"You didn't want to ruin Christmas for your mom."

"Perhaps. Or maybe I was afraid of what my father might do to me if I told her the truth. In any event, I am not proud of my actions that evening."

"You were nine years old!"

"Yes. And it was a minor transgression. However, if I had told my mother the truth that Christmas, perhaps she would have seen my father for what he really was. Perhaps she could have escaped."

"Man, you're blowing it way out of proportion."

"Perhaps. But actions, no matter how slight or insignificant, have ripple effects, Danny. Unintended consequences."

I think I understand where Ceepak's going with this.

"So you think something small we did back in nineteen ninety-six, some 'minor transgression' turned into a big, major deal for this guy Wheezer?"

"It's a possibility. 'You'll never remember. I'll never forget.' "

"Yeah."

"Try to remember, Danny. Try hard."

Ceepak stands.

"Stay here. Keep an eye on Katie. Get some sleep if you can. Try to remember."

THIRTY-SIX

Around seven P.M., Christine brings me a pillow.

Around seven fifteen, I fall asleep sideways on the couch.

Suddenly Christine is shaking my shoulder. It's morning.

"She asked for you."

"Whaa?" I forget where I am, why my breath stinks. Why is Christine waking me up? Are we even dating?

"Katie," she says and shakes my shoulder some more.

My brain sputters, I blink. It's like the grumpy superintendent inside my skull shuffles over to the circuit breaker box, flicks the switches, lights me up for another day.

"Katie," I mumble. I remember Katie.

"She asked for you."

"She's awake?"

"Come on."

Christine takes my hand and leads me into Katie's room.

Katie's eyes are open. There's a thin smile on her dry, cracked lips.

"Danny."

"Hey."

I reach for her hand. Christine nods. It's okay.

I take Katie's hand into mine and would squeeze it but I see they have an IV needle jabbed in near the thin tendons. So, I stroke her hand instead. I rub it gently, like I'm petting some newborn kitten.

There's a bunch of water blurring my eyes. I've got a lump in my throat the size of a meatball. I can't believe I'm seeing her emerald green eyes open and looking back at me.

"Danny." She sighs, closes her eyes, and smiles like she's having a really good dream.

"Let her rest," Christine suggests.

"Is she . . . ?"

"Yeah, she is, Danny. She's going to be okay."

"Promise?"

"Promise. I'll go grab you a chair. You can sit with her."

She drags a vinyl chair into the room.

"Thanks."

"She's on the mend," she says. "But she needs to rest."

About a half hour later, the doctor comes in and sees me sitting next to Katie's bed.

"How is she?" he asks.

"She, you know, recognized me."

"So I heard." He scribbles some stuff on the clipboard hanging off the foot of her bed. "That's very good news."

The doctor leaves. I resume staring at Katie while she sleeps.

Every now and then, her green eyes flutter open, focus on me, and she smiles. Then, her eyelids flicker shut and she drifts off. I think a couple of those IV bags are pumping down pain medicine, the kind that makes you drowsy. Katie should definitely avoid operating any heavy machinery for the next few days.

My mind is spinning. I wish I'd had one of those dreams last night where all is revealed. A dream where the real Wheezer stands up like in that old TV game show *To Tell the Truth*. No such luck.

Maybe one of the other guys figured it out. Probably Olivia. She's the smartest. I check the cell phone clipped to my belt. No new messages. The others have probably all gone home with their police escorts. They're sitting somewhere right now like I am, with the word "Wheezer" running around their heads like a hopped-up hamster.

"Wheezer." I whisper it. "Wheezy, Wheezer, Weasel."

It's becoming a chant, like saying the rosary, which is something I forget how to do but I remember it involved a lot of mumbling of the same words over and over.

"Wheezer, wiener, weenie, wienerschnitzel, weenie, weasel, wheezy, wheezer . . ."

"Danny?"

Katie. I must've been mumbling louder than I thought.

"Hey." I push myself out of the chair and move up to her pillow. I slide a sweaty strand of red hair out of her eyes.

"Don't," she says.

"Sorry." I take my hand off her hair. Guess her forehead hurts.

"Don't."

I'm not doing anything.

"Don't do what?"

"Don't tease Weese."

Her eyes close. She drifts back to sleep.

I remember.

Weese.

"Wheezer" is George Weese.

THIRTY-SEVEN

August something-or-other, 1996.

Summer days all kind of blur together in a lazy haze. But that one day, whenever it was, was different. Not hugely different, just different enough.

I think it sent out those ripple effects Ceepak warned me about.

It was almost the end of August, during "Back to School Savings Time." The TV was already running that Staples commercial about the "Most Wonderful Time of the Year." The old Christmas song plays in the background while a happy dad pilots his shopping cart up and down the aisles, chucking in paper and notebooks and pens and all the supplies his sad little children need before they head back to school.

What we did to George Weese that day was really no big deal. Honest. It was just one of those stupid things bored kids do, especially kids who are fifteen and sixteen. When you're that age, you never realize that some of what you do is pretty awful. I was, basically, a teenage boy trying to figure out how to become a man—I mean, besides the obvious hormone and hair stuff.

I wanted to be my own man, not just somebody's son.

My friends and I hung out on Oak Beach almost every day. We

lived in our own little world. We all had summer jobs and, like the song says, "Money got made, money got spent." We laughed and listened to music and cruised the boardwalk and chased girls we didn't even know. We were trying hard to be cool and we thought we were.

George Weese was not.

Weese was the opposite of cool. He was a loser. A dork. He was the Wheezer.

"He sits behind me in home room," Mook told us. "I swear, that big nose of his? It's stuffed with boogers. He wheezes when he breathes because the air can't make it past the booger boulders."

I remember when Weese stumbled up the beach toward our spot that day. He wasn't coming to visit us. He was just passing through.

"Here he comes!" Mook goofed. "Can you hear him?" Then Mook did this funny bit where he sounded like a donkey trapped inside Darth Vader's helmet, all raspy and asthmatic, rattling a "hee" and a "haw" with every breath. Mook cracked us up.

Weese was tall and gangly, with a farmer's tan on his forearms — the rest of his skin was basically the same goose-pimply white as raw chicken. He was one of those guys who always squinted but never thought about buying clip-ons or wearing a baseball cap to shield his eyes. And he couldn't seem to coordinate his knees with his ankles. His big floppy feet kept sliding sideways in the sand, and when he'd stumble, his glasses would slip and he'd have to push them back up the bridge of his humongous nose. Mook was right: you could hear the air whistling and wheezing and whining through his nostrils every time he breathed in or out.

To make matters worse, that day George Weese was wearing these white swim trunks with an elastic navy blue belt looped through the waistband. He looked ridiculous, like he was wearing underpants or a kitchen trash can liner with a blue plastic tie-cord.

"Nice undies, Wheezer," Mook said when Weese came close to the plot of sand we had claimed as our own that day.

It was about four P.M. I remember Jess got off duty at three, I finished at the Pancake Palace around two, everybody was done working for the day, and the six of us were basically chilling, swilling sodas, wondering what we wanted to do until it was time to head home.

Mook, our self-appointed cruise director, decided what we'd do first: we'd have some fun with a wimp named Wheezer.

He blocked Weese's path up the beach.

When Weese tried to step around him, Mook moved sideways, got in his way again.

"Where you going, Wheezer?"

Weese didn't say anything. Some girls two blankets over started to giggle. Mook loved it.

"Oops. I think they can see your weenie, Wheezy."

Weese looked down at his swimsuit. The white polyester fabric was thin, almost transparent.

"It's a teeny weenie," Mook boomed. "More like a gherkin. One of those teeny-weeny itty-bitty pickles."

Jess laughed. I did, too.

"You been jerkin' your gherkin, Wheezer?" Mook was on a roll.

"That's against beach rules." Jess stood up, dusted some sand off his red swim trunks. "Gherkin jerkin' is strictly prohibited on all public beaches."

"Yeah," I added. "It says so on all the signs. Right after 'no glass bottles' comes 'no weenie whacking.' "

Mook laughed at my new spin on his joke and we slapped each other a high-five. Jess knocked knuckles with us. I felt great. We were guys. Tough guys, topping each other, saying shit that was funnier than hell.

Becca and Olivia giggled and tried not to be obvious while they stared at Weese's crotch. Poor guy. His swim trunks weren't just white—they were two seasons too old. Extremely tight.

"You can totally see his pecker," Becca said while she pointed. "Totally!"

Olivia slapped Becca's hand down.

"Stop!" But Olivia was laughing.

"It's a teeny-weeny jelly-beanie." Becca sang it. Olivia lost it.

Katie shocked us all. She had no brothers, and I think this was, you know, an eye-opening experience for her, so to speak. She kept staring at the nubby lump located between Weese's legs.

"It sort of looks like a mouse," she said in this small, astonished voice.

"Yeah," Mook snorted. "Like Minnie Mouse!"

Katie didn't laugh.

Everybody else, however, hooted. Katie, I remember now, sort of covered her mouth, like she was horrified by what she had just let slip out and wished she could take it back.

The other girls wouldn't let her.

"Minnie Mouse!" Becca hollered. She and Olivia rolled backwards, kicking their feet, squealing and howling.

Katie flung some sand at them. "Come on you guys," she said. "Knock it off. Don't tease Weese."

"Knock it off?" said Mook. "Never!" Then he raised his hand like he was some kind of king making a speech to his soldiers. "No retreat! No surrender!"

Jess raised his arm, I raised mine. We were the Three Goofeteers. All for one, one for all.

"No retreat! No surrender!"

Weese just stood there taking it. I remember his face went pink like the sunburned patches on the tops of his shoulders.

"Like Minnie Mouse!" Becca gasped again when she finally caught her breath.

Weese backed up. Looked around. Saw that all the kids on Oak Beach were staring at him. Guys stopped tossing Nerf balls and leered like ringside drunks at a boxing match waiting for the knockout punch and wishing they could be the ones to land it.

The girls up and down the sand? Most were sitting up on their towels, leaning forward, arching their backs, laughing into cupped hands. I noticed some were looking my way. Sizing me up. Liking what they saw. I remember feeling extremely manly that day.

The adults? I don't think there were any adults on that stretch of sand. No little kids, either. I guess that's why we hung out there. Oak Beach was Teen Town. We had our own rules, our own laws, our own music—the same station, WAVY, blasting out of every boom box.

"Hey, Wheezer?" Mook said, shaking the grape soda bottle in his fist. "Think fast!"

Mook released his thumb, let the foam fly, sprayed Weese right in the crotch.

"Uh-oh!" Mook screamed. "Looks like Wheezer just got his period! Anybody have a Kotex he can borrow?"

Everybody—I mean everybody—busted a gut laughing at that one. Guys, girls, everybody. They were pointing at the purple splotch, thinking Harley Mook was funnier than anything they'd seen or heard all summer. I remember Mook took a little bow. Some of the girls near us dug into their beach bags, found tampons, tossed them at Weese.

I also remember glancing over at Katie.

Okay. Not everybody was busting a gut. She was staring at me the way my mom would whenever I did something that "disappointed" her. You know—when she saw me swipe a miniature chocolate egg out of my kid brother's Easter basket when I still had plenty in mine. Stuff like that.

"Thank you, folks," Mook said. "I'm here all week." Mook was bigger that day than Leno.

I remember other things: Weese narrowing his eyes, not saying a word. The sound as he breathed in through his mouth, wheezed out through his nose. The strong gumball grape smell, like dry Kool-Aid powder.

"Now don't go running home to tell your mommy," Mook said, moving in closer, poking Weese's bony rib cage with his empty Welch's bottle. "You do that, we'll come after you. Capeesh?"

"No retreat! No surrender!" screamed Jess.

"You can run, but you cannot hide," I added.

I swaggered up to Weese to say it because I knew those bikini babes up the beach were still checking me out and there were a couple

I hoped to impress further. Those girls weren't disappointed in me. They weren't like Katie or my mom. No, they were intrigued by my savage masculinity. Or so I thought. I guess I had a pretty vivid imagination back then.

"If I can't get you," Mook promised Weese, "my friends will!"

Weese looked at Jess. Looked at me. Then, he turned around. I could see his head tilt down as he dared a quick peek at the front of his soiled swim pants.

"Careful girls," Mook hollered and strutted back to his beach towel. "Wheezer here has a one-eyed Purple People Eater in his pants."

Katie shook her head. I think she was disappointed in all of us.

We didn't care. We swayed back and forth and sang a quick chorus of that stupid one-hit wonder: *"It was a one-eyed, one-horned, flyin' purple people eater . . ."*

Weese shuffled away. Everybody he passed pointed at his pants and hooted. Some guys shook cans of whatever they had in their mitts and made like they might spray that at Weese, too. Others yelled, "What'd you do? Piss your pants purple?" Girls shook their heads, disgusted by the scrawny doofus with the splotchy crotch who they thought should find some other piece of beach to go geek around on.

The whole deal lasted maybe five minutes. Ten tops.

Even Katie got over it.

We moved on to whatever was next. Chasing each other with squirt guns. Playing paddleball. Meeting some girls from the city who were in town for the week and looking to party. Maybe we plotted that night's beer run. Maybe we ran out of snack food items and argued about whose turn it was to hike up to the Qwick Pick and grab another bag of something to munch on.

The same old same old.

We moved on.

We forgot.

I guess George Weese never did.

• • •

I have to wonder if maybe Mook got hot waiting in his car for Wheezer. Maybe he took a couple of swigs from that twenty-ounce grape soda we found in the cup holder. Maybe Weese saw Mook knock back a few gulps and a certain purple-stained day came rushing back to him in Digital High Def and Surround Sound.

I guess we'll have to ask him.

I unclip my cell phone and punch in Ceepak's number.

He answers on the first ring.

"This is Ceepak."

"Hey," I say. "We need to find George Weese."

THIRTY-EIGHT

Coast Guard Auxiliary Flotilla 75 in Avondale, New Jersey, usually does stuff like teach boating safety to weekend sailors.

But they also have this really fast boat. A forty-four-foot, aluminum-hulled number that can do thirty-five knots. That's like forty mph. I know because Rosie, my skipper, a Coast Guard Reservist, told me so. Actually, she had to scream it because we were flying across the bay so fast—about forty mph.

When I called Ceepak, he called his Coast Guard buddies. Apparently, they were delighted to help him out by seeing how fast their new boat could go. So now I'm wearing a bright orange life jacket over my bulletproof vest, holding on to a handrail with sea spray needling my face and skimming like a flicked stone across the bay back to the island. This sea puppy's fast.

Christine will keep an eye on Katie at the hospital. So, of course, will the doctors. Ceepak said he'd meet me at the marina off Bayside Boulevard, over near Schooner's Landing—back where we think George Weese parked his white minivan, stepped out, and took two shots. One at me, one at Katie.

Rosie pulls back on the throttle. We churn up backwash, lose speed, and drift toward the dock. Ceepak is standing there to salute us on our final approach.

Rosie snaps one back.

"Throw him the line," she barks. It takes me a second to figure out she's barking at me, that I'm all of a sudden her first mate. "Throw him the dock line!"

I hoist this big coil of rope and heave it toward Ceepak. I almost fling myself onto the dock after it. Ceepak catches the line and wraps it around a cleat.

"Here's your cargo," Rosie says when I stumble off the boat.

"Thank you, Rosie," Ceepak says. "I owe you one."

"So buy me a beer."

"Will do. But not when you're on duty."

"Roger that," she says. "Hurry up. Go catch the bastard."

"Come on, Danny." Ceepak motions for me to keep up with him. "We need to join everybody over at the Weese residence."

"Did the guys find George?"

"Not yet."

I check my watch. It's 10:52 A.M. We walk faster, heading off the dock into the parking lot.

"Did they, you know, find any evidence?"

"Roger that. They tell me there's a white minivan parked in the garage."

"Green beach sticker?"

"On the front bumper not far from the lighthouse license plate."

"I thought George Weese lived out of town."

"He does."

"So what's he doing with a resident beach sticker?"

"His father cheated. Bought an extra tag, sent it to his son hoping it might encourage George to . . ." Ceepak checks his notebook. " 'Bring the grandchildren down more often.' Mrs. Weese bought George the minivan. Apparently, the Weeses are quite wealthy."

But they cheat.

To Ceepak, that's all that matters.

• • •

We pull up in front of the Weese house.

Ceepak's right: these people are loaded.

They have a humongous house, two in from the ocean at the corner of Beach Lane and Walnut Street. It's three stories tall, with all sorts of angles and extensions and different-shaped windows and jutting decks and this big sweeping staircase up to double front doors with gold-trimmed glass windows like something Tony Soprano might buy at Home Depot. I'm surprised the Weeses don't just hang a sign off one of their roofs: "Got money? We sure as shit do."

I see Kiger and Malloy's patrol car parked out front near the two-car garage at the left side of the house. I see the CSI team's Taurus, too.

Ceepak pulls in but doesn't park very well. He just sort of angles our Ford against the concrete curb with the butt sticking out into the street. Kiger is in the driveway looking like he's eager to tell him something, so Ceepak yanks up the emergency brake and basically jumps out of the Explorer. I follow along.

"What've you got, Adam?"

"Weapon and ammunition in the minivan. Rear cargo hold."

"The M-24?" Ceepak asks.

Kiger shakes his head. "Negative. Looks like a paintball shooter. You know—a big toy gun. Black plastic. Molded to look like an army rifle."

"Most likely a Tripman A-5 with reactive trigger," Ceepak says. Then he turns to me because he knows I'm totally confused. "Same as rifle number three at Paintball Blasters on the boardwalk. I checked last night. Weese wanted to practice on the same type of gun, see if he could manipulate the trigger action while gloved."

While I was passed out on that sofa outside the ICU, Ceepak was back here working the case.

A Ford Expedition crunches up the street. Chief Baines.

"What've we got, Ceepak?"

"Potential suspect, sir."

"Weese? From the Chamber?"

"His son. George."

"Do we know where this George Weese is presently located?" The chief reaches for the shoulder microphone to his radio, ready to call in strike coordinates on our sniper.

"No, sir. We've posted an APB based on witness descriptions."

"And," Kiger says, "we have his father and mother inside. Also the suspect's wife and children. Malloy's in there with them, making sure nobody tells Georgie Porgie the cavalry's coming."

"What's the prevailing mood?" Baines is curious. "Inside?"

Kiger smiles. "Pissed off, sir."

The chief nods, turns to Ceepak.

"John?"

"Yes, sir?"

"You sure about this? You sure George Weese is your guy?"

"It's where all the evidence leads, sir."

The chief checks his watch, nods his head.

"Let's go nail the bastard."

Looks like we might beat that noon deadline after all.

"This is preposterous. George would never do such a thing." This is his mother talking, naturally. She's short and chubby and chain smokes.

Two little kids bawl and screech in a playpen in the middle of the living room. One, a boy, looks to be almost two years old. The other? I don't know. I'm no good at guessing how old babies are supposed to be. I wish they had rings I could count like with trees. Maybe the little one's nine or ten months. The way it screams? Got the lungs of a twelve-year-old. Both kids have tears streaming down their cheeks and snot dripping out their noses, and it all ends up as crusty green stuff on top of their lips. There's reason to suspect the small one has a load in its pants, too. Either that, or Mrs. Weese is cooking something foul for brunch.

"Bad move, Baines," Mr. Weese says. "A one-month job never looks good on a résumé." He is peacocking around the living room in bright-yellow shorts and a sky blue polo shirt. He's also got on golf shoes so I think we more than likely interrupted his Sunday plans. His socks match his shirt and pants. Vibrant. I guess so the other golfers can see you coming from two tees away.

"George would never do such a thing." Mrs. Weese is indignant. "Never. I know my boy."

The two kids in the playpen break some kind of indoor world record and scream even louder.

"Natalia? Jesus!" Mrs. Weese turns to their mother, who's sitting slumped in an armchair. "Take them upstairs, please. Now!"

"All right," her daughter-in-law says with some kind of thick, grumbling accent that makes her sound like one of the bad guys in a billion spy movies. She could be Russian. She has dark hair and a sour face.

Natalia Weese marches across the living and scoops up her two squealers.

"Malloy?" Ceepak now says.

Mark Malloy nods. "On it." He follows the younger Mrs. Weese and the screaming kids out of the room. No one is being left alone where they can whip out a cell phone to let George know people are looking for him.

"Perhaps you should arrange for someone to help out with your grandchildren," Ceepak says to Mr. Weese. "We'll want to interview all of you, including George's wife."

"Good luck," Mr. Weese says with a curl of his lip. "She's Russian. None too bright, either. Still having a tough time with English, even after she's been here, what? Three years?"

"Lies!" Mrs. Weese now screams at Ceepak, as if shouting might make it true. "This is all a pack of lies! You don't have any evidence!"

"Yes, ma'am, we do," Ceepak says. "Your son fits the description of a young man who recently purchased seven Derek Jeter baseball cards at Aquaman's Comix and Collectibles."

"Wrong. George never played baseball."

"He never played any sports," Mr. Weese adds.

"He played those computer games."

"Those are not sports!"

"He had that soccer one!"

Mr. and Mrs. Weese scowl at each other. Then they swivel so they can scowl at us, too.

"What's with the baseball cards?" Mr. Weese asks Chief Baines.

"The sniper placed the same cards your son bought at Schooner's Landing," Baines says.

"So? Maybe he stole them from George!" Mrs. Weese says. "You ever think of that?"

"Aquaman's Comix?" Mr. Weese says. "That's Dan Bloomfield's shop. He's with the Chamber. If he's spreading lies about George . . ."

"He's leasing that space." Mrs. Weese sucks down some hot smoke. "We can raise his rent . . ."

"We sure as shit can!"

"Mr. and Mrs. Weese?" Chief Baines interrupts. "Please. Where is your son?"

There is no answer. Mr. Weese shakes his head in disgust. I'm not certain, but I get the feeling he's been disappointed with his son for some time. I say this because my dad used to give me the same kind of headshake—usually right after I did something totally stupid.

Ceepak turns to Kiger. "What about the tires? On the minivan?"

"They match." Dr. McDaniels walks into the room.

"Who's this?" Mr. Weese demands. "This is my house . . . all these people . . . traipsing in and out . . ."

"Dr. Sandra McDaniels." She extends her hand. He doesn't take it. "Pleased to make your acquaintance."

"What's this about tires?"

"The tread pattern on the minivan in your garage matches those we found over on Oak Street."

"So? What is that supposed to mean?"

"It means your son is the primary suspect in the killing of Harley Mook."

"Who did you say you were?" Mrs. Weese sounds even angrier than her husband.

"Dr. Sandra McDaniels. New Jersey State Police Major Crime Unit. I'm not really here." She holds up a big plastic baggie. "But I did find these in the back of your son's minivan, right next to the paint-ball rifle. Do either of you folks surf?"

Inside the baggie? Two neoprene surfer gloves.

"No," Mr. Weese answers, not quite getting that McDaniels's question was basically what they call rhetorical. "I golf. Helen gardens."

"Where's your son's toothbrush?" McDaniels asks.

"His toothbrush?"

"I need to collect some DNA. Lift his prints off the handle. Maybe his bathroom cup. Pretty fertile forensic fields, bathrooms. Find all sorts of human detritus. Unless, of course, your son wore gloves while he brushed his teeth, too."

Somehow, Dr. McDaniels entrance has made Mr. and Mrs. Weese realize we mean business.

"His bathroom's on the second floor." Mr. Weese suddenly sounds defeated.

"Go get what you need," Chief Baines says to McDaniels.

She winks at Ceepak and ambles up the staircase.

"Franklin?" Mrs. Weese put her hand on her chest and sighs. "I feel faint."

"Then sit down." Which he promptly does himself. She follows suit.

"We need a recent photograph," Ceepak says.

"Of George?" Mrs. Weese looks ready to cry. Instead, she lights another cigarette.

"Yes, ma'am."

"This will work," I say, reaching for a framed wedding photo on an end table.

"No. Not that one." Mrs. Weese takes it from my hands. "He looks terrible there. His mouth hanging open like that. Let me get you a better one. From my bedroom . . ."

"Adam?" Ceepak cocks his head to send Officer Kiger wherever Mrs. Weese goes.

"Ma'am?" Kiger steps forward to let George's mother know she now has an official police escort.

"What? You think I'm going to call George?"

"Yes, ma'am," Ceepak says because he always tells the truth. "That photograph? We need it immediately if not sooner."

"Oh, take whatever you want. It doesn't matter."

I hang on to the wedding shot.

Ceepak's cell phone rings. He rips it off his belt, flips it open.

"This is Ceepak. Go ahead."

We all stare while he nods, then nods again.

"Right. Thank you."

He snaps the cell phone shut.

"What?" demands Chief Baines.

"Friend of ours down on the boardwalk."

"Who?"

"T. J. Lapczynski." Ceepak turns from the chief to face Mr. Weese. "He's played paintball with your son."

"So?"

"George is on the boardwalk right now, heading for the Tower of Terror."

"Let's go," Baines says.

"Possible ten-eighty-eight."

"Jesus, he has a gun?"

"Not certain. However, T. J. says our suspect is carrying a duffel bag."

THIRTY-NINE

T he Tower of Terror is that 250-foot-tall ride in the middle of the boardwalk.

It looks like the Seattle Space Needle—a steeple of steel girders and diagonal tie beams stretching up to the sky. On all four sides are these chairs you pay good money to sit in to be scared out of your wits. There are six chairs on each side with seat belts and padded shoulder harnesses. Twenty-four folks get hauled up to the top. Twenty-four folks get dropped about 240 feet before the brakes come on. It's like paying five bucks to ride an open-air elevator and have somebody snip the cable.

I only rode the Tower of Terror once, and I think my stomach is still somewhere up there, about halfway down.

From the top, before they drop you like a rock, you do, momentarily, get this incredible view—all the way up and down the beach. You can see the boardwalk below, the ocean off to the side. On a clear day, you can see all the way out to the Ship John lighthouse on the north end of the island. If George Weese makes it to the top of the Tower with an M-24 Sniper Weapon System, he could definitely rain down all sorts of terror.

"Shut it down!" Chief Baines issues the command into his radio microphone. We run down the sweeping staircase outside the Weese house. "Shut the Tower down, now!"

Fortunately, we have plenty of guys patrolling the boardwalk on account of the big holiday crowds. Dominic Santucci, the hardass of all hardass cops, the guy who constantly busts my chops, is in charge down there. He'll get the job done. In fact, I'm sure the Tower of Terror is already frozen in mid-hoist, stranding confused thrill-seekers in their seats with nothing to do but dangle their feet and check out that view.

"Lights and sirens?" Ceepak asks the chief as we slide into our vehicle and the chief jumps into his.

"No. No noise. Just haul ass. Flashers only."

"Ten-four." Ceepak slams his door shut and snaps on the roofbar. The lights swirl their reds and blues to request that anyone driving in front of us kindly get the hell out of our way.

Malloy and Kiger will stay here with the Weeses. McDaniels and her techs will swab George's bathroom. Ceepak, the chief, and I?

We shall proceed to haul ass.

"The ride is shut down," our radio cackles. "Repeat. Tower of Terror is shut down."

"Good work, Dom," we hear the chief reply.

We're doing about 75 mph up Ocean Avenue. Ceepak grabs the radio mic. Now he's doing 75 one-handed. "Any sign of Weese?"

"Not here," Santucci comes back. "Not at Tower of Terror."

"Do you know what he looks like?" the chief asks over the radio.

"Sort of."

On the radio, we hear the chief's curt reply. "Not good enough, Sergeant Santucci!"

Ceepak gestures for me to take the George Weese wedding photo we grabbed out of its frame.

"Dom, do you have your computer up?" he says into his hand mic.

"Ten-four. Up and operational."

"Danny's going to e-mail you an image."

I use our in-car digital video camera to grab a still frame of the wedding photo. It shows an open-mouthed George wearing the same glasses he wore when he was fifteen—at least the same style. His bride, Natalia, at his side looks impassive. Kind of glum. George's own expression is difficult to read.

I squeeze off a freeze frame, punch a few keys, and zap the image off to Santucci.

"Brace yourself," Ceepak says.

I brace my hand against the dash. Inertia thrusts me forward. It'll do that when your partner goes from 75 to zero in ten seconds.

Another sloppy parking job for Ceepak. We're right near a flight of steps leading up to the boardwalk. We hop out and start running.

"Excuse me. Pardon me."

Ceepak is polite even as we shove our way through the crowd. It is a total teeming mob scene. Thousands of kids. Teenagers. College girls. Bare skin and bikinis everywhere. The place is packed. There's so much coconut oil on the breeze you can't even smell the Italian sausage sandwiches.

"This is Two," a voice crackles off our walkie-talkies. "Suspect spotted. Headed south. He is carrying a black duffel bag."

The Tower of Terror is north. George must've changed his mind when he saw the crowd of cops converging on that ride, realized the elevator wasn't going up to the top anymore.

Ceepak scans the horizon. I follow his eye line. The Tower of Terror pokes up against the cloudless blue sky to the north. We swing to the south. I see the Ferris wheel and the Paul Bunyan–size statue of a Muffler Man someone repainted to look like a giant pirate holding a treasure chest. In front of us is the Atlantic Ocean. Behind us the shops—the mile-long row of arcades, food joints, tattoo parlors, T-shirt places.

"There!" Ceepak does his three-finger point to the south and east. The Mad Mouse roller coaster. "That'd be my fallback position."

I see what Ceepak sees. The Mad Mouse is the second-tallest steel structure on the beach. The twisting track is at the end of a short pier that juts out across the beach and over the ocean. The turns on the track are tight, sharp. The track itself, narrow. It's steep in places, but you could run up it like you were running up a ladder leaning against the side of your house, no need to wait for a seat like back at the Tower of Terror. You could hop the line, knock over the kid taking tickets, scamper up the track, and be at your sniper post in no time.

There's jagged, light-bulb letters up top spelling out the words "M A D M O U S E." Each of the Ms is at least six feet tall. Weese could slip behind one, prop his rifle in the giant Ms V-shaped crotch and start picking off targets down below.

"Excuse me. Pardon me. Coming through."

We play Ceepak's hunch, work our way through the mob and head south, over to the Mad Mouse.

I see Ceepak touch his pistol. He doesn't unsnap the holster, doesn't want to start shooting, not when we're surrounded by this tight a pack of innocent bystanders. But he wants to make sure it's still there in case he needs it.

"This is Four. We've got him." Another one of our foot soldiers has spotted Weese.

"Go, Four." It's Baines. He's in his car somewhere, coordinating.

"Suspect . . . south . . ."

Unit Four's broadcast breaks up, but we catch the gist.

"Middle of crowd . . . now east . . . Swirl Cone."

Ceepak stops in his tracks. Tries to get his bearings.

"All units," Baines voice comes over the radio. "Move south. Surround suspect."

"This a drug bust?" This chubby guy in a Speedo blocks our path. He licks an orange-and-white ice cream cone, stands with one hand nestled against the belly roll where his hip should be.

"Sir, where did you purchase that?" Ceepak asks him.

"Why? Is something wrong with it?"

"No, sir. Where did you purchase your cone?" Ceepak sounds like he really, really wants soft-serve ice cream.

"Over there." The guy gestures with his cone and it drips down his pudgy fist.

"Danny?"

"Sand Castle Swirl Cones. I know it."

"Is it near the Mad Mouse?"

"Yeah. Top of the pier. Fifty feet from the roller coaster."

Swirl Cones. We heard the words in Unit Four's call. Ceepak's hunch was right. We need to hustle.

"There," I say, pointing to the glowing orange-and-white swirl cone turrets poking out from Sand Castle's roof. We weave our way down the boardwalk, reach the top of the pier.

There's a commotion by the Mad Mouse ticket booth. A wave ripples through the line like somebody is pushing and shoving everybody else.

"Watch it, asshole!" Someone screams. Whoever she is, she has a mouth on her. "Fucking asshole is cutting the line!"

"There." Ceepak points to a silhouette of a skinny man lugging a duffel bag. He is climbing over coaster cars and scrambling up the track. He's only a silhouette against the bright morning sky, but I recognize the loping gait. It's definitely Wheezer.

Now what?

Ceepak punches his radio's shoulder mic.

"This is Ceepak. Suspect is scaling Mad Mouse."

"All units, this is Baines. Move in. Move in. Mad Mouse. Mad Mouse! Move!"

Ceepak stays calm.

"Suspect appears to be carrying his weapon concealed in a duffel bag," he says into the radio. "Repeat. His weapon is still cased, he is not currently armed."

"All units, all units. Move in on the Mad Mouse. Take him down!"

The screams at the base of the ride grow louder. The people don't yet sound scared, just mad.

"Get off the track, asshole!"

The ride they've been standing in line for has all of a sudden been shut down because some idiot with a suitcase is climbing up the tracks.

"We've been waiting!" One of them shouts. "It's our turn!"

So far no one suspects anything worse than a jerk with a gym bag.

Weese stumbles on the steepest hill of the track. Slips. Almost drops the duffel bag. He pulls himself back up, holds on to the guardrails like he's climbing a gangplank, checks his grip on the bag, and continues toward the top. He's heading for those blinking Ms.

Ceepak stops. Looks left. Right. Assesses our options.

"Backtrack," he says. I have no idea why. He pivots and heads west. So instead of running toward the Mad Mouse we're heading back up the pier toward the boardwalk shops and lemonade stands and . . .

. . . Paintball Blasters. The booth is right in front of us.

Ceepak dashes up to the counter like he wants to take a quick break and pop off a few shots at that cardboard Saddam.

He grabs a rifle, yanks it hard.

"Hey!" It's the old guy in the sleeveless T-shirt. Guess he's running things this morning.

"Is this weapon loaded and charged, sir?"

"Yeah, but you can't—"

Ceepak doesn't listen. He rips the gun off its anchor chain, pulls up a chunk of plywood and a screw.

"You break it, you buy it! You hear me?"

Ceepak twists around, lifts the rifle to his eye, squints, lines up the nose notch, squeezes the trigger.

Pop.

A paint ball smacks Weese's wrist. He drops the duffel but quickly lurches forward to grab it before it falls through the track.

Pop.

The second ball bops him in the right butt cheek, knocking him off balance. The duffel falls through the space between track ties, bounces off braces and crossbeams, tumbles down to the pier below.

Pop. Pop.

Paintballs three and four splatter Weese's shins. Left then right. He spins sideways, pants wet with paint, his feet slip out from under him, he flops onto the track, slides and wobbles down the hill like one of those battery-operated Penguin roller coasters.

The Mad Mouse crowd cheers when Weese comes tumbling down.

"Line jumper!" One guy yells. "That'll show you!"

Cops swarm the ride. Two guys crouch in the little mouse cars, use the ears up front to steady their pistols and take aim at Weese.

Santucci crawls under the girders to retrieve the duffel. Another one of our guys storms up the track, weapon drawn. Weese sits on his butt, his paint-slickened hands held high over his head.

It's over. We got him.

I turn to Ceepak. Check out the paintball weapon he tore off the counter.

"Rifle number three?"

"Roger that," he says with the hint of a smile. "T. J's right. It's definitely the best."

FORTY

We watch Santucci stuff George Weese into the back seat of a police cruiser parked on the boardwalk. I never knew you could drive down the boards in anything bigger than a golf cart–style trash hauler. I've seen those scoot up and down the boardwalk before, never a cop car. Guess there's an on-ramp somewhere.

Anyhow, Weese's hands are tied behind his back with flex-cuffs and Santucci has his hand on top of Weese's head, smooshing down that country music comb-back, trying to cram him into the back seat without banging his head against the doorjamb.

"Fucking line jumper!" someone shouts. I think it might be that same girl. Everybody here thinks Weese is being hauled away because he wouldn't wait his turn to ride the Mad Mouse. We're the Courtesy Cops, the Etiquette Enforcers.

"Good work, guys." Chief Baines is standing next to us. "Damn good work!" He claps Ceepak on the back. "Fantastic."

Weese is in the back seat staring at me.

It's an unpleasant sensation. The thick lenses in his glasses magnify his eyeballs so they look swollen, bloated with anger. I can see that, just as I had feared, just as Ceepak hypothesized, our suspect hates me.

Man, he hates me a lot.

"Why don't you guys take the rest of the weekend off?" Baines now says. "Enjoy yourselves. Come back tomorrow and grab some barbecue. Heck, you're the two working stiffs who just saved Labor Day!"

"We'd like to tie up a few loose ends," Ceepak says, sounding like he won't even think about taking time off until he's convinced this thing is completely over. He told me they had a lot of ceasefires back in Iraq. The only problem? People kept firing.

"We need to interrogate the suspect, ASAP."

"Sure. Sure. We'll call his folks. See if they want a lawyer present. See you back at the house."

On the drive back to headquarters, I tell Ceepak the whole story of what happened that day on the beach. What we did to George Weese. How we humiliated the Wheezer.

He nods. He understands.

Ripple effects.

When we walk in the front door of the house, everybody starts clapping.

"Way to go, guys!"

"Congratulations."

It's pretty awesome to walk into a police station as the cops who just cracked the big case and busted the bad guy. Everybody pats us on the back, shakes our hands. Most of the "way-to-go's" go to Ceepak, but I pick up the occasional "attaboy-Danny."

We head down the hall and see Santucci.

"Where is George Weese?" Ceepak asks.

"We put him in the interrogation room," says Santucci. Then, he pops a gumball in his mouth, turns to me. "You did okay today, kid."

"Thanks," I say. "Thanks, Dom."

He crunches his gumball a couple of chomps. Waits.

I try again: "Thanks, Sergeant Santucci."

He winks to let me know I got it right that time.

"We can't talk to him yet," he says. "His parents want a lawyer in the room before they let the kid answer any questions."

Ceepak understands. "How much longer until the lawyer arrives?"

"Mr. Weese said it might take a couple of hours. Apparently, their attorney is somewhere out in the bay on his sailboat looking for the wind."

"Where's the duffel bag?"

"In the back. Dr. McDaniels and her crew set up shop in the empty office."

"Was it an M-24?" Ceepak asks.

"Yep. Loaded with those special ball cartridges you told us about. Five of them. We saved some lives out there today."

"Roger that."

They both smile. Their adrenaline drains. They're coming down off the high you get when you're ripping paintball rifles off plywood counters or chasing bad guys up a Mad Mouse.

It's all good.

"Yeah, that's him."

Young T. J. Lapczynski is with us in the viewing room. There's a one-way mirror between us and the interrogation room. We can see George Weese, but he can't see us. A cop is in the room with him, sitting in a folding chair near the door.

Weese is at one end of a long table. He stares straight ahead, his eyes fixed on the wall. I don't think he knows we're over here on the other side of the mirror studying him like he's some sort of firefly we trapped in our mayonnaise jar. Maybe he does. If so, he sure doesn't seem to care. There's a cup of coffee and a bottle of Poland Spring water sitting on the table in front of him. So far he hasn't touched either.

"That's definitely the dude who kept hogging number three."

"You're sure?"

"Totally."

"Okay. Thanks, T. J. And thanks again for the heads-up."

T. J. shrugs it off, like it was no big deal.

"I just wanted to, you know, get a shot at my favorite rifle again."

Ceepak smiles.

"So, you call my mom yet?"

"We've been rather busy."

"Call her. You guys could get, like, a ten percent discount on any dinner at Morgan's."

"Ten percent? That'll work."

"Cool."

T. J. steps aside and Dan Bloomfield, the guy who owns Aquaman's Comix & Collectibles, takes his turn at the window.

"Oh, yes. That's him."

"You're certain?"

"Definitely. It's not every day some young man strolls in and purchases seven Derek Jeters. He was belligerent about it, too. 'I only want 1996. Don't try to hustle me into buying shit I don't want.' That's exactly what he said. And so, obviously, I sold him his cards. However, I did not appreciate the way he talked to me. Sure, the customer is always right, but that doesn't give him the right to be rude and disrespectful!"

We thank him for coming in. He's the last one.

Now we wait for the lawyer.

It's seven P.M. Sunday.

Mr. and Mrs. Weese are in the lobby up front waiting for their lawyer.

Their son is in the IR, not saying a word, barely breathing.

Ceepak and I are in the empty office with Dr. McDaniels.

"We took the van to the municipal garage," she says. "Hauled it over on the back of a flatbed truck."

"To keep any tire and undercarriage evidence intact," Ceepak says.

"Give that man a gold star." She says it without her usual zip or zing.

"Something bothering you?" Ceepak asks.

"Yeah. We checked the tires. They're all the same make and age."

"No flat?"

"Exactly."

"Curious, given the path of footprints you discovered . . . ."

"Yep. So why the hell *did* he walk around the van to the passenger-side rear wheel well?"

"Good question."

"It's gnawing at me."

"We could ask him," I suggest.

They both look at me.

McDaniels glares.

Ceepak is gentler. "We might do that, Danny. We sure might."

We also probably won't.

"What about the weapon?" Ceepak asks.

"It's probably our gun. M-24. Been fired recently. I sent it down to our firearms identification people. They'll shoot it into the water tank, check out the striation marks and rifling. I figure it'll all match up."

McDaniels walks to the desk and picks up a card.

"We rolled Mr. Weese's prints when he came in. And, of course, we dusted the M-24 before sending it out for the ballistics work."

"Find anything?"

"Yep." Dr. McDaniels rubs her eyes. "Too much."

"How do you mean."

"Tell me, Ceepak. You ever put your palm print all over the school bus window when you were a kid?"

"No, ma'am."

"Of course not. You were a Boy Scout the minute you popped out of your mother's womb and asked the doctor if he required any assistance."

Ceepak smiles. He knows he can be something of a goody-goody. McDaniels is one of the few people he lets make fun of him for it.

"Well," she says, "I used to do it all the time. Used to breathe on the glass to fog it up and then plaster my paw prints all over the place. Wanted folks to know I'd been there."

"And Weese's prints are all over the M-24?"

"Everywhere. Stock. Telescopic sight. The barrel. Muzzle. I picked up two dozen clean prints."

"Interesting."

"Yeah. Particularly when you remember two things. One: he never fired the rifle today. As far as we know, he never even took it out of the duffel bag."

"And two?"

"I didn't find a single print on the paintball rifle."

Ceepak nods. "Because he wore the neoprene gloves."

"Precisely. If he's going through all that rigamarole to keep the paintball rifle clean, how come his prints are all over the M-24?"

"Well, don't forget," I say, "we found his surfer gloves in the back of the van. Maybe he forgot them when he, you know, packed his bag."

Ceepak and McDaniels both look at me again like I'm the slow kid in class.

"It's a possibility, Danny," says Ceepak.

"Yeah. It's possible," McDaniels adds. "And I could be the next Miss America. I guess that's possible, too."

Ceepak and McDaniels seem real worried.

And I don't think it has anything to do with beauty pageants.

FORTY-ONE

The lawyer finally arrived around eight P.M.

We talked to Weese for about two hours and he didn't say a word. Nothing. Nada. We asked him about his wife, the kids, Derek Jeter, the Yankees' chances his year, everything. We got nothing but silence.

He didn't even tell us his name. His parents did it for him.

"George Washington Weese," his mother said when George just sat there like he couldn't remember his name.

"We wanted him to grow up and become somebody," Mr. Weese said. "But, apparently, he had other plans."

Even his old man's ragging on him didn't snap George out of his trance. He kept quiet, kept staring at the wall.

"What's wrong?" Mrs. Weese asked when her son sat there like a spud. "Did you people torture him?" She shot that one straight at Ceepak. "Did you try any of that Abu Ghraib prison crap? I know you were in Iraq, Mr. Ceepak. You were one of those military police, like in those pictures with the naked prisoners."

Ceepak didn't take the bait.

•••

Around ten P.M., the lawyer, who had on this white polo shirt that showed off his incredibly bronzed tan, suggested we resume our "attempted interrogation" first thing in the morning.

"Oh-seven-hundred?" Ceepak said.

The lawyer frowned. "I'm no good before ten. Besides, tomorrow's a holiday."

"Maybe for lawyers," Mr. Weese huffed. "Some of us have to pay our bills—the bills our lawyers send us."

"Does ten work for you?" the lawyer asked Chief Baines.

"Fine. We'll be busy earlier, securing the party site. John? You okay with ten?"

"Ten hundred hours will work."

We trooped out of the room. George was escorted back to a jail cell. Ceepak suggested I head for home.

"Big day tomorrow," he said.

"Yeah. I'm scheduled to work security at the sound stage. Stop the girls from jumping on 3 Doors Down."

3 Doors Down, the rock band that does that "Kryptonite" song, is scheduled to kick off the big show on the boardwalk at noon tomorrow.

"I want you here," Ceepak said. "I'll address the issue of your deployment with the duty sergeant."

I said okay and headed across the bay to Mainland Medical. Katie was sleeping. I kissed her on her forehead; she smiled slightly, snuggled into her pillow, and slept some more.

"Go home, Danny," Christine, my nurse friend, said. "You look wiped."

She was right.

I drove back across the bridge and called my friends. Jess, Olivia, and Becca. They freaked when I told them about George Weese.

"Oh, *that* guy." Becca said, light dawning.

"Yeah."

"Does his nose still whistle?"

I had to admit I hadn't been paying attention.

"Fry his ass," Jess suggested. "Hang him from the highest tree."

Jess kind of forgets which branch of the criminal justice system I'm working in. Cops don't get to fry anybody, and there'd be hell to pay if we started decorating trees with dead guys, like the Surfing Santas they string up along Ocean Avenue during Christmas.

"Good work," Olivia, the sensible one, said. "But it's sad how we messed up his mind."

Olivia, of course, got it right. Like I said, she's the smart one.

I climb into my rack. Tomorrow's the big day. Labor Day.

I have a feeling, one way or another, I'll be laboring my butt off.

FORTY-TWO

*H*appy Labor Day!"

It's eight A.M.

This is one of those days when I wish I didn't have a clock radio. Mike and Larry, the local morning team on WAVY, are just too damn chipper. They've both apparently guzzled a couple of those forty-eight-ounce tumblers of coffee from the Qwick Pick.

"Big day on the beach."

"Bo yeah!"

"3 Doors Down."

"Ribs. Chicken. Pulled pork sandwiches."

"Greased pole climbing contest."

"More ribs."

"I think that's how they grease the pole."

"With barbecue sauce?"

"No. Pork lard."

"You can really pig out on the beach today, that's for sure."

My fumbling fingers finally find the off switch. If I were more than half awake, I would have found it sooner.

Time to shower and head to Qwick Pick.

Time for my own forty-eight-ounce tumbler of coffee.

• • •

10:02 A.M.

George Weese is talking.

"I want them both out of here," is the first thing he says. "Their very presence offends me."

His parents look stunned.

"Your mother and father?" Ceepak says for the video camera. He doesn't want to spare anybody's feelings, he just wants to make certain the official record reflects whom the accused is tossing out of the interrogation room.

"I have a lawyer," Weese says. "I see no need for my parents to remain."

"Son, you don't know—"

Weese glares at his dad.

"Be quiet. I am twenty-seven years old. You no longer need tell me what to do."

Mrs. Weese reaches across the table to touch her son's hand.

He snaps it back, hissing at her.

She gasps.

"Perhaps it would be best . . ."

It's all the tanned lawyer needs to say. Mr. and Mrs. Weese push back their chairs. The chair legs screech as they do.

"Fine," Mr. Weese shakes his head, looking at his son. "You are such a goddam disappointment."

George smiles. "As are you, father."

Families. Freak shows without the circus tent.

Mr. Weese motions to his wife: "Helen?"

Mrs. Weese remains seated.

"Helen?" He repeats.

She finally picks up her purse, fumbles around inside to make certain she has her cigarettes, and trails her husband out the door.

When it closes, George leans back in his chair, studies Ceepak and me. He shakes his head and smirks.

"You two. What a pair of incompetents. The Two Stooges."

"Why do you say that?" Ceepak asks, showing no emotion.

"I had to hand you *seven* Derek Jeters before you could piece together my ingenious little puzzle? Maybe I should have spelled it out in braille, you're both so blind."

Now I sort of wish we were back to the bit where George Weese wasn't saying anything.

"The Jeters?" I say. "You dropped those the day you shot Katie, am I right?"

"Danny?" Ceepak shoots me one of his looks.

"You." Weese waggles a finger at me. "You ruined my life. You and your five little friends!"

"George?" The lawyer guy puts a gentle hand on Weese's shoulder. Weese smiles. Leans back.

"Tell us about it," Ceepak says.

"About what?" Weese wants to call all the shots. For the moment, Ceepak's playing along.

"Tell us how Danny and his friends ruined your life."

"With pleasure. August twenty-eighth, nineteen ninety-six," he says, deliberately drawing out each syllable of the date, like he's relived that particular day a billion times. "Unbeknownst to me, my father had come home early from work that day. He was in the kitchen cleaning out his golf cleats with a house key. When I came in the back door, he stopped what he was doing to stare at me. As you might recall, Daniel, the front of my white swimsuit was stained purple with grape soda. The wet cloth was clinging to my skin. I know my father could see my penis. I could feel his cold stare."

He lets that hang there for dramatic effect.

" 'Jesus,' my father said. Not 'What happened to you, son?' Not 'Did somebody hurt you, my boy?' No. He invoked the holy name of his lord and savior—in disgust. Because he was examining my penis through the dampened cloth and was disappointed by what he saw. 'Go change your damn pants,' he said. Then, he shook his head. He was disgusted. He started digging out more dirt, concentrating on the cleats. He didn't wish to see how minuscule a man his son had grown to be."

Okay. This is weird.

"I wanted to say something. That my member was momentarily shrunken because it was wet and cold. That it grew substantially when I achieved an erection. But I couldn't say a word. My insufficient size only confirmed what my father already suspected: I could never become the kind of man he wanted me to be. No, sir. Not with my mouse. Yes, I believe someone once called my penis a mouse. I believe it was the little girl with the red hair. Katie. Katie the Cunt."

"Is that why you shot Ms. Landry?" Ceepak asks. "Because of what she said that day on the beach?"

"You don't have to answer that, George," the lawyer advises.

"I read all about you, Daniel," Weese says. "My father sent me your newspaper clippings. Several magazines, as well. Local boy makes good. Part-time cop cracks big murder case."

For the record, that is *not* what any of the headlines said. In fact, my name was always kind of buried about twenty paragraphs down in all the Tilt-A-Whirl case stories.

"Imagine my father, sitting in his favorite chair, reading of your heroic exploits, taking the full measure of *your* manhood, picturing the overwhelming enormity of *your* penis."

Okay. It's getting even weirder.

"Let's talk about Saturday morning at Schooner's Landing," Ceepak says.

"Oh, that was a good day," Weese says. "Saturday was such a blessing."

"How so?"

"George, again I advise you—"

"Will you please be quiet? I am quite certain my father will pay you your exorbitant fees whether you say anything or not. So sit back, relax, and enjoy the show."

"As your lawyer—"

"Does this cretin even need to be here?" Weese asks Ceepak.

"Legal representation is always advisable in these situations," Ceepak replies.

"Fine. Then just sit there and dream about all the money you're making. Now then, where was I?"

"Schooner's Landing?"

"Oh, right. I knew Katie the Cunt worked at the candy shop because, earlier in the week, I had seen her pushing a retard around the ramps in a wheelchair, taking him out for an ice cream cone. Later, I approached the same child, myself. Acted quite chummy. Even bought him an ice cream. 'Will Katie be working Saturday?' I asked him. He told me she would indeed be at the shop."

He pauses, remembering.

"And there you were as well. Two for the price of one! Buy one, get one free! No lie, free pie! Tell me, Daniel. How is Miss Landry faring? Has she had the decency to die yet?"

I don't say a word.

Ceepak leans in, elbows on table, hands coming together in a finger-locking grip. I think he's making sure his hands don't reach across the table to throttle this sick bastard.

"So you discharged your weapon at both Miss Landry and Mr. Boyle?"

"Yes. Missed him. Got her. I only wish I had more bullets. One more and I could've ended your whole Superhero career." He points a finger-pistol at me and brings down the thumb-hammer. "Bam! No more newspaper clippings for young Daniel Boyle."

Ceepak's hands slowly sink to the table. He is thinking. Weese is now silent. That smirk permanently plastered on his face. The hate making his eyes bulge again.

"Danny," Ceepak finally says. "We need to take a break. Outside."

"Are we finished here?" the lawyer wants to know.

"No."

I follow Ceepak toward the door and shoot Weese a quick glance over my shoulder.

He's staring back at me.

FORTY-THREE

Where's the chief?" Ceepak asks Gus at the front desk.

"Down at the boardwalk for the big show."

"We have a situation."

The way Ceepak says "situation," I know we're in trouble. Big time.

"What kind of situation?" Gus grabs his radio microphone, ready to call the boss on Ceepak's say-so.

"Our sniper is still at large and potentially targeting today's festivities."

"Jesus, Mary, and Joseph," Gus says. "That's a freaking situation."

"Roger that. We also need to contact Dr. McDaniels. She's staying at a motel on—"

"I got her numbers."

"Let me know when she arrives."

Gus nods and gets busy.

"Come on, Danny."

We march up the hallway, back to the interrogation room.

"What's up?" I finally ask. "What did Weese say that tipped you off?"

Ceepak stops outside the IR door.

"He said he wished he had another bullet. To shoot at you."

"He was just talking tough. Mouthing off."

"He fired twice."

"Right. One for me. One for Katie."

"The standard M-24 SWS clip holds five cartridges. Meaning there were, most likely, three rounds remaining after Miss Landry went down. Weese would know that if he were the shooter. Someone else manned the M-24."

Ceepak leads the way back into the room.

George is sitting rigidly upright, once again silent. The lawyer doodles on a yellow legal pad because I guess that's what lawyers get paid to do.

"Mr. Weese. Tell us about your partner."

"What?"

"Your partner."

Weese laughs.

"Maybe you two morons need another potty break. Maybe you shitted your brains out your asses on the last one." I catch his eyes making a swing up to the wall. There's a clock on it. "You are both so stupendously stupid. Did you check the rifle? Find any fingerprints?"

"Of course," Ceepak says. "Yours."

"Anybody else's?"

"Negative."

Weese's grin grows wider. His eyes balloon, magnified again by those nerd glasses. "Allow me to give you two boys a helpful little hint. When you find someone's fingerprints on a weapon? That means he's the one who fired it. When you don't find anybody else's? That means he acted alone."

Weese delivers this lesson as if he's talking to two-year-olds. Ceepak could care less.

"Why did you step out of the van?"

"Excuse me?"

"Oak Street. The garage. While you waited for Harley Mook, you stepped out of the minivan and walked around the front of the vehicle, went to the rear wheel well on the passenger side."

Weese's face flashes surprise. He didn't expect Ceepak to know that little footprint factoid. But he doesn't let it faze him.

"I suppose I needed to stretch my legs. The minivan provides inadequate legroom for someone of my stature."

"How'd you switch weapons? On the beach. Outside Morgan's." Ceepak zigs and zags, jumbles up the crime scenes. "How did you switch from the paintball rifle to the M-24?"

"I'm quite fast with my hands," Weese says, sounding proud. "I practiced for months."

"We know. You practiced at Paintball Blasters on the boardwalk."

"That is correct. Good work, detective."

"You wore surfer gloves."

"Who told you that?"

"It makes no difference."

"Was it that handsome lad with the spiky hair? Is he still so sullen and surly?"

"Why did you leave fingerprints on the M-24?"

"I'm sorry?"

"The gloves? How did your fingerprints end up on the rifle if you were wearing gloves?"

"Simple, moron. I took them off."

"Before you switched weapons?"

"That's right."

"Why?"

"They were extremely hot."

The lawyer? His head is flipping back and forth like he's watching Forrest Gump at that Chinese Ping-Pong tournament.

"You put down the paintball rifle . . ."

"Correct."

". . . took off the gloves . . ."

"Yes."

". . . picked up the M-24, aimed it, shot."

"That's right."

"All in a manner of seconds?"

"As I said, I'm quite speedy. Practice makes perfect."

Pop, snap, pop? Weese is no Ceepak. He's not that fast.

CHRIS GRABENSTEIN

"How tall are you?"

"Excuse me?"

"How tall?"

"Why do you wish to know?"

Ceepak digs through a stack of folders piled on the table near his elbow, finds what he's looking for, slips it out, flips over Weese's booking shot, the one where you stand in front of a scale marked off in feet and inches.

"Six feet, three inches," Ceepak says.

"Can I see that?" The lawyer says it like he's in court and needs to examine State Exhibit A or whatever. Ceepak doesn't care. He slides the photo over. The lawyer pulls out his reading glasses. "Let the record show—"

Ceepak cuts him off. "Tell me, George. How did you shoot your weapons?"

"Let's see . . . oh, I remember. I pulled the triggers."

"How were you set up?"

"Excuse me?"

"Were you prone? Standing? Did you use the bipod on the SWS?"

The look on Weese's face? I'm not sure he knows what a bipod is, that it's the little leg thingie up front to steady the nose of the rifle.

"Yes. I used a bipod."

"Where did you shoot from?"

"Different locations."

"The minivan?"

"Obviously."

"Where?"

"What?"

"Out the front windshield?"

"No, I did not shoot out the front window. The glass would be shattered if I did. Imbecile."

Ceepak smiles. "Where then? I know you didn't use the sliding door when you killed Harley Mook. If you did, all you would have hit is a garage wall and some gardening supplies."

"Brilliantly deduced, detective."

"So, when you shot from the minivan, how did you do it?"

Weese hesitates before answering. "I stepped outside the van, propped my weapon—"

"You mean weapons."

"That's right. I stand corrected. I propped my *weapons*, both of them, in the window of an open door. That's why you found my footprints. I was walking around, looking for the best shooting position. Decided to open the front door, use the window to brace myself."

"So you positioned your bipod on the driver-side window?"

"That's right."

"Did you have the paintball rifle in one hand, the M-24 in the other?"

"Maybe."

"So you were only wearing one glove? Right or left hand?"

"Both. Then I took them off."

The lawyer and I? We're both trying to imagine how Weese would look doing what he's telling us he did: juggling two rifles, balancing them on a car door, removing gloves. Playing Twister is less complicated.

"Was the window rolled down?"

"Of course."

"All the way?"

"Yes. I wanted to position my bipod on the crack where the glass goes down into the door. There's a rubber sealing-strip there. Good support surface for my bipod."

"I see."

Ceepak stops. Waits. Starts in again.

"How tall is the bottom edge of the window on your minivan?"

"I haven't a clue. Do you? Did you, perchance, take a mug shot of my minivan?" Weese seems pleased with this little zinger.

"We can."

"Perhaps you should."

"Would you agree that the driver-side window ledge is shorter than you?"

"Well, obviously."

"So you crouched down? While you balanced the two rifles?"

"Yes. I practiced at the gym. Did squats with weighted poles balanced upon my shoulders."

"Your quadriceps didn't cramp up?"

"No." Weese eyes dart left then right while he tries to remember what quadriceps are. "My thighs were fine. I did fifty squats every morning."

"Fifty?" Ceepak curls his lips and raises his eyebrows like he's mightily impressed.

"Sometimes I'd do a hundred."

Ceepak nods. Pauses. Weese smiles. He figures he's won this round, maybe the whole bout.

Ceepak finds a manila file folder in the pile of papers. Looks inside. Closes the folder.

"Mr. Weese," Ceepak says, "I try to conduct my life guided by certain principles."

"Really? I'm impressed."

"I will not lie, nor will I tolerate those who do."

"Then we should get along just fine." Weese smirks some more. "I am not a liar. And I've answered each and every one of your questions, no matter how insipid."

"I would concur," the lawyer says. "My client has been very frank and forthcoming."

"Bullshit."

I have never heard Ceepak use those two words together like that.

"Excuse me?" The lawyer is acting offended, like his dainty tanned ears aren't used to hearing such coarse language.

Ceepak stands and leans his considerable weight on his balled-up fists. He's mad enough to drill holes through the table with his knuckles.

"Everything you have told me thus far is a bald-faced lie."

"Is not," Weese says, sounding like he's six years old.

"Danny, do you know how you can tell when George Weese is lying?"

"His lips are moving." I give Ceepak the punch line to the old lawyer joke so the lawyer doesn't have to.

"I am not lying!"

"Of course you are."

"Prove it!"

Ceepak opens the folder.

"We know from trajectory analysis done at Schooner's Landing and the Oak Street location that the M-24 weapon was fired from a height between six and a half and seven feet."

"So? You just said I was six three."

"What did you do, Mr. Weese? Hold the rifle up over your head?"

"You tell me."

"Hard to aim that way."

"I leaned the rifle on top of the van."

"I thought you were squatting?"

"Sometimes."

"Behind the driver-side window, which I would estimate to be, what? Four feet off the ground?" Ceepak looks to me for some kind of confirmation.

"Four. Maybe four and a half," I say.

"Maybe I didn't use the van. Maybe, I found sniper posts . . . different places each time . . . maybe I fired off the porch there on Oak Street."

"No. Sorry, Mr. Weese. That is not what the trajectory path would indicate. See?" Ceepak slides a drawing across the table. Weese doesn't look at it.

"You figured it out wrong. Used flawed geometry."

"Why didn't we find any cartridges? Over by the porch where you now say you fired from?"

"I picked them all up."

"I see. You stood, no, you crouched in the parking lot at Schooner's Landing—"

"I was talking about Oak Street!"

"But you had to use the minivan at Schooner's Landing because there wasn't any porch. In fact, there was nothing in the trajectory path but a parking lot, automobiles, and blue sky. So there you were with a rifle propped up on the open door of your minivan. You fired your two shots, strolled around the asphalt casually picking up spent shell casings like they were cigarette butts."

"It didn't take long. There were only two."

"That's right. Only two. Even though most M-24s hold five cartridges in a single clip." Ceepak lets it hang there for a second. "When you fired, which side of the M-24 barrel did the empty cartridges eject from?"

Weese hesitates.

"Which side, Mr. Weese? Right or left?"

Weese's eyelids blink like crazy.

"Right or left?

"The right."

"Sorry. Left. And you had a fifty-fifty chance on that one. So tell me, George. Who *is* the sniper? Who are you working with?"

"I need to take a break now."

"No," Ceepak says.

"I need to take a break!"

The lawyer suddenly realizes his client is actually asking him to do something.

"We need to take a break," the lawyer says.

"No." says Ceepak. "No breaks."

Weese folds his arms across his chest, settles back into his chair.

"Uh," the lawyer says, "I think, we, you know . . . I think George is done talking . . . for a while."

Ceepak surrenders.

"Fine. Fifteen minutes."

"I need an hour." Weese says

"We need an hour," the lawyer echoes.

Ceepak looks at his watch. I look up at the clock on the wall. It's almost eleven. Weese won't talk again until noon.

Right when the party's getting started on the boardwalk.

FORTY-FOUR

C lever bastards," Dr. McDaniels says with just a hint of admiration. "Handed us one guy on a silver platter so the other guy could run free, ready to rock."

We're in the empty office with the evidence. McDaniels just finished on the phone with the state ballistics expert who did the tests on the M-24 found in Weese's duffel bag.

"Is it our weapon?" Ceepak asks.

"Of course," McDaniels says. "But that only means Dude Number Two has Rifle Number Two. Probably another M-24. They gave us the gun from the first attacks, plastered Weese's prints all over it, made us think our work was done, that we could go pig out on the beach. Bastards." Again, just a touch of grudging respect.

I also notice that the good doctor is wearing shorts and a tee shirt with some kind of Save the Dolphins art airbrushed on the front, like she was thinking about hitting the big boardwalk shindig herself since her work here was basically done.

"So, Ceepak," she says, "what do the bastards want?"

"Not knowing, can't say. However, I suspect we'll learn more at noon."

"You're gonna talk to Weese again?"

"Yes, ma'am."

"Good. Poke him in the eye once or twice for me."

"Will do."

"How can I help?"

"The van."

"It's secure in the garage."

"Let's take a second look. It might be the only place where our two shooters were together. Perhaps there's something inside we didn't catch on the first pass. Something outside."

McDaniels nods. "We'll double-check every nook and cranny. Might find some fibers. A stray hair. Something that'll help identify Bastard Number Two."

"Thanks. We'll join you the minute we're done with Mr. Weese."

"Right." McDaniels shakes her head. "Two shooters. One on the paintball gun, the other on the M-24. One to plaster the trading cards all over the place, another to do the serious shooting. Good thing they had a van. Sounds crowded."

FORTY-FIVE

We're back in the interrogation room at 11:58.

Weese sits silent

We wait.

When George Weese says "noon" he means noon.

When the big hand and little hand are finally facing skyward, he sighs.

"Touché, Officer Ceepak," he says. "Touché! Perhaps you aren't quite the ignoramus I assumed you to be. That bit with the trajectory? That was good. Hadn't expected that one."

"Who is your partner?"

"I enjoyed our little pas de deux. Did you?"

"Who is he?"

"You mean my friend? Once upon a time, when I was younger, this obnoxious beach bully sprayed grape soda on my swim trunks. He warned me not to tell anyone. Said he had *friends* who would get me even if he couldn't. Friends such as Daniel and the buff lifeguard, Jess, who, one would think, should have been duty-bound to come to my assistance that day."

"I want a name. Who is he?"

Weese shakes his head.

"Tsk, tsk, tsk, Officer Ceepak. Shame. Are you really such a male chauvinist pig? Remember: behind every great man, there is a woman. Why, I believe . . . yes . . . I believe I even handed you several clues that should have pointed you in that general direction. Perhaps my subtle allusions were a tad too sophisticated for someone of your limited abilities. The Phantom card? The first one?"

"Yes?"

"Why, I believe there was a woman standing behind the man. And card number two? The Avenger? Why, look—another woman, wreaking revenge. Third card? Another from The Phantom and our hero is standing with *another woman.* And, if you look carefully, which is something I suggest you do the next time someone so graciously drops evidence into your lap, you will notice that, yes, indeedy—the woman is standing *behind* the man!"

Weese has this shit-eating grin on his face like he's oh-so-fucking-clever.

"But none of that really matters now does it? It's high noon. All is in readiness. The multitudes have assembled on the beach and board-walk. I understand from my father that the Chamber of Commerce is expecting quite a turnout. Thousands and thousands of happy holiday revelers, none of whom, I'll wager, are particularly interested in dying today. But, alas, some may have to. For it is time for the triumph of the son! Time for the world to experience life under the son, as they say!"

"Who is she?"

"Someone quite capable of doing her job as well as I have done mine. You see, Mr. Ceepak, I did everything I could to help you catch me so you'd drop your guard and open the big Boogaloo BBQ on schedule. What a stupid name. Boogaloo BBQ."

"Who?"

"Tell me—when you were with the army, did you study much military history? Specifically, *Russian* military history?"

"Some."

"Then you must know about the legendary Lyudmila Mikhailovna

Pavlichenko, the greatest female sniper who ever lived! I'm certain you've heard of her fabled exploits, how, during World War Two she single-handedly killed hundreds and hundreds of Germans."

"Your wife?"

"Did you know that the Russians still encourage their little girls to become snipers? Oh, yes. Quite a proud tradition of it, actually."

"Your wife?"

"I met her on the Internet, you know. Russian Brides Dot Com. The new world order of mail-order brides. My father helped, paid for everything. He was rather desperate for grandchildren but feared I couldn't bed a wife on my own, not given what he perceived to be my overwhelming lack of manliness. So, he bought me a wife when I graduated from college. Some children get a year in Europe, other a flashy sports car. Me? I got a Russian virgin."

Ceepak heads for the wall phone.

"Natalia Shevlyakova Weese," Weese continues, his eyes glazing over.

"Gus? Ceepak."

"Oh, she's no beauty, I'll grant you that."

"We need to find George Weese's wife."

"Squat. Homely. Rather dour. But then again, the poor girl grew up in Kemerovo. It, I assure you, is a squalid armpit even more dreadful than fetid Sea Haven."

Ceepak concentrates on the phone, blocks out Weese. "Malloy was with the wife yesterday," he says to Gus.

"All she was looking for, like so many Russian girls these days, was a 'nice, generous, American man.' Translation? She wanted money. Preferably, cash. Hard currency. U.S. dollars."

"Have Kiger check to see if any of the Weese family vehicles are missing."

"Now, that would be stupid, Officer Ceepak, and Natalia is not stupid. Ugly, yes. Stupid, no."

"Have them run her photo past any and all rental car agencies within a twenty-mile radius."

"We're actually quite smart. Brilliant, really. You'll see. Natalia's tough, too. Scrappy. Resourceful. And, as you might suspect, she's also very heavily armed."

Ceepak hangs up the phone.

"Where is she?"

"So much of this was her idea—a way to make our American fortune while simultaneously wreaking revenge on my childhood tormenters *and* my father. Natalia is something of a tactical genius."

"Where is your wife?"

Weese glances up at the clock again.

"Where?" Ceepak barks.

Weese smiles.

"Waiting for a phone call."

FORTY-SIX

"Shall we cut to the chase, gentlemen?"

Weese leans forward, brings his hands together.

"My father and his Chamber Of Commerce cronies must immediately transfer ten million dollars to an offshore bank account, the number of which I will provide to you. Their deadline is two P.M. When certain friends of ours, certain—oh, how shall I put this? Certain Russian mobsters? When these gentlemen advise me that the transfer is complete, I will instruct them to contact Natalia on her secure satellite phone with orders not to shoot a single sunbather.

"Once the money matter is taken care of, you, Officer Ceepak, you will escort me to the airport, where I will board Aeroflot flight fifteen to Moscow. Tomorrow, when I have arrived safely and have no Russian police or KGB or CIA following me—and we'll know if they are because, as I said, we have several financially interested, high-powered friends—when I reach my undisclosed location in the motherland, Natalia will lay down her weapon and depart from these shores."

Weese has a faraway look in his eyes. Like he's been waiting ten years for this one moment. It hits me: he's the Mad Mouse. A timid, mousey guy we made so mad one day that now he's ready to wipe out an entire boardwalk full of innocent kids like maybe he used to be.

"By the way, you will never catch Natalia before she slips out of the country. She will not book passage on Aeroflot, so don't waste your time with amateur airport theatrics. Just know that she and I will one day reunite on a Baltic beach to split our share of the ten million dollars. Perhaps we'll even nibble caviar and sip vodka. Everything will be *hor-a-show*. That's Russian for hunky-dory."

Weese sighs.

"You gentlemen should know that Natalia's sniper post is well stocked with provisions. Food. Water. She can remain hidden for quite some time now that I have kept you engaged long enough for her to properly secure her position."

"What about your children?" asks Ceepak.

Weese shrugs. "My father wanted grandchildren so damn much, he can keep them. They're loathsome little creatures, actually. Filthy."

The lawyer nervously twists his ear lobe. "I'm not certain the town fathers can raise ten million dollars in under two hours."

"Of course they can," scoffs Weese. "I'm not asking for actual cash. It's all electronic banking, counselor. We can do it online. Don't forget, my father is a mortgage broker with access to all sorts of lenders willing to provide money at very reasonable rates, or so he constantly claims in his annoying advertisements. The other merchants will surely chip in because—let's face it. If Natalia starts shooting, this town will never recover. Never. Two incidents in one summer? 'Welcome to Sea Haven. Have a Sunny, Funderful Day—Unless You Get Shot First.' Not a very catchy slogan. I fear it would make a dreadful bumper sticker."

"Your wife is setting you up," Ceepak says. "She's working for the Russians. The mobsters."

Weese ignores him.

"Mr. Ceepak, you have heard our demands. Ten million dollars. If the transfer is not completed by two P.M., Natalia will start taking out targets. Scores of them. Hundreds! Why, she might even break Lyudmila Pavlichenko's world record. Trust me. My little wife packed a great deal of ammunition."

The lawyer looks like he's lost all his tan, like it all drained down to his underpants. His face is pale and white.

"Ten million dollars?"

Weese shrugs again.

"It's what the D.C. snipers asked for. Who knows—perhaps we should ask for more. The town fathers can certainly afford it. Besides, Natalia and I? We're much more lethal than those two Negroes down in D.C. Much smarter, too."

FORTY-SEVEN

Natalia Shevlyakova Weese rented another white minivan from the Avis in Avondale.

Makes sense. It's the vehicle they practiced with. Guess they'll dance with the one who brought them to the party. George Weese was right about one thing: he and his wife are pretty smart. They keep us looking for needles in haystacks—a boring white minivan in a town full of boring white minivans.

Natalia rented the white Plymouth Voyager with burgundy interior from Avis last Tuesday. Almost a week ago. So she's had ample time to find herself a prime parking space and stow her rental vehicle down by the boardwalk. She beat the crowds. Smart again.

"Will she shoot from the van?" I ask Ceepak as we drive down the block from headquarters to the municipal garage.

"Don't know. She's probably handpicked her ideal sniper post. Could be anywhere. A motel balcony. A water tank. Some other elevated spot on the boardwalk, maybe even another roller coaster. There's no way of knowing." Ceepak shakes his head. I can tell he's mad at himself. "We should have kept her under surveillance. I let her drop off my radar."

"Weese did his job," I say. "He wasted our time, didn't say a word until he knew it was too late for us to do anything, too late to shut down the beach party. He did his job."

"Roger that. Now it's time for us to do ours."

We park beside a garbage truck and hustle inside the municipal garage to see if the first minivan has anything more to tell us.

"The wife, huh?" Dr. McDaniels rolls out from under the van on a mechanic's trolley. "That would explain that." She nods toward one of her guys who's holding a plastic Baggie with a single strand of curly black hair. "Found it in the rear cargo bay. There's more on the passenger side headrest, but that only proves that Mrs. Weese was in the car with her husband."

"Find anything else?"

"Just some Cheerios and Cheez-Its ground into the carpet. Under the seat cushions, too. Kids."

Ceepak nods.

I notice two child safety seats. Guess George's son and daughter won't be throwing food at each other in this van again anytime soon.

"We need to focus," Ceepak says, checking his watch. "We have less than two hours."

I wonder if he sensed my mind wandering off to the land of crumbled Cheerios and Cheez-Its.

"It's the same old story, same old act. One step up and two steps back."

Ceepak's quoting Springsteen again. Forcing himself to concentrate.

Dr. McDaniels hauls herself up, dusts off her shorts.

"Okay," she says, like a professor rallying a drifting class discussion, "we know Who. We know Why. Now all we need to determine is How and, most important, Where Next."

"The van," Ceepak says, staring at the bland white automobile, trying to will the sheet metal to surrender its secrets.

"Just your typical kidmobile," McDaniels says. "Did I mention the half-empty juice boxes I found in the back seat? The chewed crayons? Doesn't matter. They don't give us diddly."

"Mrs. Weese purchased the vehicle for her son. Mr. Weese provided the resident beach pass bumper sticker to encourage frequent visits from his grandchildren . . ."

He trails off.

"How firm are your trajectory numbers?" Ceepak suddenly asks Dr. McDaniels.

"Firmer than your butt. We reworked them. Ten times. Our best projection comes from the parking lot outside Saltwater Tammy's because we had those two definitive points to work with. The entry hole in the plate glass window, the second hole in the bin of Red-Hots hearts."

"We have our straight line," Ceepak says.

"And our angle of impact."

"Right."

"The line took us straight out to that empty parking space. The angle took us up to an elevation of six feet, eight inches at the front end of the rectangular parking space and climbed up to six-nine-point-five at the rear."

"Suggesting the minivan had been parked there prior to the shooting."

"Only empty space in the whole damn lot," Dr. McDaniels says. "And it wasn't there earlier when Officer Boyle went hunting for a spot."

"We can surmise the shots were fired from this vehicle. The perpetrator then drove away while Danny and I tended to Ms. Landry's wounds."

"I'm certain of it," McDaniels says. "The shot came from this goddamn minivan. There's a little bit of an oil leak underneath. We could go back to Schooner's Landing, take samples of any fluids pooled in that parking space."

"No time. Won't help."

"Yeah. I know. Got my shorts dirty for nothing."

"What about the roof?" Ceepak suggests.

"The van is six-six."

"The bipod would add another two inches."

"Six-eight."

"She could have stood on the rear bumper," Ceepak says. "Rested her rifle on the rooftop."

McDaniels nods. "Steadied her shot."

We all walk around to the back of the van.

"Maybe," McDaniels says, shaking her head, disappointed at what she sees. "Maybe not. Be damn difficult."

There's a bulky bike rack rigged to the rear of the minivan. Maybe the older kid brought his tricycle with him down the shore. Maybe George and Natalia have his-and-hers trail bikes. The rack's arms poke out at least two or three feet and spread sideways. They'd get in your way if you wanted to stand on the rear bumper and squeeze off a few rounds from a rifle resting on the roof.

I think about those two screaming kids back at the Weese house. They're going to have a lot more to scream about if they wind up being raised by their grandparents when mom and dad are locked up in the state pen, that's for sure. Not only that, they'll grow up knowing their parents were cold-blooded killers.

"Poor kids," I mumble aloud. "That's a lot of crap to carry around."

"Danny, what did you just say?" Ceepak demands.

Busted. I feel like I'm back in grade school: *if you have something to say, Mr. Boyle, why don't you share it with the whole class?*

"Nothing. I was just thinking. My mind kind of drifted."

"Danny, just repeat what you said."

"I'm sorry. I know I should be focusing on the task at hand."

"Danny—*what* did you say?" Ceepak isn't fooling.

" 'Poor kids. It's a lot of crap to carry around.' That's all. I figure their two kids will have—"

"Crap. Kid's crap," McDaniels echoes, sounding like she's in some kind of trance. "Carrying it around."

"Suitcases." Ceepak sounds like he's in the trance with her. "Collapsible crib, playpen, stroller . . ."

"Bingo!" Dr. McDaniels hollers. "Guys?" she calls out to her CSI crew. "We need a ladder. Pronto! I need to be taller!"

The two CSI guys root around in the garage, push aside rakes and shovels. Something heavy and metal crashes to the floor.

"Whoops. Sorry."

More rummaging. Steel scrapes against concrete.

"Here we go."

One of the guys digs out a three-step aluminum ladder from behind this clump of signs and poles.

"That'll work," Ceepak says.

The guys set it up alongside the minivan.

"Doctor?" Ceepak offers McDaniels the first look.

"You do it," she says. "I'm afraid of heights."

Ceepak climbs up the three short steps, puts his hands on his hips, looks up and down the roofline.

"You were right, Danny."

"How tall is Mrs. Weese?" Dr. McDaniels asks up to Ceepak. "The Russian one, I mean."

"Five-two, five-one. Short. Maybe four-eleven."

"Good thinking, Boyle."

I have no idea what I've said or thought that deserves so much praise.

"It explains the foot steps," she continues. "Why Weese got out at Oak Street, walked along the side of the vehicle. Probably checking up on her."

"Definitely," says Ceepak. I still have no idea what the two of them are so excited about. "Weese seemed to have a vast knowledge of the D.C. sniper case."

"So he knew how the shooter, usually the kid Malvo, hid in the trunk," McDaniels adds. "Had that special rifle hole bored through the rear of their Chevy Caprice."

"Affirmative. Weese also intimated that he and Natalia were smarter and potentially more lethal than the D.C. team."

"He could be right," McDaniels says. "This is pretty damn clever."

"What?" I have to say it.

Ceepak climbs down off the stepladder.

"Take a look."

I climb up. Look at the roof. It's got a rack on it: Black bars running up the sides, two adjustable struts spanning the width. You could put lumber or a Christmas tree up here and tie it down with bungee cords.

"Look closely, Danny," Ceepak says. "Examine the details."

Okay. Fine. I look closer. I see dust splotches. Rain stains. The roof looks like my windshield does after a thunderstorm, speckled with dirt splats, the residue left behind when the raindrops dry. The top is freckled like a leopard skin of spattered sand-dust.

Except on one side. The passenger side.

Over there, there's a clean patch, a rectangle that covers most of the roof. The front edge is somewhat rounded at the corners.

I lean back. Take in the big picture.

Kids' crap.

Somebody used to have a cargo carrier lashed down up here to haul all the suitcases and cribs and stuff they couldn't jam into the wayback or hang off the bike rack over the bumper.

"A cargo carrier?" I say.

"Roger that." Ceepak is beaming. "Nice call, Danny."

"Any idea what make, Officer Boyle?" McDaniels asks.

"No. I've never, you know, really studied—"

"I suspect a Thule or Yakima," Ceepak says. "Judging by the rounded nose up front. Perhaps the Thule Cascade model, which is one of the largest on the market: seventeen, eighteen cubic feet. Opens on the side."

"Could our Russian friend fit inside?" McDaniels asks.

"Easily. The Thule box I'm thinking about is almost six feet long, maybe three feet wide, a foot and a half tall. She'd be cozy inside but quite capable of operating her weapon system in an efficient manner—with plenty of room left over for ammunition and provisions. Water. Food."

"Which might be why Weese walked up the side of the car on Oak Street," McDaniels says. "He wanted to make sure his honey wasn't baking inside the plastic casket while they waited for Mr. Mook. Maybe George brought Natalia a cold Coke. The sweet bastard."

"The sniper was up here?" I say. "Hidden in a cargo holder?"

"Quite clever," Ceepak says.

McDaniels agrees. "Yep. Young Mr. Weese and his wife built themselves a handy-dandy gun turret on top of the family van." No admiration in her voice this time, just disgust. "Completely innocuous. Seemingly harmless. Just another minivan with a box strapped on the roof. Only, this minivan turns out to be a minitank."

"More like an armored personnel carrier," Ceepak says.

McDaniels shrugs. "Tomato, tomahto."

I climb down.

"It also explains why we never found any shell casings," says Ceepak. "They ejected from the rifle, hit the sides, stayed inside the box."

McDaniels nods.

I wonder if this is why Natalia, the sniper with the real bullets, missed us on the beach and outside Morgan's. Maybe firing from inside a cargo carrier takes some getting used to. Maybe she was still getting the hang of it on Wednesday and Friday and only got her groove going Saturday morning at Saltwater Tammy's. By Saturday afternoon, she could place one in the center of Mook's forehead.

"I'm certain they've now attached their customized cargo carrier to the top of the rental van. Well done, Danny," Ceepak says. "Excellent work." He says that, but he looks worried. So does Dr. McDaniels.

They're both go completely quiet so I speak up again.

"What if Natalia has something up there other than an M-24 sniper rifle? What if she has a machine gun or a grenade launcher or something?"

Ceepak nods grimly.

"Exactly."

FORTY-EIGHT

W're working on the money," Chief Baines says over the radio.

Ceepak and I are driving toward the boardwalk. We don't know exactly where to go, but we know we need to be there now. It's one fifteen. Before we left for the World's Biggest Beach Party, we swung by the house. Ceepak wanted a few things: a recording of our interrogation with Weese, which a tech burned onto a CD so we could listen to it in our car; a pair of small, high-power binoculars; and the paintball gun he ripped off the counter at Paintball Blasters. I have no idea why he grabbed it, but it did come in handy when he nailed Weese up on the Mad Mouse.

"You think the damn kid is bluffing?" Baines says, his voice edgy. Every time he opens the microphone at his end I can hear a rowdy mob and snatches of music.

"No, sir. I think Weese is dead serious."

"His father thinks the boy's bullshitting us. Says Natalia is long gone and George is too much of a wuss to do anything himself."

"I don't think Mr. Weese knows his son very well or what sort of man he has become."

"Okay. Fine. What do we do?"

"Search the parking lots for any minivans with cargo carriers up top."

"Which parking lot?"

"All of them."

"Jesus, John! Have you seen this place?"

"No, sir. We are currently en route."

"There's cars parked everywhere. Half of them are damn minivans!"

"We'll try to narrow it down for you, sir."

"There's about a jillion people—men, women, children, dogs. They're crawling all over the boardwalk and the beach."

"Roger. I understand, sir. Check for open lines of fire. Clear shots from the parking lot to the boardwalk. Openings between buildings. Gaps. Concentrate on the most crowded sectors. The target-rich environments."

"What's your ETA? What's your twenty?" It sounds like the chief has a head start on a panic attack.

"Northbound on Ocean," Ceepak says flatly. "Approaching Kipper. Turning now. We should arrive in under a minute."

We're moving pretty fast. No lights. No sirens. Once again, Ceepak doesn't want the bad guy to know we're coming. Might spook the little Russian lady up in her sweatbox if we come screaming in to nab her.

"Which damn parking lot?" The chief? I think he just lost it. "There's one every block for a mile!"

"Kipper and Beach Lane."

"Hurry! We have, what? Forty-five minutes? Jesus!"

"Forty-three, sir. Keep in contact with the house. Let George Weese know the money is not an issue."

"I don't like paying extortionists. Terrorists!"

"Neither do I, sir. If we work this right, we won't have to. Keep this channel open."

Ceepak tosses the radio mic to me. I get the sense he doesn't want to waste any more time on Baines. Not now.

Public Parking Lot 4. There are eight other lots up and down

Beach Lane butting up against the boardwalk. I see several gaps, openings between the brightly painted backs of buildings. In those clear spaces I can also see the mob of seminaked bodies bobbing and weaving, moving and grooving—cool young dudes and bodacious beach babes. I can hear 3 Doors Down two blocks up at the band shell. It sounds like they're doing their biggest hit, "Kryptonite." After that, they'll probably do "Dangerous Game" or "Ticket To Heaven." They both kind of fit today.

I have never seen so many vehicles jammed into these parking lots. I look north, I look south, there's not an empty spot anywhere.

"Where?" Ceepak surveys the scene. "Where."

You never realize how many cargo carriers Thule and Yakima and Sears sell until you're wishing they only ever sold one. Everywhere I look, I see vans with boxes on top.

Ceepak punches the play button on the CD player. I hear Wheezer's cocky voice. Arrogant. So proud of his plan.

"Once the money is taken care of, you, Officer Ceepak, you will escort me to the airport where I will board Aeroflot flight 15 to Moscow."

Ceepak hits the reverse button. The digits spin backward.

"He probably told us where," Ceepak says. "He likes dropping clues. Hints."

"Yeah. Because he likes laughing at us when we don't catch them."

"Precisely."

Ceepak punches play.

"Perhaps my subtle allusions were a tad too sophisticated for someone of your limited abilities."

Weese gloating. Bragging about his big successful plan. What'd he call it? "The triumph of the son." His father would see how big and important he had become.

"Life under the son," I say out loud.

"Come again?"

"Go to that part. Where he talks about 'the triumph of the son.'"

"Roger."

Ceepak remembers. Finds it, fast.

"All is in readiness. The multitudes have assembled on the beach and board-walk. I understand from my father that the Chamber of Commerce is expecting quite a turnout. Thousands and thousands of happy holiday revelers, none of whom, I'll wager, are particularly interested in dying today. But, alas, some may have to. For it is time for the triumph of the son! Time for the world to experience life under the son, as they say!"

"What does it mean, Danny?"

"I'm not one hundred percent sure."

Ceepak tilts his wrist. Checks his watch.

"Now's a good time to give me your best guess."

"Okay. There's this booth. About two blocks up the boardwalk. 'Life Under the Son.' It's run by these born-again Christians who try to convert sun-worshippers, turn them into, you know, *son*-worshippers."

Ceepak's foot is on the gas.

"Two blocks?"

"Yes, sir. Near Halibut Street. The main entrance."

"Radio."

I toss him the microphone.

"Chief Baines?"

"Go?"

"Suggest you begin to quietly evacuate the area around the Life Under the Son booth."

"Where's that?"

"Halibut Street."

"Jesus. The band shell is up at Halibut!"

"Pull the plug."

"Come again?"

"Cut off the electricity to the band stand. Have the performer—"

"3 Doors Down," I say.

"Have the Doors inform the crowd they are experiencing technical difficulties. Let the civilians drift away. Encourage them to hit the beach. Get them down off the boardwalk."

"What if—?"

"Do it, sir. Now!" Ceepak tosses the mic back to me.

We swing into Public Parking Lot 6. I see lots of cars and vans glistening in the sun. I see a Pepsi truck. I see a tour bus. A couple of Winnebagos. A garbage truck ready to clean up all the empty Pepsi cups. I don't, however, see a minivan with a cargo carrier up top.

"There!"

Ceepak does.

He jams our Ford into park, reaches into his cargo pants, pulls out the binos and presses both lenses against his eyes. I see him slide the magnifying lever. He's zooming in.

"White van. Burgundy interior. Red Avis sticker affixed to rear window."

More adrenaline races to my heart.

Ceepak tilts his binoculars up an inch.

"Air hole in rear of cargo carrier."

I check out the line of fire from the minivan to the boardwalk. A good one. Maybe the best. A huge gap where a set of terraced steps, thirty feet wide, swoops down from the wooden walkway. There's a big "Happy Labor Day!" banner flapping in the breeze. It's the main entrance to everything. The whole deal. Beyond the steps, above the crowd, I can just barely see the tip of the pointed spindle on top of the "Life Under the Son" kiosk. It's like a weathervane, only it's a crucifix.

"If we rush the van, she'll start shooting," Ceepak says.

"Yeah. So what do we do?"

"Give me a minute."

It's my turn to check my watch. Okay. Fine. We have about twenty-nine minutes left. Ceepak can have one. Maybe two.

A horn blasts.

I look to my right. The garbage truck. My friend Joey Thalken, who usually drives the sand-sweeper on the beach for Sea Haven Sanitation, is behind the wheel. He waves at me, sees Ceepak, waves at him, too. Guess Joey T. is picking up some heavy-duty overtime hauling garbage after the big party. The way he's bouncing up and down? I think he's listening to the concert simulcast on WAVY.

"Can you drive a truck, Danny?"

"No, I—"

"Stay here."

Ceepak reaches into the back seat. Grabs the paintball rifle, checks to make sure it's charged and loaded.

"I could—"

"Stay here."

Ceepak is out the door and working his way across the parking lot. Low. Crouching down and hiding behind cars whenever he thinks he might be visible to any rearview mirrors Natalia might've set up in her sniper nest.

He scuttles over to Joey T.'s garbage truck.

I flick on the radio just as the concert dies. I mean, it loses electricity.

"Looks like we're experiencing technical difficulties on the bandstand," the deejay announces. *"Maybe the town fathers forgot to pay the electric bill this month."*

Ceepak's at the garbage truck hunkered down under the driver-side door, talking up to Joey.

Joey nods.

Ceepak does a three-finger point toward the white van.

Joey nods again.

Ceepak and Joey T. worked together back in July. Got along great. Looks like they still do.

Chief Baines must have some of our guys working the crowd in front of the bandstand. It starts to thin out.

"Hey folks, now's the time to hit the beach," the radio deejay says. *"The mayor has just officially declared 'Pig Out Time!' Right now, for the next thirty minutes only, all food down on the beach is free! So, while we wait for the juice to come back on, hit the pit!"*

I guess some people on the boardwalk brought along radios, Walkmen. People seem to hear what I just heard and drift away in droves. I see some pushing and jostling as bodies bunch up near the staircases leading down to the beach on the far side of the boardwalk.

I look right and see Ceepak scramble towards the Pepsi truck. He carries the ray-gun-looking paintball rifle at his side like he's some kind of extraterrestrial deer hunter. There's no driver in the Pepsi truck. Ceepak yanks open the big door, crawls into the cab, pulls the door shut behind him. His head disappears under the dashboard. Seconds later, I hear the engine roar, see a chug of diesel fumes puff out its exhaust pipe. I guess hot-wiring is one of those valuable job skills you can learn in Today's Army.

I hear another engine start up.

Joey's garbage truck.

I look toward the boardwalk. The crowd is pushing against itself, heading down to the beach for the free food. Natalia will have a lot fewer targets to choose from come two P.M.

Then I see him.

In his wheelchair. Jimmy. Saltwater Tammy's son. He looks to be alone and, as the crowd thins out, he also looks like a sitting duck. The bull's-eye, smack dab in the middle of Natalia's line of fire.

I open my door and remember I left my bulletproof vest at home this morning. It was soaked with sweat so I hung it over the shower curtain rod to dry. Forgot to put it back on.

Jimmy is just sitting there.

I guess Tammy brought him to the concert, left him alone to enjoy the loud, noisy parts while she went down to the beach and fixed him a plate of pulled pork.

Jimmy is in serious trouble. Target number one.

Ceepak's busy. I'm not.

I hop out of the Explorer.

If Natalia sees me, she might start shooting. She'll definitely recognize me because she's already taken a couple of shots at my face. She might want to mow me down for old-times sake.

She might mow down Jimmy, too.

I make my way forward, try to stay wide of the sniper's eyeline, try to run and crouch and hide behind cars like Ceepak did.

I need to move faster.

Ceepak drives the lumbering Pepsi truck away from the service entrance where it was parked. He turns left and heads down the parking lot lane that will put him directly in front of the minivan.

Joey T. is on the move, too. He rumbles down the row that will put him behind the van.

I see what they're up to.

Ceepak will block any shots with his Pepsi truck; the paneled sides are about three feet taller than the minivan's cargo carrier. Joey T. will box in Natalia's rear. No one will have to storm the sniper nest.

I pick up my pace.

If Natalia gets a hint of what's up, she'll start shooting, whether it's two P.M. or not. I know it. She'll nail Jimmy.

I look up to the boardwalk, see him waiting patiently in his chair, watching everybody leave, head for the beach.

No time to crouch.

Need to run.

I glance over my shoulder. Ceepak is almost in front of the van. He drives slow, tries to look like an everyday, ordinary Pepsi truck just pulling on in to make a delivery. Joey T. keeps pace, parallels Ceepak's moves.

I need to get to Jimmy before Natalia is totally blocked. If she figures out what's going on, she'll definitely go ballistic.

I dart up the tiered stairs, take them two at a time.

Jimmy scans the thinning mob, looks for his mother.

I'm twenty yards away.

"Move!" I yell at these big muscle-bound guys blocking my path.

"Make me," one of them yells.

So I barrel through them.

"Asshole!"

I stumble, scramble across the boards off balance, just waiting for a bullet to find my back.

Ten yards.

Five.

I'm huffing. My heart pounds. I leap the last three feet and grab on to the wheelchair handles.

My momentum pushes us forward.

Behind me, I hear what sounds like a string of firecrackers going off. Explosions. Fast.

Jimmy recognizes me.

I hear another quick burst of dull thuds. Something smacks me in the ribs. No. I just strained a muscle or something. I push the chair.

"Stop!" Jimmy freaks. I don't blame him.

I run and roll him up the boardwalk until we're safely in front of a store.

T. J. Lapczynski is standing there, licking barbecue sauce off his fingertips.

"Dude! Who's got the firecrackers?"

"Watch him!" I shove the wheelchair toward T. J.

"You got it."

Jimmy's still freaking. I need to split.

"Easy," I hear T. J. say. "Easy."

I run back across the boards. Need to help Ceepak.

I race down the steps, tear across the asphalt.

I don't hear any more firecrackers. No more shots.

I make it to the stalled Pepsi truck, slip around to the side, duck down, almost crawl. I slide along the side, move past the rear tires. The blacktop is sticky. Wet. Something drippy hits me from up above.

Blood?

I look up. One panel of the truck is riddled with bullet holes. Brown foam gushes out like a hot Pepsi can somebody shook then pricked with pins.

I look at the white van.

The front of the Thule cargo carrier is glowing neon green.

From inside the tube, I hear muffled curses followed by a flurry of angry kicks.

Natalia Shevlyakova Weese must be inside, temporarily blinded by the paintballs Ceepak just fired down her peephole.

FORTY-NINE

Monday night, I'm at the hospital with what's left of the Marshmallow Crew.

Jess, Olivia, Becca, and, of course, Katie.

Nobody's talking much. We're just sort of being there for each
other, like they say. I guess everybody's thinking about the Mad
Mouse. George Weese. What we did to him, back when we called him
Wheezer. What he did to Katie and, of course, Mook. What he almost
did to a bunch of total strangers.

It could have been worse.

Katie's feeling better. She sits up in her bed, pillows propped
behind her back. I brought along a take-out box of Labor Day barbecue for her. Ribs. Baked beans. Cole slaw. Corn bread. But she
doesn't eat any of it. I don't blame her. I can't eat tonight, either.

The doctors aren't sure yet if the sniper bullet did any permanent
damage to Katie's spinal cord. They do know she'll be in a wheelchair
for a while. That's cool with me. I can handle wheelchairs. Just ask
Jimmy.

Katie tells us how she listened to some of the concert on a radio her
nurse friend smuggled into the room.

"And then the power went out on the bandstand. That was weird."

"Totally." Jess agrees.

So does Becca. "Extremely random."

"You'd think they would have made proper arrangements prior to the event," adds Olivia.

Power outages. This is the kind of stuff you talk about when the important stuff you should be talking about is still too raw. It's like the weather. You can talk about it without thinking about what you did ten years back when you were a kid learning how to be cool. August 28, 1996. Oak Beach. The end of summer. The Marshmallow Crew. We have our memories. The mad mouse has his.

"You ready?" Katie asks, looking at me with her sweet green eyes, still a little fuzzy from all the drugs being pumped into her veins. "Tomorrow's the big day."

I feel like saying, Today was big enough. Instead, I say, "Yeah."

Katie smiles.

"That's right!" Becca tries to perk up the room. "Tomorrow, you can officially fix all my parking tickets!"

"Nah, he'll be too busy," says Jess. "Officially eating doughnuts. Hanging out at the Qwick Pick."

I snuffle a laugh. So does Olivia. But the mood in the room? It's not exactly elevated. A week ago? We would have immediately launched into a round-robin debate, riffing on the relative merits of Krispy Kreme versus Dunkin' Donuts, glazed versus cake. Today, we all just get real quiet again. We listen to the air conditioner humming under the window and think.

Mook. Wheezer. Weese.

Natalia Shevlyakova Weese quit firing her machine gun when those paintballs splattered in her eyes. She couldn't see so she kicked and screamed, but she didn't squeeze her trigger anymore. Her hands were busy, pounding the sides of the cargo carrier while she yelled something about "fucking American assholes."

That's when Ceepak put down the paintball rifle, pulled out his pistol, and steadied his firing stance in the open door of the Pepsi truck. I moved to the passenger side of the minivan, near the latch for the cargo carrier.

"On me," he said. Army talk. Meant to wait for his command.

He held his pistol with both hands in front of him. Aimed it down at the Thule luggage tube.

"Go," he said.

I popped open the snap, flung up the lid like I was flipping open a coffin.

"Freeze!" Ceepak yelled, jutting his pistol forward and down, ready to fire if Natalia made one wrong move.

She didn't.

She put her hands behind her head. It was over. Guess Russians are realists. Fatalistic. Must be those long, cold winters.

The first thing I noticed when I raised that lid was the stench. The trapped heat had made quite a stew in there. Gunpowder, B.O., hot urine. Seems Natalia had been locked inside her secret sauna for quite some time.

I also noticed that she had a machine gun instead of an M-24 sniper rifle. It was one of those long-muzzled jobs with a belt of pointy-tipped bullets feeding into its side. The belt was very long. If Natalia had opened fire, if Ceepak hadn't blocked her with the Pepsi truck, Salt-water Tammy's son wouldn't have been the only one mowed down. Natalia would have sprayed the whole boardwalk, might've broken that other Russian lady's record for outdoor sniping casualties.

We cuffed her and hauled her to the house. After we locked her up, we went up front to report in with the desk sergeant. He had a radio playing. WAVY. Their news update featured a short interview with Chief Baines.

The reporter asked the chief about the "slight commotion" he had heard in the parking lot earlier.

"Teenagers playing with firecrackers," Baines replied, his voice strong and confident again. "Another unfortunate consequence of—"

Ceepak and I finished for him: *"underage drinking!"*

Then, Ceepak laughed. A bigger laugh than I've ever heard him laugh before, like he was letting loose all the pressure that had built up over the past few days, letting it out in one incredible, rib-splitting rumble.

When he was done, he took a deep breath and turned to me. Shook my hand.

"You did good out there today, Danny."

"Thank you."

"Real good."

EPILOGUE

Tuesday morning. The day after Labor Day. My first day as a full-time cop.

I head to the house, figuring there are official papers to sign, W-2s to fill out, orientation videos to watch.

Instead, Chief Baines sees me, calls me into his office.

"Officer Boyle?"

"Yes, sir?"

"You did a fantastic job yesterday."

"Thank you, sir."

"Take today off. You earned it."

He salutes. I salute. That's that. My first day on the job? It's a day off.

I leave the chief's office, head up to the front desk.

"Have you seen Ceepak?" I ask Gus.

"He's off. Make-good for working the holiday."

"Oh. Right."

I check my watch. 8:15 A.M. I guess I could head home, take a nap. Katie's still at the hospital, so I could . . .

"I hear he has a date," Gus says.

"Ceepak?"

"Meeting a young lady friend for breakfast."

"Really?"

This could be fun.

"Where?"

"The Pig's Commitment. Best scrapple in town."

Now that Gus mentions everybody's favorite breakfast meat, I realize I'm kind of hungry.

I head out the door.

Rita Lapczynski, the pretty thirtysomething waitress from Morgan's Surf and Turf, is sitting by herself in a booth sipping coffee from a curve-handled mug.

Great. Their first date and Ceepak stands her up. My man has much to learn. Perhaps I can teach him. I have more experience in modern dating etiquette. Might be the one area where I'm the Zen master and he can be Grasshopper.

"Hello, Danny," Rita says when I walk to her table. "Have you eaten yet?"

"No."

"Sit down then."

"You all alone?"

"I sure am." She sounds chipper. Happy about it. "Sit down."

"Okay."

"Have you ever had the blueberry pancakes here?" she asks.

"Sure. You ought to try them. The blueberries are baked into the batter, not just, you know, clumped on top."

This is kind of awkward. It's like I'm on a date with Ceepak's date.

"I know," Rita says. "That's what I had."

"Oh. You already ate?"

"We finished a while ago."

"You and T. J.?"

"And John."

"Ceepak?"

She laughs. "Does everybody call him by his last name?"

"Most everybody."

"Ceepak," she says it out loud, trying it on for size. "I just hope he doesn't start calling me Lapczynski. Doesn't have the same ring. Lapczynski."

"No," I laugh. "Guess not."

Rita looks rested this morning. Her eyes don't seem so sad or weary.

"Is Ceepak still here?" I ask.

"Mmm-hmm." She gestures over her shoulder toward the kitchen. "Out back. You should go say hey."

"Yeah."

I stand up.

"You want me to order those pancakes for you when the waitress comes by?"

"That'd be great. But please—no scrapple."

"You don't know what you're missing," she jokes.

"Yes, I do."

She smiles and I walk past tables crowded with happy tourists talking about how much fun they had on the boardwalk yesterday. I see Mayor Sinclair over in a corner table. A mob of local merchants drops by to congratulate him on the Labor Day celebration's success.

I head into the kitchen, pass the sputtering griddles, smell the sizzling bacon. My empty stomach urges me to stop and devour a skillet or two. Instead, I head out the door.

I see Grace Porter, hands on hips, staring at the back wall of her building.

"You gentlemen do excellent work," she says.

"Thank you, ma'am." It's Ceepak.

"Thanks." And T. J.

They both have paint rollers on poles and are working pink paint over the pig cartoon, covering up the blue paintball splotches T. J. put there earlier.

"Good morning, Officer Boyle," Grace says to me. "Why aren't you on duty?"

"The chief gave me the day off."

"Excellent. Did you eat breakfast?"

"No ma'am."

"I'll bring out a basket of muffins."

She heads inside.

"We're almost finished with the second coat of pink," Ceepak says.

"You need a hand?"

"No thanks. T. J. and I have the situation pretty well under control."

"We're cool," says T. J.

"Hey, thanks for looking out for Jimmy yesterday," I say to T. J.

"No problem. Jimmy's cool."

"Yeah."

"Did you know T. J. designed his own arm tattoo?" Ceepak says. "He's quite talented."

"I just, you know, like to draw and stuff."

"He's awesome. Going to redraw the cartoon lines on the pig for us. I'm afraid I'd make a mess were I to attempt such intricate work."

"It's easy," T. J. says. "All in the wrist." He picks up a can of black paint and starts working in the lines, carefully restoring the big pig to its former glory. "See?"

"It's all good. Real good."

Watching the two of them, I am, of course, reminded of another Springsteen song. I guess Bruce wrote it about his dad. He could've written it about Ceepak though if, you know, the two of them had ever met:

> *Well so much has happened to me*
> *That I don't understand*
> *All I can think of is being five years old*
> *Following behind you at the beach*
> *Tracing your footprints in the sand*
> *Trying to walk like a man*

Like I've said before, John Ceepak has a code he tries to live by.

He will not lie, cheat, or steal. He will, however, leave some damn decent footprints for you to try and trace in the sand.

Even if you're a young kid like T. J.

Or an older one like me.

BONUS CHAPTERS

Don't miss **Whack-a-Mole**, the third book in the
John Ceepak series.

ONE

I 've never been what you might call an "over-achiever" but at age twenty-five I've already done the worst thing any human being can possibly do.

John Ceepak, my partner, tells me I should let it all out. Get it off my chest. Make what the priests used to call a full and complete confession.

Fine.

I'll do like Ceepak suggests.

It all starts with this stupid ring he found.

TWO

Last Sunday. Six fifty-five A.M.

Bruce Springsteen is on the radio reciting my most recent résumé: *"I had a job, I had a girl, I had something going, mister, in this world . . . ."*

I'm sitting in The Bagel Lagoon waiting for Ceepak. He lives here. Not in the restaurant with the bagels—upstairs in the apartment on the second floor.

"She said Joe, I gotta go, we had it once, we ain't got it any more. She packed her bags, left me behind . . . ."

The Boss is laying it on thicker than a slab of walnut cream cheese. Says he feels like he's *"a rider on a down-bound train."*

I can relate.

Katie's gone.

She said, "Danny, I gotta go." Okay, it doesn't rhyme as good as it might've if my name was Joe like the guy in Bruce's song. Katie, my ex-girlfriend, moved to California. Grad school. Left town in March.

I hope California is as nice as Sea Haven—this eighteen-mile-long strip of sand-in-your-shoes paradise down the Jersey Shore. I hope it has boardwalks and miniature golf and fresh-cut fries and a fudge forecast that's always smooth and creamy like it has been at Pudgy's Fudgery for the past seventy-five years, at least according to the sign flapping out on their sidewalk near the Quick Pick Fudge Cart.

On the radio, Bruce is done singing the blues.

Me, too.

At exactly seven A.M. every Sunday, the Reverend Billy Trumble shoves all rock 'n' roll off the air. He's been doing seven A.M. Sundays on WAVY for nearly thirty years.

"Friends, do you think it is early?" his smooth voice purrs. "Trust me—it is later than you think. Judgment Day is nigh . . . ."

"Turn it off," hollers Joe Coglianese from the back of the shop. He and his brother Jim run The Bagel Lagoon. Joe's in charge of stirring the pot where the bagels bob in boiling water. Jim mans the counter. It's the middle of July and already 80 degrees outside. It feels hotter if you factor in the humidity, plus the steam rising up from that humongous bagel vat. No wonder Joe is the grouchier of the two Coglianese brothers.

Jim snaps off the radio.

I tear another bite out of my bagel.

Ceepak should be joining me any minute. We're both cops with the Sea Haven P.D. and, even though it's our day off, today we are men on a mission.

Ceepak, who's like this 6'2", thirty-six-year-old Eagle-Scout-slash-Jarhead, found something he thinks is valuable buried on the beach while he was sweeping the sand with his metal detector.

This is what Ceepak does for fun when there are no *Forensic Files* or *CSI* reruns on TV. He's even in this club: The Sea Haven Treasure Hunter Society. It's mostly geeks and geezers, guys who strap on headphones and walk the beach like the minesweeper soldier in every bag of green plastic Army men—who, come to think of it, are now chocolate-chip-camo-brown because they've been to Iraq and back, just like Ceepak. They hunt for Spanish doubloons, abandoned Rolexes, rusty subway tokens, discarded paper clips—anything that makes their detectors go beepity-beep.

Anyway, a week ago, Ceepak dug up a ring from P. J. Johnson High School up in Edison. Class of 1983. Inside the ring he found an inscription: B. Kladko. Ceepak being Ceepak, he investigated further and came up with a Brian Kladko who, indeed, graduated from PJJHS in 1983 and still lives somewhere nearby. We're going up there today to take his class ring back to him.

After Katie split, I fill my weekends as best I can.

While I wait, I check out the early-morning crowd. It's mostly tourists from New York and Philadelphia, making them experts on both bagels and cream cheese. They swarm into The Lagoon ordering their favorite combos, forgetting they came down here to try new stuff, like Jersey blueberries or Taylor Pork Roll.

The door opens and all of a sudden it's like somebody walked in with a load of last week's lox in their shorts. A lot of noses suddenly crinkle, mine included. Phew.

"Something's fishy around here," says the big guy who's just come in. "Look no further. It's me!"

"Me" being Cap'n Pete Mullen. He runs one of the deep-sea fishing boats over by the public marina, and he's been taking tourists out after tuna and fluke for so long his clothes all smell like they've been washed with Low Tide-Scented Tide.

"Whataya need, Pete?" asks Jim, the bagel brother behind the counter.

"Baker's dozen. Got a charter going out this morning."

Cap'n Pete has a walrus mustache that wiggles like a worm on a hook. He grins at a kid who's staring at him, watching the lip hair twitch. "I'm Cap'n Pete, laddie. But you can call me Stinky. Stinky Pete."

The boy laughs. So do his folks.

"You run a fishing boat?" asks the dad.

"Sure do."

Pete is good. He comes in to buy breakfast and ends up hooking and booking more clients. I'm sure before their week in Sea Haven is over this fine family of four will be strapping on life vests and heading out to sea on the *Reel Fun* — Cap'n Pete's forty-seven-foot Sportfish.

Jim scoops up an assortment of bagels from the bins and hands the bag to Cap'n Pete.

"Well, I best be shoving off." He chops a salute off the brim of his admiral's cap to the little kid. He sort of looks like the Skipper from *Gilligan's Island.*

Now he shoots me a wave.

Grins.

"Hey, Danny — have Johnny give me a holler. I missed the last meeting."

I'm in mid-chew so I nod and wave. To hear Ceepak tell it, Pete is the unluckiest of all his treasure-hunting buddies. The guy's never found anything under the sand, although occasionally he manages to reel in an interesting boot or tire on his fishing lines.

I chomp off another bite of bagel and eyeball the couple that just stormed in. Studying people is a habit I've picked up working with Ceepak. He's always sizing folks up, trying to decipher their *real* story, the one they're trying to hide.

The fiftysomething guy is wearing what I call *preppy nautical:* untucked polo shirt, khaki slacks, Docksiders without socks.

His slightly younger wife has on a wide-brimmed straw hat anchored with a scarf strapped tight under her chin. Her coffee can-size sunglasses make her look like she has gigantic ant eyes. I figure she's trying to hide from the world. She also seems to be having trouble with the menu. Keeps staring up at the chalkboard, where things aren't all that complicated. The Bagel Lagoon? Basically, it's about bagels.

"Honey?" The husband is hoping to nudge his wife toward a decision.

"Do you have toast?" she asks.

"No," says Jim. "Bagels."

"Eggs?"

"She'll have a raisin bagel," says the husband.

"I don't like raisins."

"Fine. Make it a plain."

"I don't like plain, either."

"Well what *do* you like?"

Obviously, these folks came down the shore to put a little sizzle back in their marriage. I'm glad things are working out so well for them.

"If you paid more attention, you'd know what I like!" The wife steps closer to the counter, farther away from her husband.

"I'll have a poppy," she finally says.

"Anything on it?" asks Jim.

Her eyes go back to the menu board. There are six different kinds of cream cheese and four kinds of butter, if you include peanut. This could go on for hours.

I turn and stare out the window.

Well, well, well.

Here comes Rita. Down the side-of-the-building staircase from Ceepak's apartment.

Over the past year, my partner has struck up a romance with a lovely local lady named Rita Lapczynski. She's a single mom, about thirty-five, who has this huge swoop of blonde hair, which, if my detective's instincts do not deceive me, currently features a pillow dent on the left.

Interesting.

Rita comes into the bagelry.

"Morning, Jim."

"Rita! How you doin'?"

"Yo, Rita!" Joe in the back gives her a big wave of the wooden paddle.

"The usual?" asks Jim.

"Yes, thank you."

"One Salty with a schmear. Coffee light."

"Excuse me. My wife was next," says the preppy husband.

"I'm sorry," says Rita.

"Honey?" says the husband. His voice sounds patient. His eyes, however, are in a hurry. "We are on a schedule . . . ."

"Do not rush me, Theodore!"

Jim goes ahead and fixes Rita her bagel.

Rita is humming to herself. A little smile crosses her face. I guess she spent the night upstairs because her son T. J. is on vacation—up in New York City, staying with an aunt who lives out in Queens. In fact, I know Ceepak paid for the bus tickets. My partner's running a reverse version of The Fresh Air Fund—sending a shore kid up to the polluted city.

Jim takes Rita's cash, keys the register, and hands her back her change, which she drops into the tip cup. Rita waitresses over at Morgan's Surf and Turf. Those who live by tips are always the best tippers.

Finally, she sees me.

"Hey, Danny."

"Hey, Rita. How's it goin'?"

"Fantastic. Looking forward to hearing about your adventures up in Edison."

"Okay."

"Take care now. Have a great day!"

"Sure."

I watch her head toward her car. Then I count to five.

Right on cue, Ceepak comes through the door. So that's how it works: she slips out first, he sneaks down a minute later. Clever.

Now an important thing to know about John Ceepak is that he lives by this very strict, very rigid moral code. It's easier to explain than to follow. Ceepak will not lie, cheat, or steal, nor tolerate those who do. It's a holdover from his fourteen years in the Army. The West Point Honor Code. This morning, I plan to use it against him. Big time.

The wife in the insectoid sunglasses decides she doesn't really want anything for breakfast—except maybe a new husband—and hurries out the door fumbling with a pack of cigarettes. Hubby follows.

"Good morning, Danny," Ceepak now greets me. He's as bright and chipper as usual. The dimples in his cheeks seem a little more animated this morning, but his hair reveals no pillow wrinkles. Then again, his buzz cut is way too short to dent.

"Have you been waiting long?" he asks.

I smirk. "Long enough."

"You had breakfast?"

"Yeah."

"Awesome."

Here comes the fun part. "So—did Rita spend the night?"

"Yes."

I act *amazed*.

"Really?"

"Yes. Ready to roll?" Ceepak's still smiling. No guilt. No shame. No bullshit or cover-up. Just the simple, unvarnished truth.

Apparently, it really does set one free.

Two hours later we're at the food court of the Menlo Park Mall outside Edison, New Jersey. We're sitting in plastic chairs at a table near the Cinnabon counter. The scent of warm dough and cinnamon swirls through the air like invisible frosting—it smells even better than sticking your face inside a box of Cinnamon Toast Crunch cereal. Trust me. I know. I've done this.

Ceepak puts a little clear plastic bag on the table. The ring.

"I can't believe you found it!" says Brian Kladko.

It's your standard high-school ring. Big cut stone in the middle of a gold band. The school's coat of arms inscribed on one side, Latin words nobody still alive can translate on the other.

"Where'd you guys say you were from?"

"Sea Haven," says Ceepak.

Kladko doesn't pick up the ring. He drums the cellophane window on his big Cinnabon box. Take-out breakfast for his family.

"Where exactly is that?" he asks. "Sea Haven?"

"Down the shore," I say.

He nods. Smiles. Fidgets with the box flaps. "Okay. Sure. Near Asbury Park, right?"

"Further south."

"Okay."

He looks at his watch. The ring with its big red rock is still sitting there, all alone in its tiny plastic pouch, stranded like the pimply girl nobody wants to dance with at the prom.

"Well, thanks for driving all the way up here and all."

He stands.

"Sir?" says Ceepak, pointing to the table. "Your ring?"

"Oh. Right. Duh."

"We hope you'll come visit us in Sea Haven again," says Ceepak.

"Yeah. Why not? Be nice to see it."

"You've never been?"

"No. Don't think so." His voice sounds a little shaky.

"Interesting," says Ceepak. "Then I wonder how your ring wound up buried on our beach?"

"Guess you'd have to ask Lisa."

"Lisa?"

"My old girlfriend. I gave the ring to her. A long, long time ago."